Memories

SASHA GREENE

This book is for all the key workers who gave so much
during the COVID-19 pandemic.

We can never repay what they did, but we can remember
and honour them.

Author Note

I never planned to write a sequel to Happiness and Trust, but when the COVID-19 lockdown came in March 2020 I was working on a new three part series and found myself unable to write anything due to worry and stress about what was happening. I realised the only way I might get back to it was to write a story about the situation, even if it would never be published. I started wondering about Steven, who appears in Happiness but had split with his wife before the book even started. What if a lockdown situation forced them back together? How might it come about? I wrote about forty thousand words, broke my writer's block and put it aside, thankful that it had done the job.

Three years later I was working in the library and decided to dig it out to see how bad it was. I had expected it would be all doom and gloom but to my surprise some bits were really funny. The friend I was with heard me laughing out loud and said, 'You should publish that book.' So here it is.

This book contains discussion about miscarriage and depictions of dementia and I have tried to write about these as sensitively as I can. The latter half of the book is also set in the first few months of the pandemic lockdown and if you don't want to be reminded of that time then this book is probably not for you. But I've loved writing Steven and Chantelle's story, because I think it shows that in the middle of what seems like impossible difficulties love can still somehow find a way.

PS. Support your local library! They're awesome.

Prologue

'I need to leave.' Chantelle had spent a sleepless night and though she lay on her back, watching the morning light making shadows on the wall, she knew her husband was awake beside her.

Steven rolled over and curved his body around hers. 'It's still hours before you have to be at work. You should go back to sleep.'

'No, Stevie.' It wasn't just the weight of his arm that she could feel constricting her chest. 'I need to leave you. I can't do this any more.'

He pushed himself up onto an elbow, staring at her. 'What do you mean?'

'I mean all this.' Chantelle sat up in bed, pulling the covers with her. 'My mum is dying of cancer and I desperately need your support. I realise you might not be that able physically yet, but have you ever bothered to even get a meal out of the freezer for when I get home from the hospice? Or put a load of laundry in? You just sit around doing nothing all day, eyes fixed on the TV.'

Steven sat up too, and as the duvet fell away a pang went through Chantelle at how much his body had changed since the accident. But it wasn't his body that she really cared about. It was the state of his mind. 'You need to give me a break, Chaz. It's only been six months. Hell, it's only been three since I got out of hospital and I nearly died the day that bastard ran me over. So forgive me if I'm still trying to process that.'

'I know. And I'm sorry. But I really don't feel like your wife. I'm just a carer, for you and for Mum, and if we're talking about breaks, I need one too. Your mum's taken on extra shifts to make up for your wages and she's coming home exhausted as well. And every time I bring this up we end up shouting at each other and nothing changes. I'm literally at my breaking point.' She would not cry. She would do this like a rational adult having a logical conversation.

Steven looked at her for a few long seconds and then lay back down, facing away from her. 'Go on then. Just leave.'

'You don't want to fight for this? For us?' Chantelle felt shock run through her body. In all the years she had known him they had argued and fallen out and made up, but he had never let her down.

'What's the point if you've already decided?'

She couldn't argue with that. Couldn't say that she wanted him to beg her to stay. To tell her that things would change. Fifteen minutes later she was on the front doorstep with two suitcases at her side and her marriage in tatters behind her.

Chapter 1
Three Years Later

'Police are after you.'

The voice was right next to his ear and Steven almost lost his grip on the pull-up bar, barely managing to save himself with a shoulder-jolting grab for stability.

'Fuck's sake, Jim, don't come up behind me like that. Almost landed on my arse.' Steven dropped to the ground and swung around to look at the gym owner. 'So where are they?'

'Told them to wait outside. Didn't want people thinking you were in trouble.' Jim frowned, scratching his stubbled chin. 'You're not, are you?'

'Not that I know of.' The last time Steven had been in contact with the police was over three years ago, in circumstances he didn't like remembering. 'I'll go talk to them, see what they want.'

He grabbed his towel and slung it around his neck. It no doubt looked silly and pretentious but his jacket was in a locker in the changing room and he would need some protection against the cold November chill. Hopefully this wouldn't take long.

The fresh air was a welcome change after the slightly sweaty smell of the gym. Steven had expected two police officers but there was only one, although a quick scan of the car park showed her colleague waiting in a nearby vehicle. He warned himself to stay polite, although he could feel his skin rapidly cooling in the icy wind. 'What can I do for you?' The officer turned her head at the sound of his voice and he found himself looking up into the face of his ex-wife.

'Chaz?' His mouth fell open, the cold forgotten. He hadn't seen Chantelle since the day she had left their flat and she definitely hadn't been with the police then. Her high-vis jacket gleamed in the light that shone from the doorway and her blonde hair was pulled back at the nape of her neck into a no-nonsense bun. She was still just as beautiful as he remembered.

'Hi, Stevie. Sorry to interrupt you, but we were passing and I needed to talk to you. You've been ignoring my calls.'

'Oh. That was you?' He flushed guiltily as he thought of the ten or so that had gone unanswered in the last week. 'Sorry. I still don't pick up unknown numbers. Not after Mad Max got his friends to call up and shout abuse at me for three months without a break.'

Her perfectly shaped eyebrows rose. 'Unknown number? You deleted me from your phone?'

'Safety measure. In case I was tempted to drunk dial you at two am some night.' He could feel one side of his mouth lifting, which surprised him. 'Anyway, how did you find me? Did you track my phone somehow?'

Chantelle laughed, a hand going up to her mouth. 'You've been watching too many crime dramas. I called your friend Pete this afternoon and he told me where you'd be.'

'Oh.' Steven shifted, aware that his muscles were rapidly stiffening up. He waited for her to say more, listening to the sounds of the rush hour traffic grinding by on the main road. 'Sorry, but I'm freezing my tits off out here. What's up?'

Chantelle glanced down at his thin shorts and close-fitting t-shirt and nodded. 'It's OK, I don't have much time either. We only came down to swap a car and we've got to get back. It's about your mum.'

The police car workshop was at the end of the road, Steven remembered. Then her words penetrated into his brain and a thrum of adrenaline shot through him. Didn't the police come round when someone had died? *Relax*, he told himself as his heart started to race. This clearly wasn't a formal call.

Chantelle must have seen the thoughts in his face, because she reached out to touch his arm briefly. 'Don't worry, this isn't official business. She's fine. I mean, she's not fine, that's why I'm here. But she's not dead, or in hospital or anything.'

'That's good.' Steven shivered, half with the cold and half with relief. He had never had an easy relationship with his mother, but the thought that something might have happened to her cut him deeper than he had expected.

'I'm afraid it's still pretty bad.' Chantelle's mouth twisted. 'She's got dementia. She's been hiding it well, but last week Jules finally had to fire her from the takeaway and he won't have her back.'

Steven felt his shoulders slump as the news sank in. 'But she's only just reached her sixties. How can that happen?'

Chantelle shrugged. 'Bad luck, I guess. I've been trying to persuade her to go to the doctor but she keeps insisting she's fine. Jules said he tried to hang onto her as long as he could but she's made too many mistakes.' She lifted a hand to fiddle with the aerial on her radio. 'To be honest, I thought you knew. It was just something she let slip last Friday that made me realise you didn't.'

Steven rubbed his face with his hands. 'Shit. This couldn't have come at a worse time. I've got it full on at the moment trying to sort out my new business with Nick.'

Chantelle sighed. 'Look, I know you don't get on well with Irene, but she is your mum. I think you owe it to her.' She checked her watch, looking over at the police van. 'Really sorry, but I've got to run. Donny will never forgive me if we get into trouble. Just go and see her, OK? Then you'll understand.' She was gone before he could collect his brain together enough to reply.

It was too late to go back to his workout routine. A hot shower helped thaw out his muscles and by the time he was done his mind was made up. There was no point worrying about anything until he had seen the situation for himself and the sooner he went the better. Sitting in the changing room with a towel slung around his waist, he called Nick.

'Is that you finished?' His housemate's voice was cheerful. 'Should I get the curry orders in?'

'Nick, something's come up. Order me my usual, but I won't be back until-' He checked his watch. 'Maybe half eight?'

'Is everything OK?' There was concern in Nick's voice.

'Aye, I'm fine, it's something with my mum. I'll tell you everything later. Just need to go check on her.' He started grabbing things out of his locker.

'You sure? I mean, Jade's here, but we could wait for you if you want. Or is there anything we can do at all?'

'Thanks, but I'm good.' Steven brushed off the offer. 'I'll see you both later. Looking forward to that bhuna, OK?'

It took him about thirty minutes to get across town on his bicycle, which in rush hour was a pretty good run. At least it made up for his interrupted workout. The time it took to lock up his bike to a lamp post and swap his cycling socket back to the regular one was a welcome opportunity to get his breathing under control before he knocked on the familiar brown door.

A shout came from the hallway. 'Who is it?'

There was no spyhole, and even though he kept offering to have one put in then she always refused. It was only one of the many things they had argued about over the years.

'It's only me, Mum.'

'Oh.' There was a note of surprise in her voice, but the lock turned and the door opened. He didn't know what he had been expecting, but the sight that met him wasn't it. She was dressed in a smart outfit, not a hair out of place, and the hallway looked as neat as it usually did.

'Stevie.' Her voice sounded puzzled as she shut the door. 'Was I expecting you? Because I'm off out soon with Brenda, she's taking me to the bingo. It's not really my thing, but she goes every week and she said she wanted a bit of company this time.'

That was her upstairs neighbour, Steven remembered. The cottage flats looked like semi-detached houses but were actually split into two separate levels. 'No, don't worry, you haven't forgotten. It's just, well, Chaz told me you were...'

He suddenly found he couldn't say it to her face. 'Chaz told me you weren't well, and I thought I'd swing by and check up on you.'

'Oh.' She smiled at him and gave him a quick peck on the cheek. 'That's very kind of you, love. But I don't know what she's talking about. I'm fine. I've got time for a quick cuppa before I go out, if you'd like to stay.'

'Sure.' Steven was puzzled. She did seem fine, and as he followed her into the living room, everything looked normal. The house was clean and tidy, and in the next twenty minutes she successfully managed to make a cup of tea and hold a coherent conversation. She brushed off his questions about her job, saying that they had let her go because business wasn't that great. So what was Chantelle talking about?

Another knock on the door interrupted them just as he was taking his last swig of tea. 'Oh, that'll be Brenda.' His mother got up. 'Thanks for dropping by, love, it's kind of you to check up on me. Will I see you again soon?'

Steven was so wrapped up in his own thoughts that he found himself agreeing absent-mindedly. 'Aye, sure.'

'Hi, Brenda. You'll remember Stevie.'

Steven turned a smile on the neighbour but was met with a glare that was colder than the chilly night outside. This one was taking no prisoners and he wondered what the hell was going on. He swallowed nervously and made his escape. 'You two have a good time tonight.'

As he cycled back home he was still puzzling over what had just happened. He would trust Chantelle with his life, but at the same time his mother seemed fine. Wasn't dementia supposed to make your memory bad? He hadn't seen any evidence of that at all.

Nick must have heard the key in the lock because by the time Steven had hung his bike on its hook inside the entrance of their ground floor flat he was standing in the doorway to the living room, a concerned look on his face. 'Is everything OK?'

Steven placed his helmet on its peg. 'I'm not sure, really. Let me get some dinner inside me and then I'll tell you all about it. It's been a bit of a weird evening.'

'We wrapped your takeaway in Nick's Arctic coat, so hopefully it should still be warm.' Jade came to stand beside her partner, placing an arm around his waist. 'If not then bung it in the microwave.'

'Cheers, guys. Really appreciate it.' It didn't take long to tip everything out of the foil containers onto a plate and then Steven retreated to his favourite big red armchair and started shovelling food into his mouth. It was only when he was more than halfway through the plate that he began to slow down.

Nick finally switched off the TV and broke the silence. 'So what's going on with your mum?'

Steven finished his mouthful before he continued. 'Chantelle. My ex. You won't have met. She came to see me at the gym. Turns out she's been trying to call me all week because she says Mum's got dementia.'

'Oh shit. That's bad.' Nick swung his feet down from the wooden coffee table. 'So is that why you're late? You went to check up on her?'

'Aye. On Mum, I mean. Chantelle's working tonight.' Steven let out a mirthless huff of laughter. 'Can you believe it? She's with the polis now.' He loaded up another forkful and shovelled it in.

Nick laughed. 'I don't know if it's because my parents spent so long in England, but I still can't get used to the way people here say the word police. It makes me feel like I'm in a gangster film or something.' He made shooting motions with his hands. 'The polis is coming! Run fae yer lives!'

Jade elbowed him in the ribs. 'That was a terrible attempt at a Glasgow accent. You're embarrassing yourself.'

'Sorry.' Nick pressed his hands together and bowed to each of them in mock apology. 'So does she?'

Steven was still distracted by thoughts of Chantelle. It had been a shock to see her standing in front of him and the uniform had been even more of a surprise. 'Does she what?'

Nick rolled his eyes. 'Your mum. Have dementia.'

'I don't know, that's the thing.' Steven set his empty plate down on the table. 'She seemed fine. And Chaz said she'd been fired from her job, but my mum's story is they let her go because they needed to cut costs. So I really don't have a fucking clue what's going on.'

'It does come and go though, I think.' Jade scratched her head. 'One of my grandads got dementia. Some days he'd seem perfectly fine, then others he'd forget to eat anything at all. It almost started off a family feud at one point, because in the beginning my mum wouldn't believe it was happening. It eventually turned out that by some stroke of luck she always went to see him on his good days.'

Steven considered this. 'It was weird. She did seem totally fine. Although she was nice to me for at least twenty minutes, which isn't her usual style. I guess I'll just have to talk to Chaz about it. She must have some reason for worrying about her.' He yawned. 'Anyway. Nothing I can do about it tonight. Turn the TV back on and let's watch that film after all.'

He did take a few seconds to send a message to Chantelle but a couple of hours later she still hadn't replied, or even seen it. She must still be working. Normally he was dead to the world as soon as his head hit the pillow but tonight his brain stubbornly refused to cooperate. The conversation with Chantelle kept replaying in his mind, and especially the moment when he had looked up into her face. She had always been a smidgen taller than him, and the thick soles of her safety boots only added to her height. He hadn't minded about that one bit, in fact he considered himself lucky to have snagged someone as amazing as her at all. Going from childhood friends to husband and wife was a bit of a cliche, but it had been one of the proudest moments of his life when he had watched her walk down the aisle with all their friends and family about them. It was only after his cycling accident had left him fighting for his life in hospital and ultimately with an amputated leg that their relationship had started to spiral inescapably downwards.

It was about a quarter past midnight when a sudden glow from his phone lit up the darkened room. *Did you check inside the kitchen cupboards?*

He puzzled over the message for a few minutes, then realised she might be waiting for an answer. *No.*

Her reply was almost instant. *Might be a good idea.*

For the next couple of minutes it looked like she was typing another message, and he braced himself for a long explanation, but what came through was surprisingly short. *Just let me know if you need me, I'll do all I can to help.*

Thanks. He typed back. *I will.*

Chantelle could feel the beginnings of a headache starting. She crawled into bed and shook two pills from the pot on the nightstand, relishing the feel of the cosy duvet above her. The second part of her shift had been pretty tough, not helped by the fact that Steven had been in the back of her mind for most of the evening. She knew she had probably come across as uncaring. Asking how he was or about this new business he had mentioned would have been the normal thing to do, but she had been worried about staying for too long when they weren't really supposed to be there and also thrown by how strong the urge had been to step forward and wrap her arms around him. Still, he had shown no interest in her new job and barely any in his mother, so they were even on that score.

She took a deep breath and let it out slowly, massaging her head gently. Joining the police was originally something she had done to fill the void left by the ending of her marriage, but it was actually one of the best decisions she had ever made. If she could pass her probation next year and graduate to being a proper officer she would finally feel like she had achieved something worthwhile. It was strange how one thing led to another. If it hadn't been for the circumstances of Steven's accident and all that time trying to get compensation from the man who ran him over then she never would have talked to the police inspector who had encouraged her to join. Silver linings came with every cloud.

She curled on her side, hugging one of the pillows. Even now she still missed Steven's warm shape in the bed beside her. She hadn't slept well since they'd split, which was probably another silver lining too. Doing shift work was so much easier if you had broken nights already.

Closing her eyes and willing oblivion to come didn't usually help, but she still tried it. She had made the right decision, both with her career and her marriage. Her job made her feel like she was making a difference, and by leaving Steven she had moved on from a situation in which she had no hope of doing that. Some people never changed.

She sometimes felt guilty for not telling him about their miscarriage, but then, what difference would it make? At least they hadn't been forced to try to patch up a failing relationship just for the sake of a kid. She hugged her knees to her chest. Two years old. It would have been two years old by now. It still seemed strange to think about that.

'Don't get stuck in what might have been.' She spoke the words softly, as if by saying them aloud they might have more power to convince her. It was the only way to live, especially with her job. She did what she could and moved on, which was exactly what she was going to do with Steven. Closing her eyes, she lay and waited for the darkness to overtake her.

The next morning her head felt gummy, as it always did when she resorted to painkillers. She made herself some toast with jam and migrated as far as the sofa, the banality of daytime TV about as much as she could handle. Another shift awaited her at two, but at least she had free time until then.

Chantelle normally relished her lazy mornings before a late shift, enjoying the simple luxuries of her spacious one-bedroom flat, but seeing Steven had affected her deeply, no matter how much she tried to convince herself otherwise. Sighing, she reached for her phone and did what she always did when something was bugging her.

Her sister answered on the second ring. 'Hey. What's up?'

'How do you always know?' Chantelle felt a smile cross her face and could already feel her spirits lifting. The two sisters had always been close, but the support that Sarah had given her over the last three years was really what had kept Chantelle going.

'Know what?' Sarah sounded puzzled.

Chantelle swung her feet up onto the sofa and leaned her head back against a cushion. 'You asked what's up.'

'Oh. That was just a general greeting.' Sarah laughed. 'But I take it something is actually up?'

'I finally caught up with Steven last night. He wasn't taking my calls so I had to track him down.'

'Well, at least you've done your bit. And it's more than a lot of people would do.' She could tell Sarah was trying to comfort her, but then why did the comment not leave her comforted one bit?

'Yeah, I know.' Chantelle rubbed her forehead with her free hand. 'But it meant I got to see him, Sarah. Which with hindsight was such a bad move because I realised I still have feelings for him. And that makes me hate myself because I'm also still really angry at him.' The sigh from Sarah on the other end of the phone was enough to convey everything Chantelle had expected as a reaction. 'I know, I know. I'm an idiot. But it took all the moving on I've been trying to do since I left and smashed it into smithereens.'

'Hang on, I'm going to switch to video.' Sarah came up on the screen, her face drawn in a concerned frown. 'Don't beat yourself up about it if it's the way you really feel. Even though it might be annoying there's no point being in denial.'

'Urgh! Annoying is about right.' Chantelle balanced her phone on top of a cushion so she could grab her second piece of toast. 'Why am I still like this after such a long time? I was really hoping I'd moved on. I mean, I've kept in touch with Irene because she's been like a mother to me, but I really thought I'd be over him by now.'

'It isn't that surprising, if you think about it.' Sarah yawned massively. 'Sorry, it's not you that's boring, Effie kept me up half the night. She's asleep now, the little demon.'

'Is she alright? Is it just the normal baby stuff?' Chantelle loved her two month old niece, but the little one did have a powerful set of lungs on her.

Sarah laughed mirthlessly. 'She's fine. It's me who's suffering. I'm sure it wasn't this bad the first time. Anyway, we were talking about you. I was saying it wasn't surprising because it will have been the first time you've seen him since you moved out, right?'

'That's true.' Chantelle hadn't thought about it that way. Her failed marriage was another thing that she wasn't proud of, but it had been the only way forward at the time. Staying with a person was useless if it meant falling apart herself. 'I still wonder if I could have done more to keep us together.'

'Marriages are meant to be a union of two people, Chaz.' Sarah sighed. 'And you were definitely doing all the emotional lifting in that relationship by the time you left. I'm not saying things should be perfect, and I appreciate what Steven went through after the accident, but sometimes, just sometimes, everyone needs to show up and do their best, and I don't think he was even doing that.'

'Thanks, Sarah.' Chantelle found tears beginning to form in her eyes. 'It really means a lot to hear you say that.'

'Any time.' Sarah blew her a kiss. 'Oh, that's my free time over, Effie's just waking up. Would you like to see her?'

'Of course. Let me give her a wave.' Chantelle pulled the screen closer so she could see. 'Oh, look at her sleepy little eyes! So cute. You would hardly suspect she's demon spawn at all.'

The two sisters laughed together and Effie made the little creaky noise that meant she was happy too. Chantelle took a deep breath and let it out again slowly. Life was OK. It really was. She would do her best to forget about Steven and move on.

Chapter 2

Steven was still wondering what to do about the situation with his mum when he got to work in the morning. It was always a familiar routine: say hello to the porter, climb the two flights of stairs and make himself a coffee before settling at his desk. He had taken this job in desperation to get out of unemployment but had found it such a pleasant place to work that he had ended up staying, even though the job bored him to tears. They called him office admin, but the reality was that he did practically anything. Making arrangements for meetings, ordering stationery supplies, dealing with the landlord and organising the office Christmas party were all part of his responsibilities. It had been slightly overwhelming at first but now he could do it with half his brain. Lately this had been a good thing because he was full of plans for his new business, but now it only left him with time to worry.

If Chantelle was right then they definitely had a problem, because his mother was clearly hiding things and wouldn't take kindly to him interfering. So what to do? He considered his options. The coming weekend was supposed to be for catching up with Nick about final preparations for the business launch and how things were going. Even though it was months until the first trip away, both of them wanted things to go perfectly and there still seemed to be so many details to sort out. But maybe he could spare a few hours.

He sent his mother a text. *Shall I swing by for tea on Sunday?*

It didn't take long for him to get a reply. *Sure, that would be lovely. Shall I make something?*

The thought of her cooking terrified him and it was nothing to do with dementia. She had started working at the Indian takeaway when he was fourteen and the swap from her disastrous attempts at dinners to bringing home leftovers had been like stepping into some kind of heaven. He quickly typed back. *I'll get a takeout on my way.* And that was as much as he could do for now.

He put her out of his mind, but that just gave space for Chantelle. She had clearly moved on with her life since they had split and if he was honest with himself he was a tiny bit jealous. She had a new job that she obviously enjoyed while he was stuck in this office. Not for much longer though, hopefully. Setting up a social enterprise to take elderly and disabled people out into the mountains had been Nick's idea, but Steven had thrown himself wholeheartedly behind it. Steven was desperate to get back into something closer to his former job doing outdoor adventures for kids and Nick was hoping to get away from a nightmare boss, so they both had an interest in making things work.

But Chantelle... Steven took a swig of his lukewarm coffee and gave up pretending. He was still just as much in love with her as ever. Which was all the more reason to avoid her; there was no point embarrassing himself when she clearly didn't care for him in that way any more. It shouldn't be that hard. Unless he bumped into her at his mum's place then he was unlikely to see her.

He ditched the coffee in the sink with a symbolic flourish and turned his mind towards the problem of where to put a meeting now that a client was bringing four extra people.

'Right, so how many weekends do you think we can actually run next year?' Steven looked down at the paper calendar which was laid out on their coffee table. With freezing rain lashing down outside summer seemed a long way away but they had to get planning now or things would never be ready in time.

Nick frowned. 'It's tricky. A bit of an unknown really. As you know, our funding application for the minibus is dragging on and I don't have any idea when they're going to make a decision. I don't know if it's us being set up as a social enterprise instead of a charity that's thrown things off, or the fact that we're all so young, but there's nothing we can do about that now. It's out of our hands. At least it means I've got more time to finish getting my minibus licence. I couldn't get a test date until January.' He set a cup of tea down on the table. 'Here you go.'

'Cheers.' Steven pulled it towards him. 'So until we know we've definitely got the bus we'd better to stick to small groups, aye? People who have their own transport.'

'Yeah, I guess so. I wouldn't want to have more than two or three to one anyway, depending on the disabilities of course.' Nick sat down on the other side of the table. 'Which gives us four to six people max. Unless we hire in help.'

Steven cradled the mug in his hands, enjoying the warmth that was seeping out of it. 'What about Jamie? Is he in on this, or is he too busy doing his own stuff?' Jamie was a long-standing friend of Nick's who ran an outdoor business in Fort William.

'He's in, if we want him to be. He says as long as we let him know well in advance he'll make the time. Apart from Easter, unfortunately. Apparently he's already got something booked for that. And we can use any of his equipment that we want. I think a couple of weekends in his kayaks sounds like a great idea.'

'So we are only doing weekends then, not weeks?' It was important to get this all thrashed out.

Nick nodded. 'I was even thinking perhaps some day courses as well, in locations not far from Glasgow. We could do a week, but I feel like it's more important to be a bit cautious. It is our first year after all.' He helped himself to a biscuit from the stash on the table. 'Besides, for anything more than a day we're going to have to sort out accommodation, and that's tricky. Proper accessible accommodation is incredibly hard to come by and usually gets booked up way in advance. That's why I want to get this sorted as soon as possible.'

All the extra factors made things so much more complicated, Steven thought. 'But I guess it's not everyone who will need that kind of stuff. People like me, for example, are going to be fine without any kind of special accommodation arrangements.'

'Yeah, but people like you are probably going to be away off climbing the hills by themselves, unless they're right at the start of their recovery. They won't need us at all. I'm thinking more people in wheelchairs, those with visual impairments, elderly people with mobility issues, that sort of thing. If we're really going to call ourselves inclusive we have to be prepared for almost everything.' Nick crunched into his biscuit, sending crumbs splattering across the table. He brushed them away with a sleeve. 'Sorry. Didn't mean to make a mess there. But those two rugged wheelchairs

Archie's family gave us the money for should be finally with us just before Christmas, so that's really exciting.'

'So what's the plan? Choose some dates and put them in the diary?' Steven felt a flutter in his stomach at the thought they might actually be going for it.

'I guess so. Jamie's said he'll advertise for us on his website, and Jade says there's definitely some interest at the care home.' It was taking elderly people out on trips around Glasgow which had first given Nick the idea for all this.

'It was nice to see Jade the other night, I feel like I've not seen her for ages. Or not properly.'

Nick shrugged. 'She's incredibly busy trying to finish off her book. She was really worried about people accusing her of making money off her sister's death, but she's had quite a few offers and the one she went for is working in collaboration with a youth mental health charity. I would say I've barely seen her so excited, but the truth is I've barely seen her at all. She says the bad winter weather is the perfect excuse for writing. I'm almost considering asking her to move in with me so at least we see each other when we're sleeping.' Nick laughed, reaching for another biscuit. 'No, I am exaggerating a bit. We're all good. And she's said that if we need any text for a website she'd be happy to write it.'

'You're joking about moving in but that's actually not a bad idea, you know. I wouldn't mind if she did.' Steven decided it was time for a biscuit of his own.

'You sure you wouldn't?' Nick sounded slightly dubious.

'Course not. I love Jade. I'd be happy to have her in. Especially if it means you two pay a bit more towards the bills.' He flashed Nick a sly grin.

'Ah yes, I knew you'd have some sort of ulterior motive.' Nick's face lit up.

'I'm only joking. But seriously, sure. She can move in any time you like. And while we're on this topic, how are you really?'

They both knew that his question was more than a casual one; a couple of years previously Nick had gone through a patch of bad mental health which had ended in him having to be rescued when a solo trip into the mountains had gone down the pan. It had changed them all in small ways and now their circle of friends always ensured they made space for an answer when they asked each other how they were.

Nick shrugged. 'I'm OK. Winter is always a hard time for me, especially in Glasgow with everything so grey and miserable. But planning things like this definitely helps. I can't help thinking that if we're successful we might eventually be able to go full time. Then I can get away from my nightmare boss and you can finally quit that brain-numbing job you've got.'

'It's not that bad.' Steven frowned. 'At least the people are nice.'

'Oh come on. You're wasted in that place and you know it. Anyway, right back at you, how are you?' Nick waggled his finger towards his friend's nose.

Steven batted it away. 'I don't know, if I'm honest. This thing with my mum has thrown me and I just don't know what to do about it.'

'You know all the guys are here for you, right? If you need anything all you have to do is ask.' When Steven nodded reluctantly, Nick put a hand on his shoulder. 'I mean it. Anything you need, we're here. We've got your back.'

'Yeah, yeah, I know.' Steven grasped Nick's hand, feeling himself getting slightly emotional. 'Trouble is, I don't have a fucking clue what's going on yet. But when I do find out I'll let you know. I promise.'

'Great.' Nick bent over the planner again. 'Now, let's get these dates sorted out and we can decide what we want to do. Oh, and Jamie suggested we might even like to do a winter weekend. How about skiing one day and some low level walking the other?'

'Not with my skiing as shite as it is.' Steven grimaced. 'We've got to be realistic.'

'There are people we could hire in who can help us with lessons I guess. We should consider it at least. So tell me, which weekends do you think would be best?'

Steven couldn't help feeling nervous as he knocked on Irene's front door. Look in the kitchen, Chantelle had told him, so that would be his first move. Then he would have to confront her somehow. He kissed his mum on the cheek in greeting. 'I got Chinese like you asked, hope you like it.' Did she look thinner than normal? Or was he imagining things?

'Great, I'll get some plates. You go sit down.' She took the bag from him before he had time to protest.

'I'll come with you, get something to drink.' Steven followed her through the archway which connected the kitchen to the living room. 'Have you got any juice?'

Irene looked uncertain for a moment, a frown crossing her face. 'I'm not sure. I usually have some in. I think it might be in one of the cupboards.' As Steven reached for a knob she put out her hand. 'No - not that one -'

Her voice trailed off as a ream of paper crashed out of the cupboard, fluttering all over the kitchen floor. She quickly knelt down and started to pick it up. Steven lowered himself down to help her and couldn't help noticing that most of them were empty envelopes and all of them had been scrawled upon. He glanced at one as he picked it up. It looked like a shopping list with random food items on it. The second one had a list of names. Himself, Chantelle, Jules and Brenda were all on it, and even his father, plus a few other names he didn't recognise. The third one was a list of supermarkets. Puzzled, he looked across at Irene. 'What is all this?'

She frowned at him. 'If you've come here to criticise the state of my house you can get out, tea or no tea.'

'But Mum.' Steven realised how much he sounded like a disgruntled teenager and started again. 'Chantelle said you've been forgetting things. She's worried you've got dementia.'

'That girl has no business poking her nose into what's going on in my life.' Irene got to her feet and banged a stack of paper onto the kitchen counter. 'And you're a fine one to talk, you never even remembered my birthday this year.'

She had unwittingly betrayed herself with that comment, Steven realised. He did distinctly remember her birthday, mainly because they had argued at the barbecue he had arranged for her in the back garden. He remembered because he still felt bad about it. He stood up as well so he didn't feel like he was at a disadvantage. 'Chantelle just cares about you, Mum. She only told me because she was worried about you.'

Irene slammed a fist on the counter top, making him jump. 'Oh, so that's why you're round here after all this time, pretending like you care, is it? You'll be putting me in a home next, trying to claim that I'm losing my mind.' Her finger pointed towards the door. 'Get out.' She knelt down and started picking up more papers, then, when he didn't move, she looked up at him. 'You think I'm not serious? Son or no son, there's no way I'm going to take that kind of shit from you. Just go.'

Steven found himself paralysed by indecision. He could go, hope she calmed down a bit and deal with things later. But there was a real chance that she meant what she said, and if that was the case he wouldn't get any further than the front door next time. He knelt down next to her and put a hand on her arm. 'Mum. You know that Chantelle loves you and would never do anything to hurt you. I love you, hard as it might be to believe that after I've been such a shitty son to you these last few years. Why won't you let me help you?'

Irene glared at him for a few more seconds, then a deep sigh escaped her and she sat back against the washing machine, some of the papers still clutched to her chest. 'Chantelle's right. I have started forgetting things, Stevie. At first I thought I was imagining it, but now it's got too bad to pretend.'

She placed one piece of paper carefully on the floor, and arranged another neatly on top of it. Another three followed and he was starting to wonder if that was all he would get out of her when she spoke again. 'To begin with it was things like my keys, my purse, but lately I've been forgetting people's names, and on bad days I can't even remember whether I've eaten or not. My short-term memory is getting really terrible.'

She touched his outstretched leg briefly. 'I'm sorry I lied to you. The real reason why Jules got rid of me was because I screwed up a few too many orders. Well, many too many orders really.' A wince crossed her face. 'He kept trying to get me to go to the doctor's to sort things out, but I was too proud. In the end he gave me an ultimatum: either go, or he would have to let me go. I walked out. You know I don't like anyone pushing me around like that.'

Steven knew exactly what she was referring to; his father hadn't been an easy person to live with. There was still guilt inside him about missing him when the man had left, even if all the time he'd known exactly what his mother was going through.

He still missed having a dad, if he was totally honest. Not his dad specifically, but someone he could depend on from time to time. Someone who could help to sort out this mess. He knew he had Nick's offer of help, but it wasn't the same. His shoulders slumped. Just when he thought he was starting to get his life back on track, something like this got dumped on him. He pointed to the neat stack of envelopes that was now sitting under Irene's right hand. 'So what's with all of those?'

Her eyes darted back and forth as if she was trying to find something in the rest of the papers that littered the tiles. 'That orange book.' She pointed and he lifted it up, flicking through a few of the pages. It was more scribbled bullet points in handwriting he could barely read. Places she'd been on holiday. TV programmes she'd watched. 'I read on the internet that a good way to remember things was to make lists. It said that you should also write things that mattered, so that you can go back to them later when your memory gets worse. I started in the book, but it soon got filled and I meant to get another one, somehow never got around to it. So I grabbed whatever I could find when I thought of another thing I should write down. I meant to get some sort of filing system sorted out, but never got around to that either.'

He lifted up the list of names. 'So glad I made the list of people who are important to you.'

She only managed a weak smile at that, but then it was a fairly weak attempt at a joke. 'You've always been important to me, Stevie. I might not have been good at showing it, but you've always been the most important person in my life.' She paused as if something had suddenly struck her. 'I wonder if that's partly why your dad left; he could see as soon as you came along that I was always going to put you first.'

'No, he left because he was an asshole, Mum.' Steven raised his eyebrows. 'He left because he cared more about his new girlfriend than the eighteen years you spent together.'

'Relationships are tricky, Steven, you know that.' There was a slight reproach in her voice.

'Don't I just.' Steven grimaced, thinking of his own failed marriage. 'But this is not about our love lives. It's about you. You need to go to the doctor, Mum. If you don't do something then you're going to get thrown out of this flat.'

'I know.' She touched his leg again, a gentle squeeze this time. 'I'm just so afraid, you know? I get that it sounds stupid, but something is stopping me from going. I think I don't want to hear what they're going to say.' He saw a tear roll down her cheek.

'I'll go with you.' He swivelled himself round so he could put his arms around her. She rested her head on his shoulder, and neither of them spoke for a couple of minutes.

'You know I realised Wednesday that something was up because you were actually nice to me?' Steven tried to put some humour in his tone and must have succeeded somewhat, because a proper laugh escaped her this time.

She raised her head, patting his chest gently. 'Have I really been that bad? Is that why you never come and see me?'

'I don't know, Mum. You always seem to make me feel that I'm not good enough.' This conversation was getting a lot deeper than he had expected.

'Oh Stevie.' She put a hand up to touch his cheek gently. 'I just know you're capable of amazing things if you set your mind to it. All I've tried to do is to encourage you to achieve.'

He didn't know what to say to that, but a few nice words weren't going to take away all his frustrations with her. He pulled himself up by the edge of the kitchen counter and then reached out a hand. 'Come on. I'll help you organise these papers later. Our food'll be getting cold.'

Chapter 3

Steven checked his watch as the front door closed behind him. It was late, but not too late to see if Brenda would talk to him. She hadn't been in the neighbourhood more than a year or so but had obviously taken a shine to Irene. He rang the bell, feeling as if he was going to see his least favourite teacher at school.

As soon as he saw Brenda's face he blurted out the first words that came to mind. 'I didn't know.'

The closing door stopped, and then slowly opened again. 'I didn't, I swear.' Steven looked at the older woman standing there, arms crossed. 'And she would have hidden it anyway. She pretended everything was fine on Wednesday when I came over.'

'If you were around more often you would have noticed.' Brenda's tone was still harsh, but she already looked less angry.

'Seeing as you are around more, you'll know what a pain she can be sometimes.' It was a risky move, but only total honesty would save him now.

Brenda surprised him with a laugh. 'Well then. You'd better come in.'

As they discussed the situation Steven felt his shoulders unwinding slowly. Brenda had been helping as much as she could around her job, but was also coming to realise that there were limits to what she could do. However she was a goldmine of information about where to get help.

'My dad had it too, passed away a few years back. These sort of things happen when your parents get older.' Brenda dug out a leaflet from a green folder and passed it over to him. 'That's a carer's charity; call them when things get too much and they'll let you have a rant. But having it happen to Irene is a crying shame. She's barely ten years older than me.'

By the time he got up to leave they had a strategy worked out where Brenda would make sure Irene was eating properly at least once a day and Steven would get the ball rolling on arranging some extra support. Brenda followed him to the door. 'Don't you have any relatives who could pitch in to help?'

Steven shook his head. 'She's got a sister somewhere down south, but I don't think they've spoken in years.'

'What about that girl who comes round sometimes? Would she be willing to help a bit?'

Steven should have known that would be her next question but even so he wasn't prepared for it. His hesitation must have shown in his face, because Brenda reached out and touched his shoulder gently. 'What is it?'

'Where to start?' He huffed out a slow breath between his lips. 'We used to be married and now we're not.'

'Ah.' Was that pity in her tone, or a hint of judgement? He couldn't really tell. He was expecting another question, but she just stood there, looking at him steadily.

'I'll talk to her.' He lifted a hand and rubbed the back of his neck. 'It's, well, she's got a busy job these days. She's with the polis now.'

'I can contact her, if you want.' Brenda shrugged. 'If she's working shifts like me then she'll be off most times when you're at work. It could all fit together quite well.'

'It's OK.' Steven sighed. 'I'll do it. We do need to talk, really.'

'Well, you've got my number. I'll do what I can. Give me a shout if you need anything.'

'Will do.' He gave her a salute as he left.

Steven tried to use his cycle home to get his thoughts in order, feeling pretty overwhelmed by the situation. Talking to Brenda had been really helpful, but had also made him realise the full scale of the task ahead. He would just have to focus on one thing at a time. First thing tomorrow he would call the doctor and make an appointment. Then once that was done everything would follow on from there.

He swung himself off his bike in front of the gate. The main trouble was, the only way for his mum from here was downwards. A lump in his throat seemed to be choking him and he couldn't breathe. Panicking, he looked over at the living room where the light was on. That meant Nick was home. His friend. He took a deep breath. He had to remember that. He had good friends who would help him through this somehow. And he had to square things with Chantelle too. Better to do that sooner rather than later.

It was hopeless trying to get hold of Chantelle, but after three days of them missing each other she finally managed to get through to him. He went out to the back of the office by the bins to get a bit of privacy and tried to think about how to begin. He hated asking people for favours. And this was Chantelle, which made it even worse.

'Hey.' She sounded as uncomfortable as he felt.

He needed to get this over with. Best just to come out with it. 'Would you mind looking in on Mum regularly? She really needs all the help she can get. We're going to the doctor next week to check it really is dementia but all the signs are there so we're going to have to deal with it somehow.' *Well done*, he congratulated himself. *Make it about her and not about you.*

'I guess.' She didn't sound annoyed at the request, which was a start. 'I'll have to fit it in around my shifts, so it won't be that regularly, but I'll do what I can.'

'Thanks.' He hesitated. 'Just try to make sure she's eating properly, OK? Brenda and I have made up food packages with the day and meal name on them so she can keep track easily of whether she's eaten or not, but I'm worried she might get them mixed up, or switch the box lids or something. If you wouldn't mind checking when you go in that she's up to date it would be great. We've also sorted her out with a filing system for her lists so she'll hopefully be fine with that too.'

'Great. Sounds like a plan.'

He hesitated again. There were so many things he wanted to ask her, but didn't know where to start.

'So how are things?' He mentally kicked himself. That was such an dumbass question.

There was silence on the other end of the line for a while and then Chantelle finally spoke. 'Look, Stevie, I love your mum and I'm really happy to do things for her, but you don't have to pretend you care about me because of that. Three years is a long time. You've changed. I've changed. So let's just get on with our lives and accept things the way they are.'

Wow. Talk about a put down. He had meant for his question to be a lead in to a proper conversation, but she had made it clear that she wasn't the least bit interested.

'You're right. I need to get back to work anyway. But Chaz?'

'Yeah?'

'Thanks. For caring about Mum. I really appreciate it and I'm sure she does too.'

'Yeah. Well. She's been there every day for me since my mum passed. So I'm not giving up on her now.'

This must be as hard for her as it was for him, he suddenly realised. Possibly even more, because Chantelle and Irene had worked together for years. They had become even closer when Chantelle's own mum had started to get sick.

He started to speak but it was too late; Chantelle cut him off. 'Look, I really need to go. I'm at Sarah's place and I don't get to see her that often these days. I'll keep you posted if I think your mum needs anything.'

'Sure. Sure. Thanks.' And she was gone.

Chantelle's sister eyed her as she cut the call. 'Don't tell me he's roped you into looking after her.'

Chantelle rolled her eyes. 'Don't look at me like that. I'm not looking after her, I'm just going to pop in occasionally to make sure she's OK. She's only a couple of streets away from me so it'll be easy for me to do it on my way to or from work.' Sarah said nothing, but the look on her face was one that Chantelle was very familiar with, and although she knew it came from a place of love, it still got under her skin. She reached out and put a hand on Sarah's shoulder. 'Look, you don't have to older sister me any more. I'm an adult now and I'm quite capable of running my own life. Irene's been like a mother to me, even after Stevie and I split up, and it doesn't seem right to give up on her. What he's asked me to do is no more than what I've been doing already.'

She reached out to pick up a toy train from the floor. 'Could we just enjoy our time together? I feel like I hardly see you and the kids since you and Simon moved out to Cumbernauld. I know it's only half an hour away, but sometimes it feels like it could be on the moon. Little Effie's growing so fast, and Aileen is like a proper person now she can talk.'

'I just feel like he's hurt you enough, that's all. Don't give him a chance to do it again.' Sarah swapped Effie from her breast to her shoulder and patted the baby's back gently.

'Don't worry about me.' Chantelle shrugged. 'All that's in the past. I'm married to my job now. It's all I need.'

She laughed and Sarah joined in too. 'I'm so glad you've found something that you love doing. I can't wait to get back to work either, to be honest. Kids aren't quite as stimulating as patients.'

'Yeah. Although at least the hospital work prepared you for all the messy stuff, right?' Chantelle made a face.

'Nothing prepares you for having kids. It's totally amazing and totally terrible all at the same time.'

Aileen came trailing into the room with her blanket, eyes still sleepy from her afternoon nap. Chantelle swept the three year old up and put her arms around her. 'Did you have a good sleep?'

Aileen nodded. 'I dreamed I was riding a dragon!' Her arms stretched expansively. 'Mummy, when can we get one?'

The two sisters' eyes met above her head. Chantelle's said, *have you not told her that dragons aren't real?* Sarah's stricken look showed that she hadn't yet had the courage to let her daughter down.

'You'll need to wait until you're older, sweetheart.' Chantelle ruffled Aileen's hair. 'But in the meantime, do you want to watch the film again?'

'Yay!' Aileen wriggled off her lap and went to fetch the remote control.

Chantelle knocked on the door to Irene's flat. The last few weeks she had popped in regularly and it made her remember how much she liked spending time with her. A lot of things had been disrupted in the last year or so as she had struggled to get used to her new job. Trying to maintain any sort of routine was a challenge.

'Who is it?' Irene's voice came from behind the door.

'It's Chantelle. I've got some food for you. Jules sent me over with some boxes from the takeaway.'

'Ah, lovely.' The lock clicked and Irene welcomed her in with a hug. 'How are you keeping?'

'I'm fine.' Chantelle handed her the blue plastic bag. 'Here you go. He said it's your favourite.'

Irene took it through to the kitchen. 'Let me get some money for you. Now. Where did I leave my purse?'

'I didn't pay for it.' Chantelle held up her hands. 'Jules said it was a present. For you.'

'Oh! That rascal. I told him I'm not a charity case last time. And now he sends it with you because he knows that if he turns up at the door then I'd give him the money.'

'He still likes you, Ma.' The word came out unconsciously and she bit her lip. She had purposely stopped calling Irene that the day of the split with Steven, to create the distance she needed, but being in this house brought back so many memories it seemed she was regressing to when she had lived here. She patted the rough papered wall of the kitchen gently as she thought about those times. This house had so often been full of family and friends and laughter. It seemed sad that those times were gone.

Irene either hadn't noticed Chantelle's slip, or she didn't mind. She was busy unpacking boxes. 'Well, you're going to have to stay for dinner, there's so much here. Will you do that for me? I don't like to see all this going to waste.'

Chantelle thought of her own bare fridge and how she had actually planned to make a return trip to the takeaway on her way back home. 'Not late, because I'm working an early tomorrow, but we could maybe catch an episode of something.'

'I'm binging one of those American cop shows at the moment on catchup. Are you OK with that?' Irene took some plates down from the cupboard.

Chantelle didn't mind; they were sufficiently far from the realities of her job to feel like fantasy. 'Perfect.'

They sat beside each other and Chantelle put her feet up on one of the footstools. She loved the cosiness of this living room, with its big blue sofa and the small dining table which was hardly ever used for food. 'This is great.' She looked across at Irene. 'I still really miss my mum.'

Irene paused, the remote in her hand. 'I'm not surprised. I lost mine when I was about your age and I still miss her sometimes.'

'Really? You never told me that. How did she die?'

'A heart attack. Gone in seconds, which was tough for us but I'm happy that she didn't suffer like your mum. Cancer is an evil disease.' Irene pressed more buttons then passed the remote across with a sigh. 'Could you give me a hand with this? I was hopeless with it even before I started losing my mind.'

Dementia was a pretty evil disease too, Chantelle thought, but she didn't say it aloud. It seemed almost normal, settling down for a takeaway in front of the TV. It took her back to the happy times that she had once spent on this sofa and she didn't want to spoil that feeling. She flicked through the selections and had just pressed play when there was a knock on the door. 'I'll go.' Chantelle put her plate aside and stood up. 'Are you expecting someone?'

Irene frowned. 'Pause it, won't you?' She waved a hand towards the TV. 'The first two minutes is always the most important.'

Chantelle was expecting Jehovah's Witnesses, or possibly Brenda, but when she opened the door it was Steven on the step. She felt the same blip of adrenaline that she always did when a serious call came in at work and took a breath, telling herself not to be ridiculous. Of course he would pop round to see his mum. And they would need to be friends - at least of a sort - if they were going to care for Irene properly. She waved him in, closing the door behind him. Tried to ignore the way her body reacted as he moved past her in the hallway. He still wore the same deodorant and she was thrown back to the last time they had been so close to each other, here, in this very flat. The day that she had left him. The three years she had spent living with Steven and Irene had been the happiest time of her life. But they were both different people now. Still, she could at least be civil with Steven. For Irene's sake.

'You didn't tell me he was coming over.' Chantelle settled back on the sofa, looking accusingly at her former mother-in-law.

'Oh dear. I must have forgotten. You know what my memory is like these days.' Irene looked away, but not before Chantelle caught a glint in her eyes. She had been set up. Was Irene hoping that the two of them would get back together?

'Go get yourself some food from the kitchen, Stevie.' Irene waved towards the door. 'There's more than any of us can eat. And put the kettle on for a cuppa while you're there.'

And of course Irene had engineered that Steven and Chantelle were sitting next to each other on the sofa, just like they had done when they all lived together. It was too close for comfort and she was intimately aware of the small movements he made as he sat beside her. Crime shows had never been his thing and she wondered at his tolerance for them now.

As soon as the credits rolled she got up, unable to tolerate the closeness any more. She needed to find a new man, that was the problem. Almost three years without sex was obviously making her so desperate that she was actually attracted to her ex.

'I need to get off.' She stooped and kissed Irene's cheek. 'I'll swing by later in the week.'

'So soon?' Irene looked disappointed.

'Yeah. Like I said, I've got an early shift tomorrow.' She usually hated getting up early, but this time was grateful for the excuse.

Yes. Sex. That would do her good. As she walked back to her own flat she nodded to herself. Or even a relationship, if she could find the right man. Someone thoughtful. Who would make her feel special. Maybe she should finally try internet dating. Sarah had been urging her to do it for ages and it was time to move on.

'Mm, that food was good, I've really missed it.' Steven rubbed his stomach, relishing the feeling of being slightly too full. 'Probably a good thing that I'm not here more often though, it would be a nightmare for my waistline.' Starting from scratch on his fitness after the accident had been tough and he was much more careful about his diet now.

Irene had been unusually quiet as they had washed the dishes and put them away, and when she didn't even smile at his comment he knew that something was bugging her.

He hung the tea towel back on its peg. 'Is everything alright?'

Irene leaned back against the counter and folded her arms. 'Why did you split up with Chantelle? You never talked about it at the time. Like a bear with a sore head if I ever tried to ask.'

He shoved his hands into his pockets, knowing he should have seen this coming. 'I screwed up, Mum. Lost the plot after I came out of hospital and by the time I realised it was too late.'

He shifted to put his back against the fridge, suddenly realising how tired he was. Sitting on the sofa and being in such proximity to Chantelle but knowing that he was unable to touch her had been a real test of willpower. Twice he had almost reached out to put his hand on her thigh without thinking and had only just rescued himself in time. It was being back in this flat with all its memories of the time they'd spent living here together that was screwing with his mind.

'Would you take her back if she asked you to?' Dementia was changing his mum, but not only for the worse, he realised. Before, she had avoided any direct questions. Always tried to skirt around anything serious. Never talked about her feelings. Never asked about his. He kind of liked her this straight up and open.

'In a heartbeat, Mum.' The thought made his insides twist painfully. 'I've loved her ever since the day we met.'

'You remember that far back?' Irene seemed surprised.

'Come on, I was twelve. That's almost an adult.' He was mostly serious; the situation with his parents had made him grow up fast. 'I remember the day as if it was yesterday.' The thought made him smile. 'It was just after Dad left. You remember, he walked out a few days after I started back at school that year.'

His mother sucked in a breath. 'God, that was such a difficult week. I was so relieved he was gone, but so angry he'd abandoned you that I didn't want to show you how happy I was. Also, I was terrified that he might be coming back. He'd left us before a few times when you were much younger, although he was usually back within a few days.'

His dad had not been shy with his fists, especially after an evening in the pub. It hadn't all been one-sided though, his mother had given as good as she got sometimes. He still remembered one particularly nasty incident with a frying pan that had left his dad reeling. 'I was relieved too, Mum. But still angry at him. I skived off school that day and went to hide at the back of the playing fields. And found Chaz doing the same. Except her dad had left for a different reason.'

Chantelle's grief at the death of her father had put his own situation into perspective and for the twelve year old

Steven the thought that his dad was not totally gone had been a small comfort. They had been inseparable since that day, even though some of his classmates had mocked him for being friends with a girl.

'It's sad, both her parents dying so young.' Irene put the glass in the cupboard. 'I guess at least she still has her sister.'

He felt an accusation in the words that was probably only in his head. 'There's nothing I can do, Mum. The past is the past and we can't go back. She's made it clear that she doesn't think of me that way any more.' He leaned across and kissed Irene on the cheek. 'I'd better get off, I've got work in the morning. I'll see you soon.'

Chapter 4

Steven came out of his bedroom, feeling a bit self-conscious in his new orange shirt. It was the first time they'd got their walking group of friends together for a while and he was excited about it. The excuse was Nick finally passing his minibus driving test, but they were well overdue in any case. He needed something to look forward to these days; although Christmas and New Year had been an unexpectedly joyous time of family celebration then his mum's behaviour had grown ever more challenging over the last couple of months and it would do him good to take his mind off things for a few hours.

He was surprised to find Jade curled up on the sofa in her pyjamas. 'You not coming?'

She shook her head. 'Didn't want to spoil your bros night out. I know how much you get on with Sean and Pete and you haven't seen them for ages.'

He frowned at her. 'That's not like you.'

Her forehead crinkled slightly. 'Well, since I've moved in with you guys I don't want Nick to feel like I'm crowding him out. I want him to know I don't always have to be around.'

Steven laughed at the ridiculousness of her fears. 'Just the other day he was complaining for the gazillionth time that you're spending so much time on that bloody book he never gets a look in. And Pete's bringing David, so if you want to make a WAGS - sorry, WAPS - splinter group when we're there then you can do that.'

'It's fine. I got another round of comments back from my editor last week and there's so much to do...' Her voice trailed off and she looked at him with a small smile. 'I'll go and get some proper clothes on then.' She stood up and punched his shoulder gently. 'Thanks, Stevie.' Heading towards her bedroom she stopped and grinned at him. 'You said WAPS. Is that really a thing? Because I so want it to be a thing.'

The evening started well, but a couple of hours later Steven was staring glumly into his empty pint glass. 'I think I'm going to have to move in with my mum.'

Nick rested his elbows on the table. 'I thought you'd sorted out care for her? Is it not working out?'

'They've given her disability benefit, but apparently things aren't bad enough yet for her to qualify for carers.' Steven rubbed his face with his hands. 'The last two months with Brenda and Chantelle and myself all pitching in it's kind of been working. But Brenda said she found her sitting out in the garden last night in her jammies, had to take her back to bed. Apparently Mum said she was out for a cigarette, but she hasn't smoked in years.'

There was silence while the others digested the news and he could see they were all wondering what to say.

'Couldn't you ask the council for a place in a care home?' Pete drummed his fingers on the table. 'I know it sounds a bit cruel, but might it be better for everyone? Some of them are great.'

'Not sure if that's really an option. Brenda said she knows a couple of people who are in our local one and the reports aren't good at all. I know Jade speaks very highly of Sunnyside but that's miles away in Clydebank. I can't rip her out of the community she's lived in most of her life.' Steven turned to Nick. 'The only thing is, that means you'd be left looking for a flatmate.'

Nick ran a finger inside his collar, looking slightly embarrassed. 'Jade and I have liked living together so much we've been talking about maybe getting a place of our own. We didn't want to bring it up because we thought you had enough on your plate, and also with starting up the business I was wondering if we should take on the risk, but if that's the way things are going we'll just go for it. So it could all work out.'

'OK. So it's settled.' Steven stood up. 'I'm buying the next round.'

'I'll come with you, carry the drinks.' Pete rose to go with him.

The pub was busy and the line at the bar was a couple deep. 'Are you sure you want to do this?' Pete spoke quietly into Steven's ear, his eyes keeping watch for their turn to be served. Steven had known Pete for a long time and he had always been the voice of reason to Steven's lust for adventure. 'It's a big commitment. You've already got work, and you've got loads of stuff coming up over the summer. Is it not going to all be too much?'

Steven shrugged. 'I don't know. But I don't really see that I've got a choice. I refuse to put her in a place where she won't be treated like a human being. Maybe later, if I really can't cope, but otherwise I just need to try my best. I'll give you a shout if things get too much.'

'Yeah. With all of us pulling together I'm sure we'll manage.'

'I appreciate your offer. The problem is, she's pretty suspicious of new people. She's already refused to open the door to the cleaner once because she didn't remember who the woman was. I had to pin up a photo of all of them right by the door so that Mum can take a look at it and double-check.'

He felt Pete squeeze his shoulder gently. 'Put our photos up by the door too and we'll all drop in to see her regularly. Even if you're there, it will take the weight off you sometimes. Are you sure she won't lose her benefits from you moving in?'

'No, I've checked, so I'm holding my breath on that. But even if we do I think I'll still be able to manage. The rent on her council flat is less than what I'm paying for half of the one I'm sharing with Nick and Jade.' Steven was still scanning the bar and saw one of the staff nodding at him. 'Come on, we're up. Let's forget about this for now and enjoy our night out.'

Things were never like people thought they would be, Steven reflected three weeks later. The general thought was that when you moved back in with your mum you would be having home cooking and your laundry done and all that sort of stuff. The reality was so different. Not that she didn't try, but she had always seemed to have a gift for being able to turn even the most delicious ingredients into something bland and tasteless and dementia seemed to make her choice of ingredients even more erratic. Curry powder in a fruit salad hadn't actually been that bad. But when she managed to shrink his favourite jumper the day after ironing one of his cycling jerseys into oblivion, he realised he had to say something.

'You need to stop this, Mum.' They were sitting on the sofa with breakfast TV turned low in the background, while the reporter talked about how China was dealing with an epidemic of some new virus. It was depressing news at best and Steven was glad to be able to drag his mind away from it.

'Stop what?' Irene looked at him with puzzlement on her face as if she thought he meant watching the TV.

'Stop doing this.' He waved a hand towards the kitchen. 'Trying to cook. Doing my laundry. Doing my ironing. I'll have no clothes left if you carry on like that.'

She held up her hands. 'I'm sorry about that, Stevie. I'll buy you new ones.'

'It's not about the clothes, Mum.' Well, it was, but admitting to that would make him feel petty and small. What sort of man shed tears over the loss of a jumper? Even if it was the one that Chantelle had bought him on their honeymoon? 'I just feel, I don't know, a bit crowded. Moving back in with my mum at twenty-six is not what I expected to be doing. I'm a grown man now. I'm used to doing my own laundry and cooking my own food.'

'But I want to take care of you.'

'I don't need anyone to take care of me. Besides, you never did all that when I was here before. Your cooking was always terrible. Sorry, Mum, but it has to be said. You have many talents, but cooking is not one of them. And ironing too. I remember you burned Dad's shirts on more than one occasion.'

'That might not have always been an accident.' Irene sounded half embarrassed and half triumphant.

Steven looked at her speechless for a few moments and then started to laugh, all his irritation gone in an instant. 'Well, bugger me.' He leaned over and gave her a kiss on the cheek. 'I love you so much.' Then he put a hand on her shoulder. 'But I'm still better at ironing than you. You need to leave me to it and find something else to do.'

'I'm going stir crazy sitting in here. I need to do something.' To anyone else her voice would have sounded petulant, but Steven knew her well enough to hear the undercurrent of fear.

'So get out and do something. Go for a walk. I'm not stopping you.'

'What happens if I get lost and can't find my way back? I don't want to be that person, Stevie. The woman with dementia who gets brought back home by the police. I couldn't stand the shame.' Her eyes were wet now and Steven felt a bit guilty for pushing her so far. Still, these were conversations that needed to be had and they should have been through this ages ago. The thought only added more guilt to his plate. He was good at dealing with his mum when she was cold or angry at him. But this more emotional version of her, the more raw, real person, threw him off.

'I can program your phone so that it always shows you how to get home, Mum.' Steven offered up a small prayer of thanks for modern technology. 'Then you'll never get lost. Unless you lose your phone. Then I really can't help you.'

'Don't be cheeky, Stevie, or I'll take my hand to your behind like I did that time you were caught stealing apples from the churchyard.' She raised an eyebrow, her eyes glinting with humour. It had been the only time she had ever walloped him, while at the same time giving him a stern lecture about not taking other people's stuff. At eight years old it had left a strong impression on him.

Steven snorted, relief flooding him about the upbeat turn in the conversation. 'You wish. I'd like to see you try it.'

They stared at each other for a few seconds and then both dissolved into laughter. 'Oh Stevie, I don't know what I'd do without you.' Irene sat back into the cushions. 'But I do need to do something with my time. Otherwise I will go crazy.'

'Ask Brenda to take you along to help out in the food bank. I'm sure they'll be glad of an extra pair of hands.' Steven didn't know where that idea had come from, but he thanked his brain for coming up with it.

'Are you sure they'll want me?' Irene's tone was uncertain again.

'Of course they'll want you, Mum. They'll be rushed off their feet right now. It's February and it's cold. People are having to choose between heating their houses and feeding their kids. In fact,' he checked his watch, 'why don't you go and talk to her now? Or write it down on your list to do later. I need to get off to work.'

Irene was already scribbling in the little black notebook that never left her side. 'I'll leave it a bit in case she's still asleep. I used to know all her shifts off by heart but I've lost track of them now. It's a great idea. Thanks, love.'

He grabbed his bag from next to the door and then came back to kiss her on the cheek. 'You want me to do your phone thing now?'

She looked up at him with a joy on her face that he realised he hadn't seen for a very long time. 'Would you? I've been longing to go up to the woods.'

Chantelle eased herself slowly onto the sofa with a cup of tea, her face aching. That guy had really managed to give her nose a good bash before they had got a proper hold of him. The girlfriend hadn't been too happy either, screeching blue murder out of an upstairs window, but luckily she hadn't tried walloping them too. Chantelle's only consolation was that the guy would now not only be charged with intent to supply drugs, but also for assaulting a police officer. She touched her nose gingerly and winced, then instantly regretted moving her face. Yes, not broken but definitely painful. She'd probably have two black eyes in the morning. No doubt her colleagues would waste no time before starting on the panda jokes once she got back into work.

She sat for a while, reviewing what had happened and trying to work out if she could have done any better. This was an important part of her probationary training; reflecting on how she could improve and making sure she didn't make the same mistakes twice. She was determined to pass her final assessment and migrate to being a full police officer. The alternative was unthinkable. There was no job she wanted to do more.

Her mobile rang and she groaned, realising she'd left it in the kitchen. For a couple of seconds she considered leaving it, but she needed to sort out some food anyway before she crashed into bed. Careful not to bend over, she got up and padded in to get it.

Her heart leaped when she saw it was Steven. *Don't be ridiculous. Chill out.* Much to her dismay she was starting to behave like a lovesick teenager.

She swiped the screen. 'Yo. You alright?'

'Not really.' Steven's voice sounded strained on the other end. 'Are you busy?'

'Depends on your definition. Is something wrong?' She closed her eyes and prayed that it wasn't.

'Mum slipped when she was getting out the shower and she can't get up. I can't get her up either.'

Chantelle stifled a sigh. He wouldn't ring her unless he was really in a bind. 'Have you used that lift technique I showed you?'

'I've tried, but the angle she's fallen at is all wrong. With my gammy leg I can't get the leverage.' Steven sounded more angry than worried and she wasn't surprised. He would be raging at how his disability was holding him up.

'What about Brenda?' As soon as the words were out of her mouth she knew they were useless; the neighbour would have been the first one for Steven to call.

'Gone up to visit her sister in Oban. Won't be back until Monday.' A frustrated sigh came down the line. 'Really sorry to call you like this but you're the only one I know of that she wouldn't mind seeing her in this state.'

'Just gimme ten minutes and I'll be there. I have to put some real clothes back on.' With a sigh of her own Chantelle disconnected and walked into the bedroom.

She only bumped her nose once while changing which was definitely a win, but she made sure to swipe a couple of painkillers before she went out the door in the hope that it would ease the dull throb.

Steven must have been waiting behind his front door, because it opened as soon as she knocked.

'Hey.' He looked her up and down and she instantly remembered her earlier comment about the clothes. Had he thought she was naked? That was something she didn't want to think about.

'So what exactly happened?' She followed him inside, shrugging off her coat and hanging it on a peg.

'She was having a shower when she slipped and fell. She says her hip's painful but it doesn't feel like it's broken. And the same for her wrist. But painful enough she can't push herself up or get herself out of the bath. I've tried to help but the angle she fell at is really weird and I can't get a good purchase.' His t-shirt was wet, as if he had been rolling around in water. She pushed those thoughts from her mind as she followed him to the bathroom. 'How long ago did this happen?'

'About half an hour. I've covered her with a couple of towels so she doesn't get cold and she says she's fine, but I can tell she's embarrassed.'

He turned to face her and as he did so he recoiled in surprise, seeing her in proper light for the first time. 'Fuck me. What happened to your face?'

Damn. The bruising must be starting to come out. 'Someone caught a swing at me this afternoon.'

He put out a hand as if he was going to touch it and she reached up to fend him off. 'Don't. It's fine. But if you come anywhere near it I may have to kill you.'

He stared at her for one more second and then seemed to remember why she was there. 'Come on. I'm hoping with both of us we can somehow get her out.'

'Hello, Mrs M.' Chantelle tried to inject some humour into her tone as she surveyed the carnage in the bathroom. 'Been practising your freestyle diving again?' Steven was right; with the tiny size of the room this was going to be a real challenge. Irene had fallen with her head towards the taps - how she hadn't cracked her skull open on them was a real miracle - but she was trapped behind the fixed shower screen and there was no way to grab hold of her without actually physically being in the bath. Unless they dragged her out by her feet, but that would take a lot of strength too. No wonder Steven hadn't been able to manage.

'Hello love.' Irene was also attempting to stay cheerful but Chantelle could see that she was almost more frustrated than Steven, if that was possible. 'Sorry to be such a bother at this time of night.'

'Don't you worry.' Chantelle bent down without thinking to move the bath mat out of the way and gasped as stars seemed to explode in front of her eyes. She quickly sat down on the toilet lid, hands flapping around her face as she waited for the throbbing to subside slightly. As she surveyed the scene, with Steven hovering anxiously in the doorway, she found herself starting to giggle.

'What the hell is so funny?' Steven glared at her.

Chantelle waved a hand in his general direction. 'Aren't we a right sight? She can't stand up,' she pointed at Irene, 'and I can't bend down. And you,' she went off into another wave of laughter, 'you can't do either.'

There was a titter from beside her as Irene saw the funny side of the situation too, and soon Steven's deeper laughter joined them. That set Chantelle off again, and it was a good few minutes before she could pull herself together.

'Right, enough of that. Let's get practical about this.' Chantelle pulled a wad of toilet roll off the holder and cautiously dabbed at her eyes. 'There's no way Stevie and I are going to be able to get you out of there, not with the state that I'm in tonight. We've got to call the fire brigade.'

'Oh Chantelle. Really? The whole street will be laughing at me.' Irene's face looked suddenly pained. 'Is there nothing you can do?'

Chantelle reconsidered the situation. 'We could try filling the bath, see if it would lift you up a bit. It'll take a while, but it might be our best option. It will also let me check you're not too badly injured before we get you out.'

'Let's do it.' Irene sounded very relieved. 'I don't mind how long it takes.'

'Stevie, why don't you go make us all a cuppa while we're waiting?' Anything to stop him worrying.

He disappeared thankfully. The bath filled quicker than Chantelle expected, and as she had hoped the extra buoyancy gave them the help they needed. After a quick check to make sure that nothing was too badly damaged, she and Steven managed to slide Irene into a sitting position on the edge of the bath and from there helped her hobble as far as the living room. It was not without some effort though; by the time they had finished Chantelle's front was dripping wet and she wished she had thought to bring a change of clothes. The bitter February wind would rip right through her. She sat on a stool and sipped at her tea slowly. Maybe if she postponed the trip back for a few minutes it would give her a bit of a chance to dry off.

It was as if Steven had heard her thoughts because he pointed into his bedroom. 'Go take some of my clothes. You can't walk back like that in this weather.'

'We've got to decide what to do about Irene first.' Chantelle was too busy prioritising.

'You may have hauled me out of that bath like a sack of potatoes, but don't talk about me as if I'm an object.' Irene wagged a finger at her. 'I'm fine. The only thing really damaged is my pride. And yes,' she added, as Chantelle opened her mouth again, 'I do promise to go to the hospital tomorrow if anything doesn't feel right.'

There wasn't much else she could say to that. 'Yes ma'am.' Chantelle saluted her theatrically and stood up to go into the bedroom. She had braced herself for the fact that any clothes she borrowed off Steven would smell of him, but she hadn't expected the room to look so much like it had when they had shared it together. All of her stuff was gone, of course, but the furniture was the same and the bed cover was the one she had left for him, if slightly more faded than she remembered. Taking a deep breath, she crossed to the cupboards. Even her socks had been soaked. She was going to need a full change of clothes, although she could probably get away with keeping her underwear on.

It didn't take her long to find a sweatshirt and some joggers that must have been long on Steven because they fit her almost perfectly. That would do to see her back to her flat. But she couldn't seem to find a new pair of socks. She perched on the edge of the bed, conscious of what had happened last time she tried to bend down, but when she opened the top drawer of the bedside table she was startled to find her own face staring back at her.

Chapter 5

Chantelle looked at the photo for a couple of seconds and then lifted it out. She remembered this one well; she had lovingly stuck a copy of it into their wedding album, which was still sitting in a box at her place because she hadn't had the courage to throw out something that was so much part of her history. This photo had been taken on their wedding day, but wasn't a formal pose at all. The photographer had managed to snap them when they thought they were between shots, and the way that they were looking at each other still took her breath away.

The wedding had been small - they hadn't been able to afford anything else - but they had booked a function room in a hotel for the reception and Jules had done the food at cost price. The day had been mainly grey but an unexpected break in the clouds had given them the opportunity to take photos in the hotel garden. Everyone had teased them about the way that she was taller than Steven, and she had jokingly picked him up for a comedy pose. The photographer had caught them just as Chantelle had set Steven back on his feet and they were looking at each other and laughing.

She traced one finger gently down the bride's veil and stroked her cheek. Six years ago. It was hard to believe that she was the same person as that twenty year old woman. Although really, she wasn't. Too much had happened since then. But it seemed a strange place to keep it, right next to the bed like that. Was it just in there because he couldn't find a better place to put it? Or did the location mean something?

There was a gentle tap on the door and she shoved the frame back and pushed the drawer closed with a bang, rising from the bed guiltily.

'Are you OK?' That was Steven's voice.

'Yeah.' She went to the door and opened it. 'Just can't find any socks.'

'Oh.' He looked down at her bare feet for a second, then stepped past her and went to the bedside table. 'Bottom drawer in here. I ran out of room in the cupboard.'

'You always did like your clothes.' It was true; when they had been together she had been the one wearing the same jumper for a week while Steven always made sure he had a freshly pressed shirt every day.

'Yeah, well.' Steven shrugged. It had been something she had managed to tease him about back in the day, but tonight it looked like he wasn't going to take the bait.

'It was a joke.' She went to poke him in the ribs, but then realised that it was a mistake to get so close to him. The world sort of disappeared, and she found herself getting closer, and then...

Chantelle jerked away, grabbing the socks he held in his hand to save her from doing something stupid. With any luck he wouldn't have noticed her weird behaviour. 'Thanks.' She retreated into the living room and sat down next to Irene to put them on.

'Oh, there you are.' Irene gave her a big smile. 'I wondered where you were.' Her gaze focused on Chantelle's outfit. 'Isn't that Stevie's sweatshirt? Why are you wearing it?'

'My clothes got wet, Ma. When we dragged you out of the bath.' All this was too much for Chantelle. First her nose, then the tribulations in the bathroom, and now a reminder that the woman she loved was in difficulties. 'I need to go.' She did, before she broke down, and this was for real. She couldn't afford to cry, in a very practical sense, because blowing her nose in the state that it was would be murder. She shoved on her shoes and grabbed her jacket from its peg by the door, blowing a kiss at Irene. 'I'll see you soon.'

The cold air cleared her head as she walked home, and though a couple of tears did drip down her face she managed to stave off a full-blown attack of the weepies. Enough was enough. She would carefully engineer that Steven was out when she visited Irene in future and she would sign up to that dating website tomorrow. But in the weeks that followed she couldn't bring herself to even install the app on her phone. And she couldn't help wondering about the wedding photo.

It was Thursday evening and Steven was at the supermarket, trying to decide what to buy. He would be spending the whole weekend with his mum and he wanted to make it feel special. Jamie and Nick were going to be away with their first set of holiday-makers but it was a small group so there was no point all three of them going. They had drawn lots and Steven had lost. Still, word had got around already and they had a good number of trips booked after Easter. He was going to have to speak to Brenda soon to work out a strategy to cover those dates. Irene wasn't getting any better and her bad days were getting worse. Just yesterday she had called him by his dad's name, although she had corrected herself immediately, horror in her eyes.

His phone ringing interrupted his thoughts and he pulled it out; it was Nick's name on the screen. 'Hey. Everything OK?'

'Where are you?' Nick sounded slightly worried.

'I'm in the supermarket. Trying to decide if it's worth paying extra for proper parmesan.' He snorted. 'Can you believe it? This is my life now. Debating over the merits of various cheeses. I mean, would-'

'We've got a crisis, Stevie.' Nick interrupted him. 'Jamie's ill.'

'Woah, woah. Wait a minute. That can't be right. Jamie's never ill.' It was true, possibly because the guy spent so much time outside. 'What happened?'

'He says he's got some sort of stomach bug. He swears he'll feel better by tomorrow but I just don't know. Two out of the three have health conditions where any kind of gastric issues would cause them serious problems. I haven't seen him since last weekend, so I'm pretty confident I'm not infectious. We've still got the ski instructors lined up for the Saturday morning but I can't do all the rest on my own. We really need two people. I'm wondering if we should cancel.'

'Oh shit. No. We can't cancel.' Steven picked up a packet of cheese in his hand and put it back, then realised a woman was staring at him. He really shouldn't be fondling the cheese if he didn't mean to buy it. Or perhaps it was because he was talking loudly into his phone.

He retreated around the corner of the aisle, taking refuge near some cut-price cereal. 'We can't cancel. We've already paid for the accommodation Saturday night and there's no way we'll get it back at such short notice. That stuff isn't cheap.' He rubbed his eyes tiredly. 'Why is this happening to me? It feels like the universe hates me or something.'

'I'm sorry.' Nick's voice was suddenly weary too. 'I know this was meant to be the start of all our hopes and dreams. But the only way we can do it is to find someone else who knows how all the equipment works. Are you sure you can't come?'

'I can't, Nick. It's dangerous to leave Mum overnight these days. She keeps leaving the gas cooker on and stuff like that.' He wished it wasn't true, but he had to face up to the facts. Life as a carer meant making tough choices.

Nick was silent for a few moments, then he blew out a frustrated breath. 'It's shit timing with the other guys being down in London. Can't you ask Brenda to keep an eye on her?'

'She's working all weekend too.'

'What about Jules?' Steven could tell Nick knew he was clutching at straws.

'Friday and Saturday nights are his busiest times. He often doesn't finish until way after midnight.' He did know someone a lot closer to home who had the weekend off. Who would probably say yes if he asked her really nicely. He tried to push that thought from his mind, but it kept coming back. He so did not want to ask his ex-wife to give up the weekend she'd planned to spend with Sarah and the kids. Not when she'd said she hadn't seen them in ages.

'Do you have any ideas?' Nick was still on the other end of the line. 'Because if not I need to get on with phoning round people and giving them the bad news. And get used to the fact that we've thrown four hundred quid down the drain.'

Steven groaned, because he knew what he was going to do. Even though he shouldn't. 'Don't cancel. I might have an idea.' He knew it wouldn't really help, but he still bought some flowers.

Chantelle was surprised when she heard the doorbell ring. She looked out of the window to see Steven standing on the doorstep. Not only that, he was holding a big bunch of pink roses. Her curiosity spiked and she pressed the button to let him in.

He appeared in her doorway, looking slightly shame-faced. 'These are for you. Because I need a favour.'

She took the flowers automatically, then looked at his face, instantly working out what he meant. 'Oh no. Not happening. So not happening. You can't ask me to do that.'

'Please, Chaz. Jamie's ill. I need to go up to Glencoe this weekend. Otherwise we'll have to cancel the whole thing.'

'No no no.' She held up a palm towards his face. 'Don't do this to me. This is going to be my weekend with my family. Simon's looking after the kids on Saturday afternoon while Sarah and I go to the spa. Do you know how long it is since I got a massage? I mean, do you?'

She was angry at him for even asking her. She had told him what her plans were for the weekend and she was supposed to be relaxing. Much as she loved Irene, looking after her was not relaxing. And her anger increased when she realised that she felt guilty for refusing. 'Fuck you, Steven, for even asking. Piss off and leave me alone.' She felt bad about the words as soon as they were out of her mouth, but being harsh was the only way she could think of to push him away. 'Don't look at me with those sad pleading eyes of yours, trying to make me feel guilty. I have a right to take some time for myself.'

He nodded. 'You're right. It was wrong of me even to ask. I'm sorry.' And before she could reply he was gone. It was only then that she realised she was still holding the flowers and she went to fling them down onto the kitchen sideboard in disgust.

Still fuming, she called Sarah to have a rant. 'Do you know what Steven just did?'

'What did he just do?' She could hear the humour in Sarah's voice at her lack of a greeting.

'He's had some sort of crisis and came round to ask me if I could take care of Irene for the weekend while he's away. I told him to fuck off. This is our weekend and I won't let anyone spoil it.'

'He came round?' Sarah sounded...wait. Did she sound impressed?

'Yeah. With flowers. Can you imagine?' Chantelle was still disgusted about the way that he had tried to bribe her. She wasn't even really a flower person. Although she did have to admit the pink roses looked pretty gorgeous.

'With flowers? How terrible. Was it a big bunch?' Sarah was definitely making fun of her now.

'Yeah, a pretty big bunch, yeah.' Chantelle found herself fondling the petals of one of the roses and she jerked her hand away as if she had been burned. 'But that's not the point.'

'I could ring the spa and see if they could add another one.' Sarah's voice was thoughtful.

'You...wait. Are you honestly saying we should accommodate him?' Chantelle was confused. Was her sister sticking up for Steven? 'I thought you hated him.'

'I don't hate him. I'm pissed off that he obviously doesn't value you, but it wouldn't hurt to give Irene a bit of a good time.'

'What about our day trip on Sunday? I thought we were going out to Loch Lomond?' Chantelle was trying to get her brain into gear.

'I was already planning to ring you about that. I'm not sure the weather on Sunday is that great and I was going to suggest we scrap going out for board games at home. But we could bring them over to Irene's and play there. Her living room is bigger than ours.'

'But...' Chantelle could feel her brain trying to catch up with itself. 'Are you sure you're OK with that?'

'Look, you're family. And from what you've said about Irene, it's clear that she's family to you too. So if making a few small changes to our plans will put a shedload of good karma back into this screwed up world, then I'm happy to do that. Because I love you.'

Chantelle felt her heart swell with affection for her sister. 'Thanks, babe. I love you too.'

'I'll leave you to go and call Steven and I'll let you know once I've checked everything with the spa. Oh, and one more thing?'

'Yes?'

'Make sure you cash that favour in later on down the line.' Sarah laughed and hung up.

Steven hefted his green rucksack into the boot of the car.

'Is that the last one?' Nick stood up from where he had been trying to rearrange things in the back so he could see out of the rear view mirror. He stretched his back out with a groan.

'Aye.' Steven nodded. 'I never thought that there'd be so much shit to cart around. I'm glad we're renting skis and stuff up in Glencoe, otherwise we'd never get it all in.'

'I feel exhausted already.' Nick slammed the boot firmly closed. 'Trying to rejig this weekend to work without Jamie has been a nightmare.'

'Yeah, if it hadn't been for Sean lending us his car we would have been screwed.' Steven patted the top of the vehicle fondly. 'And that friend of your dad bringing down the tuffchairs in their van. What is it, his mate's cousin's wife's sister or something?'

Nick laughed. 'I lost track. The important thing is that it'll be done. And we're going to have a great weekend.' He paused. 'Tuffchairs. That's not a bad name for them. Did you come up with that?'

Steven grinned. 'I got tired of calling them rugged wheelchairs, it's a bit of a mouthful. But Mum might have said it first.'

'How is she?'

'Don't ask.' Steven waved a hand at him. 'You're only going to bring all the guilt back about leaving her with Chantelle this weekend.' He pulled open the passenger door roughly. 'Time to go and get this over with. Forecast says heavy snow on higher ground this evening, so we'd best be getting up there in case the roads get difficult. Sean's not got winter tyres on this thing.'

Nick settled himself into the driver's seat. 'You're right. But can you try to enjoy this too? Because this could be the beginning of the rest of our lives, and I want to make sure we have fun.'

'You're right.' Some of the ever-present tension in Steven's shoulders fell away. 'Let's get this show on the road.'

They were just reaching Crianlarich when large fat snowflakes began to fall.

'You know what this means?' Nick grinned sideways at Steven.

Steven felt his mouth lifting to match. 'Tomorrow's skiing is going to be awesome?'

'Bang on.' Nick thumped the steering wheel excitedly.

'I'm still worried about my endurance levels.' Steven bit his lip. 'You know I've been practising in the snowdome, but I've not done an all day session yet. I'm worried about how I'll hold up.'

'Don't.' Nick reached over and squeezed his shoulder gently. 'We are kind of spurious tomorrow with the instructors being there, so once we've got everyone sorted we can always leave you in the café for a bit while we carry on.'

'That's true.' Steven smiled gratefully at him. 'Spurious? That's a fancy word. I think Jade's rubbing off on you.'

Nick rolled his eyes. 'Thank fuck her swearing isn't rubbing off on me too.'

Laughter filled the car from both of them and Steven poked Nick gently in the shoulder. 'Very funny.'

'At your service.' Nick flashed him another wide smile.

There was a thick layer of white on the ground by the time they reached the car park at the ski centre. Steven put his prosthetic back on and got out of the car, careful not to slip on the ice. 'Are we getting this lot into the pod first, or should we go for something to eat?'

'I vote food first. I'm starving.' Nick shut the driver's door. He checked his watch. 'And they might stop serving soon.'

The cafe was busier than Steven had expected with it being so cold, but he realised a lot of the people would have seen the weather forecast too.

'It's going to be packed on the slopes tomorrow.' He nudged Nick as he spotted a couple vacating two tall bar stools in one corner. 'I'll go grab those. Get me a burger or something. And lots of chips.'

'Aye aye, captain.' Nick disappeared towards the food counter.

He was back in a couple of minutes with a box of cutlery and sauces, paper ticket clutched in his other hand. 'They said they'll call our number when it's ready.' He perched himself on the other stool. 'So how does it feel?'

'How does what feel?' Steven had been watching another couple in one of the comfy sofas by the fire. They looked so happy together it sent a pang of loneliness through him. Then he gave himself a mental shake. He was here on the side of a mountain with one of his best friends and the weather was supposed to be glorious tomorrow. How could life get better than this?

Nick had noticed the focus of Steven's gaze. 'It's nice to see two people who are so obviously comfortable with each other.'

'You mean unlike me and Chantelle?' Steven couldn't help bitterness creeping into his tone.

Nick flushed. 'I didn't mean that at all. Sorry. It wasn't a dig at you.'

Steven slapped himself gently on the cheek. 'No, I'm sorry. I'm making this about me when it really isn't. I'm just finding all of this a bit hard to deal with, really. I honestly thought I'd managed to move on from my marriage and everything that happened surrounding my accident, but I was clearly delusional.'

'I think trauma works like that, though.' Nick leaned an elbow on the counter next to them. 'I was talking to Nadeem when he was here at New Year and he said that helping Jenny through what happened to her also brought back things for him. And I know being around me was sometimes hard for Jade after everything that went on with her sister. So all you can do is give space to this stuff and be kind to yourself.'

'Kindness. Aye.' Steven smiled at Nick. 'You're very wise for your twenty-four years.'

'I've grown a lot in the last couple of years, but I can't say I have all the answers.' Nick shrugged. 'Although I've decided it's my mission to enjoy life as much as possible. If you don't know how long you've got then why waste it?' He turned his head. 'And speaking of that, our number's up. I got us the special venison burgers with extra chips.'

'Magic.' Steven flexed his fingers together, feeling a bubble of excitement finally flow through him. 'Bring it on.'

Chapter 6

Chantelle eased herself into the hot tub beside Irene and reached for her plastic champagne glass. 'Oh, this is wonderful.' She took a sip. 'Where's Sarah?'

A hand tagged her on the shoulder. 'Right behind you. Are you going to make some space for me?'

'Don't be ridiculous, there's plenty.' But Chantelle scooted over a little bit closer to Irene, to give the couple across from them a bit of clearance.

Sarah sploshed in beside her. 'That massage was heavenly. Tell me why I don't do it more often.'

'Because we'd all be bankrupt before we know it. It was pretty amazing though.' Chantelle looked over at Irene. 'Sorry we couldn't get you one, but all the slots were gone.'

Irene shook her head. 'I'm happy with my pedicure, and the nice woman also gave me a bit of a foot massage, so I didn't totally miss out. She offered to paint my toenails for me when we're done in the pool, but I didn't see the point when it's the middle of winter. Who's going to see them apart from me?'

'Steven will see them, now that he's living with you.' Sarah had a wicked glint in her eye. 'And anyone else you bring home for a night of wild lustful sex.'

'Sarah!' Chantelle jabbed her sister in the ribs, but Irene was laughing.

'Not much chance of that, I'm afraid. I think those days are behind me now.'

'Sorry.' Sarah rolled her eyes. 'I seem to have sex on the brain at the moment. Maybe it's because I'm not really getting any.'

'Nothing wrong between you and Simon, is there?' Chantelle frowned.

'No, we're all good really.' Sarah sighed. 'It's partly having two small kids, by the time we get them to sleep we're so exhausted that all we can do is crash out on the sofa. But it's not just that.' She bit her bottom lip. 'I know that it was months ago, but since Effie was born I can't help feeling that something feels different down there, in a way that it didn't after Aileen.'

'Well, it was a caesarian this time, so I wouldn't be surprised.' Chantelle nudged her sister gently with her shoulder. 'And sex isn't only about the obvious, you know. Just touching places can feel pretty nice.'

Sarah leaned closer to murmur in her ear, aware that the couple across from them was now listening to every word. 'I know. It's just that one of my favourite places for Simon to touch was my boobs, and since I've had the kids sucking on them for hours on end that doesn't feel the same either.'

'OK, that's definitely TMI.' Chantelle smiled at Sarah to make sure she knew it was a joke. 'It sounds like what you both need is some proper alone time, so you can find out what you both still like.'

'I'd be happy to look after the kids for a few hours one afternoon.' Irene spoke over the noise of the bubbles. Then her face fell. 'What am I talking about? I can barely look after myself these days, let alone two kids.'

Chantelle looked briefly at Sarah and saw her nod slightly. 'That's a great idea, Ma. I'll help you out and we can take them somewhere nice.' She reached unseen in the water and found Sarah's hand, squeezed it in thanks. Then, tired of the emotion swirling round in the air, she decided to have some fun and raised her voice. 'What you need to spice up your life is a couple of sex toys. That vibrating butt plug Tania bought me last week is sensational.' Chantelle watched as the face of the woman opposite changed from avid interest to sudden horror and she climbed quickly out of the pool, muttering something to her partner, who followed soon afterwards.

'Butt plug?' Sarah looked at her. 'And who the fuck is Tania?'

Chantelle stretched out her legs across the hot tub. 'Just thought I'd create a bit more space in here. They had entirely too much interest in your sex life.'

'Too bloody right. Tania would be horrified.' Irene's comment set them all laughing.

'You are evil.' Sarah smiled at Chantelle. 'What would you have done if they'd asked you for a recommendation?'

'Ran a mile, probably.' Chantelle drained her glass and set it on the side. 'Shame I'll never know if their aversion was to the sex toys itself, or the idea that I might be a lesbian.'

'You're not, are you?' Sarah's tone was curious. 'Now that you've said it, I don't think we've ever discussed that sort of thing.'

'Well, obviously not a lesbian, based on past history, but bisexual? I don't know.' Chantelle shrugged. 'I'd always assumed I was entirely straight as I was never attracted to women, but then there is one of my female colleagues I have kind of got a crush on. But I think it's more because she's incredibly kind and good at her job and I sort of want to be her, or be with her, rather than actually sleep with her, so I don't believe it counts. You know that sort of person who being around just feels like coming home? Like a warm comforting blanket that will always be there for you.'

'I feel that way about you, babe.' Sarah's gaze was serious now.

'Oh, stop it.' Chantelle pushed her away gently.

'No, I mean it.' Sarah grasped her by the shoulders so she couldn't look away. 'You have this presence about you. And you're kind, and funny, and you're always there for the people that you love.'

'Too right.' Irene chimed in.

'Thanks, babe.' Chantelle kissed her sister gently on the cheek. 'I love you.'

'I love you too.' Sarah's eyes were bright. 'And we should do this more often. Not the spa, of course, because like you said, we've got to eat once in a while, but spending time together, just us girls. I've missed that since the kids have come along.'

'It's a deal. Although an afternoon alone for you and Simon is definitely first on the priority list.'

'OK.' Sarah leaned back and reached for her own glass. 'I wonder if he might actually like a vibrating butt plug?'

'Well, that's for you to ask him.' Chantelle shrugged. 'Although, do me a favour?'

'Yeah?'

'I definitely don't want to know the answer to that.'

The three women's laughter pealed around the room as they lay back in the tub.

Steven fumbled with the door key, his fingers numb with cold as the freezing rain pattered down on his jacket. The last two days had been great, despite the biting February wind, but all weekend he had been thinking about Irene and Chantelle. Nick had dropped him off on the way home, telling him not to worry about unloading the kit. He had wanted to buy Chantelle a present to say thank you but everything he had seen had either been too kitsch or too personal so he had settled for food to make dinner. A lot of food. His guilt had overwhelmed him and he had definitely bought more than three people could actually eat.

He could hear shouting coming from inside the house and dropped his bags on the doorstep while he wrestled with the key. What was going on? It sounded like some sort of argument. The shrieking continued as he opened the door, but he could also hear laughter. It sounded like a lot of people. Maybe they had the TV on.

'No, Auntie Irene, move your panda in a line.' A very young-sounding voice had him even more puzzled. He rounded the corner to find a motley crew spread out around the metal coffee table, where a board game was spread out. Sarah and Irene were sat on the sofa with Aileen between them, while Simon lay on the floor, guarding a crawling baby that seemed to be trying to make a break for it.

Chantelle was sitting on the rug. She looked happy and relaxed, so happy that he hesitated, knowing her tense awareness would snap up the moment she realised he was there. Instead of her usual firm ponytail or standard work bun her hair was coiled into a loose knot and several strands had escaped, curling themselves around her face. She looked gorgeous and something twisted inside him, knowing what he had thrown away. He could have been a part of this. A proper part of her family. He felt a pain in his chest that was almost physical.

At his sucked in breath they all looked up, with the exception of the baby, who obliviously continued on its quest towards the TV.

'Oh, you're back.' He couldn't miss the tone of disappointment in Chantelle's voice. 'Sorry, with this shitty weather there was no point going anywhere, so we thought we would bring the party here. You're back a bit earlier than we expected.'

'Here, you take the sofa, you look shattered.' Sarah moved to sit by Chantelle on the rug. Unconscious or not, it was a clear sign that she was by her sister all the way.

'Thanks.' He dropped down with a satisfied sigh. 'It was pretty tiring. But great.'

'What did you do?' Simon had rescued the baby by now and was bouncing it on his knee.

'We got some people to take them skiing at Glencoe, that was one of the exhausting bits. I'm still getting used to skiing with one leg. And then out for a low level walk today.' He leaned his head on the back of the sofa. 'The snow was amazing though. They had a big dump on Friday and the weather was gorgeous yesterday. A bit rubbish today though. That's why I'm back a bit early.'

Aileen jumped off the sofa and went to clamber on her mother's legs. 'Mummy, who is that man?' Her whisper was as loud as a normal voice, and everyone laughed.

'That's Uncle Stevie, love.' Sarah put an arm around her daughter. 'Last time he saw you then you were in Mummy's tummy. It's a long time ago.'

'A very long time. I'm three now.' Aileen held up the right number of fingers in Steven's direction.

Steven nodded approvingly. 'That's pretty impressive.'

'Be nice to him, and he might show you his mechanical leg.' Sarah pretended to whisper back to her daughter.

'What's a 'canical leg?' Aileen's eyes widened.

Steven rolled up his trouser leg, while Aileen drew near to have a look. 'Can I touch it?'

'Sure.' He was impressed by her manners. Most kids - in fact, most adults too - thought nothing of grabbing it whether it was on or off his body, or even trying to manipulate it to see how it worked. He was very protective of it though; it had cost him a small fortune, bought with his compensation payout after the accident. But it was worth every penny. He didn't know exactly how much tech was actually in it, but even simple things like being able to change the flexibility and shock absorption settings on the knee enabled him to do a much wider range of activities in a much better way than the standard one he had been issued with at the beginning.

Aileen fingered the red metal gently. 'Are you a robot?' The eyes looking up at him were hopeful. Only in a kid's world would bionic be exciting.

He shook his head. 'No, just a normal human being.'

'We should probably be going.' Sarah began to push herself off the floor.

'Please stay.' Before he had opened the door Steven had thought there was nothing he wished for more than to disappear into a hot bath, but now he wanted to soak up the cosy atmosphere just a little longer. 'We stopped at the supermarket on the way back and there's shedloads of food in those bags. Dips and stuff, and mince to make bolognese sauce. Give me a minute more to sit down and I'll get on with things.'

'Well, bolognese is Aileen's favourite...' Sarah looked at her husband uncertainly.

'Go on then.' Simon shrugged. 'I'll help Stevie get the dinner together if you don't mind looking after Effie.'

'Give her to me.' Irene held out her arms. 'I'll take her off you for a few minutes.' She grabbed a toy off the floor and settled Effie on her knee.

'There's wine and beer in the other bag, if anyone wants some.' Steven pushed himself off the sofa and went to grab it.

'Ooh. Sounds great.' Sarah looked hopeful. 'Simon, do you mind driving us home?'

'I suppose so.' Simon did his best to look put upon, giving a theatrical sigh.

Steven laughed. 'I don't think they're buying it, mate.'

'Yeah, he knows he has to say yes because I gave him a lie in this morning.' Sarah waggled a finger.

Chantelle shifted on the rug. 'Not for me, thanks. I'm working early tomorrow.'

'Thought you might say that, which is why I bought you this.' Steven pushed a bottle of non-alcoholic beer into her hands.

Chantelle took it, looking at the label. 'Oh.'

Her voice was slightly strange and he knew which memory had sprung into her mind. The night they had been out to the German beer cellar in town. They had been to a club afterwards, and, intoxicated by the music and too much drink, had decided to walk all the way home. He hadn't been intending to, but he had proposed to her as they were walking back along the canal in the moonlight.

'You want me to chop these onions?' Simon's voice interrupted his thoughts.

Steven blinked; for one moment the room had faded away and he had been back there as Chantelle looked down at him, with his blue bomber jacket around her shoulders to keep off the chill. They had danced all the way home after that, laughing as they twirled along the deserted streets.

'Aye, sure.' Steven looked across at his former brother-in-law. They had enjoyed cooking together, back when it was only the four of them. Before things got complicated by children and other stuff. 'I'll get the carrots.'

By the time the parents left with one sleeping baby and a very sleepy three year old it was well into the evening. Steven moved to do the washing up, but Chantelle stopped him. 'You go get yourself a shower. You look totally wiped. Irene and I will do it.'

'Are you sure? You look pretty tired too.' He tried not to seem too eager to take up her offer, although it was true. He had taken a few hairy tumbles on the ski slopes and there were definitely parts of him that were feeling sore.

She looked across at him and for one moment he felt like pulling her into his arms and resting his head on her shoulder. Then his mother's voice interrupted them. 'We'll be fine. I haven't forgotten how to do dishes yet.'

'OK. I'll see you in a bit.'

Chantelle was gone by the time he re-emerged. He tried to tell himself that it was because she needed to get an early night, but he couldn't shift the sneaking feeling that she was avoiding him.

Chapter 7

The following Saturday was bright and sunny and Steven rolled out of bed with an excitement he found hard to suppress. He and the rest of the boys were picking Nadeem up from the airport and then heading on into Edinburgh for the kilt fitting for Nadeem's wedding.

Steven was just finishing the final mouthful of his lunch when he heard the car horn beep outside. He stooped to kiss his mum on the cheek. 'That's me, Mum. Got to go. I'll make sure I bring you a picture.'

He nodded at Brenda. 'Are you sure you're going to be OK? I might not be back until late.'

Brenda looked up from her knitting. 'We'll be fine. We're going to bingo tonight.' Seeing him still hovering, Brenda waved her hand in a shooing motion. 'Go on, off with you. Don't keep them waiting.'

'Aye. I know.' Steven grabbed his bag.

Brenda followed him to the door. 'You've got to learn to let go sometimes, Stevie.' Her voice was low, so Irene wouldn't hear. 'She's her own person. You can't keep her protected in cotton wool forever.'

'I know.' He rubbed his face, sighing. 'I'm trying. But it's hard. It feels almost like being a parent.'

The car horn beeped again; obviously Sean thought he hadn't heard the last time. Brenda patted him on the arm. 'You get yourself off to Edinburgh. And have a good time. It's been ages since you were out with the lads. So make sure you enjoy it.'

'Thanks, Brenda. You're a star.' He turned and made his way down the path, feeling a million times lighter.

Sean's tiny red car made him smile, and not just because it had rescued them last weekend; it always seemed a wonder that it could actually carry them all. Nick and Pete had stuck themselves in the back, leaving him space in the front, for which he was really grateful; the three doors meant it had been hard to get into the back even with two fully working legs. This was their walking group and they had been on so many trips last summer just like this. He felt some of the anxiety easing from his chest. Nineties music was pumping out of the speakers, and all three of them were doing cheesy dance moves while they waited. They waved enthusiastically as soon as they saw him.

He eased himself into the front seat. 'So what's the plan?'

'Deem's plane lands in just under half an hour, so we'd better get a move on.' Sean pulled away from the kerb as

Steven fastened his seatbelt. 'Plan is to pick him up and then head straight into Edinburgh.'

'Where are we going to fit him in?' Steven eyed up the small space left in the back seat. 'Should we chuck him in the boot?'

'Oh, we'll manage.' Sean grinned. 'This car is bigger than it looks.'

There were enthusiastic hugs all round as Nadeem appeared. In the end, after a couple of minutes of deliberation, it was Steven who took off his prosthetic and climbed into the back seat, while Nadeem squashed his tall frame into the front.

'Always good to be able to disassemble yourself. Very handy for situations like this.' Steven found his spirits lifting enough to make a proper joke. These four guys were his family, really. And he totally loved them.

'I can't believe we're going all the way to Edinburgh just for a kilt fitting.' Pete sounded fondly exasperated. 'Wouldn't any old kilt place do for the wedding?'

'We've been through this already.' Sean sounded like a resigned father and it was totally appropriate; as the driver of their little band he had always fallen into the role of organiser. They all had things they were good at. Pete was the one who came up with exciting ideas about where to go next. Nick was great at creating amazing picnics. Steven normally provided the comedy, but today his heart wasn't fully in it. It reminded him too much of how his life had changed since his mother's diagnosis.

'Yeah.' Nadeem nodded, oblivious to Steven's thoughts. 'I kind of said the same thing to Jenny, but she wouldn't hear of it. I barely managed to persuade her not to tailor-make all of our outfits but she's got enough to do with making her gown and the bridesmaids' dresses alongside all the orders she's got for regular customers. Besides, a trip to Edinburgh means I have the chance to catch up with some of my family, which is always a bonus.'

'Is her business doing really well then?' Pete was now sitting in the middle, squashed in between Steven and Nick.

'Amazingly. She got a commission from some woman who heads up a massive pharmaceutical company and then after that everything seemed to explode. She'll be moving into a proper studio space next month.'

'So this guy we're going to visit, is he a clothes designer too?' Steven couldn't help asking. He had always wanted a tailor-made suit. He knew it might seem shallow to like clothes so much, but he didn't care. It wasn't only about the outside. A well-fitting outfit made him feel different inside too.

'Yup.' Nadeem sounded pleased. 'This guy's a friend she made through an event she went to last year. I've seen his website and the stuff he does looks amazing.' He pulled out his phone, tapped a few times and then passed it backwards.

'Ooh.' Steven scrolled through the photos. 'Looks pretty swanky.'

'Yeah. That's why we had to come so far in advance of the wedding; I know it's not until the end of the year but he's got a big collection coming out so it was the only time he could squeeze us in.'

'Gimme a look.' Pete grabbed the phone.

'Wait. I hadn't finished yet.' Steven tried to grab it back, only to get an elbow in the ribs as Pete held it away with his other hand.

'Oi! I'm not two inches wide!' Nick had his face pressed up against the window. 'Give me some space!'

'Children! No fighting in the back, or none of you are coming to the wedding!' Nadeem raised his voice. 'You'll be sent to bed with no devices!'

They all collapsed into laughter.

'I thought you weren't going to get married? What changed your mind?' That was Pete.

Nadeem shrugged. 'I wasn't bothered, but Jenny was the one who actually proposed. Surprised me one night when we were walking along the canal and I couldn't really say no.'

Steven thought about his own moonlit proposal and winced. He could only hope that Jenny and Nadeem's marriage turned out better than his.

Steven stood in front of the large mirror, smoothing his hands over the kilt. He could hear the other guys laughing and joking next door as they waited to take their turn. He had been expecting a traditional bold tartan, but this was much more of a subtle design. The stripes were more of a hint than a proper checked pattern, and instead of a heavy sporran there was an in-built pocket at the front. He never would have thought that it would work, but the way it was cut actually made it look good. No, not just good...it looked sexy. He twisted a little so he could examine the back, and then sighed, remembering the last time he had worn a kilt.

'Good sigh or bad sigh?' Nick had come up behind him, wearing exactly the same. The jackets were also a masterpiece; they were very similar to a traditional one but with some subtle alterations which seemed to put some kind of magic into them. Or possibly it was the amazing fabric.

Steven turned to look directly at him. 'A bit of both, probably. I look damn good in this getup. But then I can't help thinking about the last time I was in something like this.'

'Your own wedding?' Nick guessed.

Nick had only moved to Glasgow two years ago so had never known him as a married man. It felt weird, thinking about it. That there might be people who had never known him at his happiest point. Steven nodded. 'Aye.'

Nick's arm snaked round his shoulders and he pulled him into a sideways hug. 'I'm sorry, man. You want to talk about it?'

Steven shrugged and turned back to the mirror, pretending to study his outfit again. 'There's not much to talk about. I screwed up. Lost the love of my life. I still regret it.'

'Can't you talk to her? Might she not take you back if you tell her what you told me right now?' Nick looked hopeful. 'They're some pretty powerful words.'

'I don't know.' Steven sat down on one of the leather stools and rubbed his face with his hands. 'I've been seeing a bit more of her recently because she's been coming across to see my mum and I hate the way she looks at me. She's kind of jumpy whenever I'm around. As if I'm invading her space somehow.'

'Ouch.' Nick winced. 'I think all you can do is be yourself. Be honest with her and see what happens.' He sat down on another stool opposite, leaning back against the wall. 'I'm hopeless with relationships anyway, so don't let me give you advice. It always seems like a miracle that Jade is willing to put up with me.'

'Woah.' Steven covered his eyes dramatically. 'You can't sit down like that, you'll be flashing anyone who's opposite you. Have you not worn a kilt before?'

Nick laughed. 'Not really, my family was never into them. So what do I do? Put my knees together like this?' He struck a very camp-looking pose.

'You could.' Steven was glad of the opportunity to laugh. 'But really, you're better off doing this.' He showed Nick how to tug a bit of the kilt to make a pool between his thighs. And that was when the others joined them.

'Hey! I hope that's consensual touching,' Pete called out.

Nadeem wagged his finger. 'He has a girlfriend, you know.'

'Piss off.' But Steven's voice was full of laughter too.

They all stood for a moment in front of the mirror. 'Well, gents, we look pretty damn gorgeous. They'll all be swooning at the wedding.' Nadeem nodded approvingly. 'It's time we went out on the town.'

'Wait.' Steven reached for his phone. 'I promised Mum a photo.'

'That photo had better make it nowhere near social media, otherwise Jenny will kill me.' Nadeem wagged a finger at him. 'She wants to keep it a surprise.'

'No fear of that. It's only for Mum. It's not going anywhere.'

In the end they got a proper group shot taken by one of the staff, and Steven took the phone, looking at the five of them, arms around each other and faces in wide smiles. These people would be there for him, no matter what happened, and that thought was very comforting. 'Cheers, guys. Let's get these off and go get some beers in.'

The evening panned out just as they had planned; a few drinks and a curry at one of Nadeem's favourite places. But at some point the conversation turned to the story that was increasingly in the media; the coronavirus outbreak.

'So do you think that people's worries are realistic? I mean, there's only been a few isolated cases in the UK so far.' Steven was finishing off his last forkful of rice and he put his plate down with a happy sigh.

'Deem's the best person to ask. His company does medical logistics.' Pete pointed a thumb in that direction.

Nadeem ran a hand through his hair. 'I honestly can't tell because I'm not really involved in that side of the business any more since I switched to running our charitable foundation. I know we've been trying to stockpile supplies - you know, gloves and masks and stuff like that - just in case it's needed, but I'm still hoping they'll manage to track and trace everything and isolate the cases. I've been doing my best to help the charities we work with to prepare themselves.'

'I hope so.' Nick grimaced. 'If we get a lockdown situation like they've had in China we can say goodbye to our budding business. There'll be no tourism if people can't travel.'

There was silence while everyone contemplated the idea.

'It's impossible to tell.' Sean shook his head. 'There's no point worrying about things we can't control.'

'Yeah. You're right.' Pete nodded. 'Anyway Deem's here and we should make the most of it. We don't get to see him that often.' He turned towards him. 'You sure you don't want to move back to Glasgow?'

Nadeem laughed. 'I'm doing pretty well sampling everything London has to offer at the moment. And Jenny's business is best off in London so I'm happy to make whatever sacrifices she needs.'

Nadeem really was in love, Steven realised. His thoughts turned to his own marriage, which had started much the same and then gone so badly wrong. Maybe Nick was right. Perhaps he should talk to Chantelle about how he felt.

It was after midnight by the time Sean dropped Steven off at his front door. Brenda had fallen asleep in front of the TV, and Steven gently woke her and gave her effusive whispered thanks as she made her way out. He quietly opened his mother's door to check on her and smiled as he heard soft snoring coming from her bed. He studied the figure lying under the covers for a few seconds, thinking how small she looked, and a fierce protectiveness swept over him. She had spent a good part of her life trying her best to bring him up as well as she knew how. Defending him from his father. She needed to be his priority now.

He closed the door softly and went to have a wash in the bathroom, making sure he took good care of his stump. It throbbed fiercely, as it often did if he spent all day in his prosthetic. While he massaged cream into it gently he considered the conversation with Nick again. Talking to Chantelle would get everything out in the open and then he could be sure of how she felt. He would try to have a proper conversation with her next time he saw her. But as the next couple of weeks went by and she became increasingly evasive about her movements, it became clear that she was actively trying to avoid him.

Chapter 8

Chantelle jerked out of sleep, her heart pounding. In her dreams she had been chasing through a garden and a loud crash as someone dived through a window had woken her up.

Except...she could still hear shouting. A woman's voice, and it sounded as if it was coming from her living room. Had someone broken in? The single glazing on the ground floor windows would be easy to smash if someone really wanted to.

A quick check of her watch told her it was just before three in the morning. She eased herself out of bed silently, grabbing her phone and slipping into her running shoes. Her t-shirt and shorts made her feel unprotected, but it was better than nothing. Still, she wasn't going to go for any heroics; if there was someone in her house then she was definitely calling for some backup. She punched in three digits, knowing that if she did one touch was all it would take to dial 999. The torch on the phone also gave her some visibility in the darkness.

'Hello?' She tried to make her voice sound confident. 'Is anyone there?'

The shouting continued. Chantelle exited into the hallway, hearing the noise grow louder. She rounded the doorway to peer into the living room and her eyes were hit with a scene of devastation.

Someone had thrown a brick through the large bay window, smashing a massive hole in one of the panes. As if that wasn't enough, a large empty bottle of bleach lay in the middle of the floor. As it had flown it had spattered all over the room, leaving nothing untouched. Sofa, curtains and carpet were all dripping with liquid. She was just about to press the button on her phone when a second crash made her jump and she knew what it was straight away. Another brick had gone through her bedroom window. She shivered as she imagined what might have happened if they had done that room first, and then winced as she thought of what a bottle of bleach would do to her favourite bed cover.

It didn't take long to dial the call in and the operator promised there was someone on the way. It was time to get out of here and try to work out what was going on. Chantelle rescued her keys, coat and grab bag from beside the front door and eased quietly out of the back door of the close. A short walk down the back lane would bring her out the side and hopefully out well away from whoever had thrown the bricks. As she peered around the corner of the building she could see that there were other lights on now and people looking out of their windows. No doubt some of her neighbours would also be calling the police.

The street lights illuminated a youngish woman who stood yelling up at her windows. The words were partly blown away by the wind, but she caught the words 'bitch' and 'boyfriend'. Another woman was tugging at the first one's arm, no doubt trying to get her friend away before the police did actually turn up. There were numerous faces peering out from behind curtains both in her own building and the flats across the street, but no-one had dared to venture out.

Chantelle bit her lip. If it was only one person she would have been happy to tackle things on her own, but having two of them there made things more complicated. She remained where she was, at a safe distance. It wouldn't be long before at least one of her colleagues turned up.

She wasn't wrong; it only took a couple more minutes before blue lights rounded the corner and two officers piled out of a car. The woman was someone she knew well and she vaguely recognised the man who was with her, but she couldn't place his name. If she remembered right he hadn't been with them long.

The two young women seemed to deflate as soon as they saw the police and the one who had been shouting sat down on the low wall and burst into tears while the other tried to comfort her. Chantelle made her way over to the group. 'Hey, Karen.'

The female police officer looked around and Chantelle could see her connecting the dots. 'Hi. Is this your flat?' She pointed at the broken windows.

'Yeah.' Chantelle shoved her hands in the pockets of her jacket. 'I didn't see her do it, but I assume you'll find her fingerprints on the bottles of bleach that she chucked through the windows.'

The crying woman had looked up at the sound of Chantelle's voice and suddenly lunged towards her, fists flailing. 'That's the bitch! The one who got my Tommy in the jail.' If it hadn't been for her friend dragging at one arm and the male police officer hanging onto the other then she might have reached Chantelle, but she was quickly subdued and handcuffed and placed in the back of the police car.

'Do you know this woman?' Karen seemed surprised.

Chantelle shook her head. 'Not directly. I arrested her boyfriend a few weeks ago. Intent to supply. But how she found out my address I have no idea.' It wouldn't have been too hard though. You didn't spend your whole life living in the same area and working at the local takeaway without people getting to know you.

Another two officers turned up with a van and took the woman away to custody and Chantelle had just finished giving a statement when a car screeched to a halt behind them. It was unmarked and Chantelle braced herself to deal with another situation but relaxed when she saw the driver. It was one of the sergeants from her station.

'I thought I'd come and check up on you.' Chantelle saw his eyes make a quick scan to ensure she was unhurt. 'Are you OK?'

'I'm fine.' She was fuming, but that wasn't his question. 'Luckily she chucked the one through the living room window before she did the bedroom.'

He looked over to the two other officers. 'Do you need any help?'

'I think we're fine.' Karen nodded decisively. 'We've got what we need from a few of the neighbours and Chris and I are going to wait for the joiner to turn up.'

The sergeant turned to Chantelle. 'It'd be better if you didn't go back in because we'll need to take pictures tomorrow but I can rescue you some things if you need them.'

She shrugged, wanting to offer help but knowing that procedure would stop her from doing so. 'I've got my grab bag, I can do without the other stuff until tomorrow.' She suddenly felt self-conscious, standing there in her skimpy shorts without her uniform.

He gave her a wry smile. 'A grab bag, hm. Taking too much of the job home, are you?'

Chantelle straightened her shoulders. 'I've been doing this for years. My dad was in the army. A Sapper.' Mentioning him brought a wave of emotion over her and she sucked in a breath. The events of tonight had obviously hit her harder than she had realised and now that the adrenaline was starting to seep away she could feel her composure starting to wobble.

The sergeant kept on looking down at her. 'I'd love to be able to get you the day off tomorrow, but with numbers as they are I'm afraid that's never going to happen. Can I give you a lift anywhere?'

She quickly considered her options; there weren't many. Her sister's flat in Cumbernauld was a good half an hour away, even at this time of night, and she would be camping on the sofa, which meant no sleep once the kids woke up. Most of her other friends were the same. She thought about Steven and his spare bedroom, only a few streets away. A place where she could sleep until her shift started tomorrow afternoon. But could she really do that? And did she even want to?

She realised her colleague was waiting for her answer. 'I've got a friend who lives just around the corner. I'll see if I can stay with him.'

'I'll drive you there.' He waved away her protestations about walking and she thankfully climbed into the passenger seat, giving a quick thumbs up to Karen and Chris, who were still talking to the other woman.

Two minutes was all it took. When they pulled up outside the house the sergeant looked at her. 'You know she's unlikely to get remanded, but I'll see if I can make sure she gets some decent bail conditions so she's not going to bother you. I only wish that you could stay a bit further from where she lives.'

Chantelle frowned, considering what he had said. 'She doesn't live around here though, I'm sure she had an address on the south side. The property we lifted her boyfriend from belongs to his parents.'

The man's eyebrows rose. 'I'm impressed you remember all that.' He nodded firmly. 'That might make things a bit easier. And you said the second brick fell onto your bed? Let me see what I can do.'

She tried to say goodbye but he insisted on waiting while she went around the back and knocked on Steven's window, careful to do it quietly so she didn't also wake Irene. The curtain was pulled back and Steven's face went from puzzled to shocked when he found her standing outside. The window opened. 'Chaz? What happened? Are you OK?' He spoke in a whisper.

She nodded. 'I'm fine. But I can't say the same thing about my flat. I need a place to stay. Would you mind?'

'Let me just get my prosthetic on and I'll be with you.' He disappeared and she went back around to the front door, giving her colleague a thumbs up as she did so.

It was only another minute before the door opened. 'Come in.' Steven was still whispering. 'Fuck's sake, what happened?'

'Some crazy woman put a couple of bricks through the windows of my flat.' She kept her voice low too. 'I'm fine, but my place is a mess. She went for a couple of bottles of bleach as well. God knows how much will be rescuable. I'll have to find out tomorrow.'

He took her into the living room. 'Surely the stuff in the cupboards will be OK?'

She shrugged. 'I'm hoping so. Only issue is, I had my laundry hanging out in the living room. Most of that will probably have to go. And the landlord's going to shit himself when he sees the furniture and the carpets.'

Steven looked around. 'I'd put you in the spare bedroom but it's totally overflowing with junk. I can clean it out for you tomorrow, if you need to stay longer, but the sofa's probably going to be the best option for tonight.'

'Don't worry, that'll be fine.' She was just relieved to have a place to stay that she knew would be safe. The damage to her flat had shaken her more than she cared to admit. She expected some violence on the job, but to have it follow her home was really unsettling.

He went into the spare room and came out with an armful of bedding. 'Here you go.'

It only took a couple of minutes for them to make up the sofa into something resembling a bed. Chantelle sat down on it thankfully.

She had expected Steven to disappear, but he remained standing in front of her, his eyes full of concern. 'Are you OK? You're literally shaking.'

She was, she realised, and wrapped her arms around herself. 'It's been a bit of a rough night.'

'I'll go put the kettle on.' It didn't take long before he was back, pushing a steaming mug into her hands. 'Here you go. I've bunged loads of sugar and milk in it.'

She sipped at the hot liquid gratefully. 'Thanks. I really needed this.'

He plopped down next to her on the sofa. 'So what happened exactly?'

Steven's eyes were wide by the time she had finished relating the night's events. 'Wow. So will your landlord expect you to pay for the damage?'

Chantelle shrugged. 'I'm hoping the insurance will cover it. But I'll find out tomorrow morning.'

Steven shook his head, still trying to absorb what had happened. 'I can't believe someone would do that. I remember I always used to tease you about your grab bag, but never again.' Chantelle looked at him and burst into tears.

'Hey. Hey.' He gathered Chantelle and her empty mug into his arms. 'You're safe now.'

She sighed. 'I know. I just miss Dad. And Mum. I wish they were here.'

'Aye.' He took a deep breath. 'I do too. I mean, I never met your dad, but I loved your mum. She was amazing.'

'They were wild about each other, I remember that. I thought it was disgusting as a kid. If I'd only known he was going to go so soon.' Chantelle leaned back and he let her go, watching her turning the cup around in her hands.

'You couldn't have seen what was coming. No-one gets the privilege of knowing that.' He longed to reach out and touch her hair, but the time for comforting her like that had gone when she had pulled away.

'Yeah. I know. But I could have expected it, with him being in the army and all that. I guess I never realised the danger he was really in. Who would have thought he would die on a training exercise before he ever got out to Afghanistan?' She looked up at him. 'I guess that's the bit that hurts the most. If he'd been blown up by an IED or shot by a sniper or something, it would have been tough, but I would have accepted it. But that bridge bit that crushed him - it was someone's decision to place it down at exactly the wrong moment. Someone who should have been looking out for him.'

'I'm sure that person still feels guilty about it.' It was the only thing Steven could think of to say.

'Yeah, I know.' She shifted on the sofa. 'I need to get some sleep. I've got a shift starting tomorrow afternoon and I desperately need to be on the ball for it.'

'Sure.' It was his cue to disappear. 'Sleep as long as you like, it's Saturday tomorrow so I'm not working. Mum might come out, but I've put a small TV in her bedroom now so often she lies in there and watches stuff in the mornings.'

'Thanks.' Chantelle gave him a grateful smile. 'I really appreciate it.'

Steven jerked open his eyes. He could have sworn he'd heard something, but when he listened it was all quiet. His watch told him it was just before six and he rolled over with a groan. No doubt his mum would be up and wandering around somewhere. He grabbed his crutches and crept quietly down the corridor, but when he peered cautiously into her room there was an unmoving shape in the bed. That was strange. Had Chantelle got up for a drink or something? But a similar peek into the living room showed her sprawled out on the couch. Her arm was flung up above her head in the way she always used to sleep when they were together. He couldn't help a smile as the memories came flooding back. She had always been a space hogger. He would often wake to find part of her draped over him, and one time she had even whacked him in the face by accident as she turned over in bed. They had made a joke of it for ages afterwards.

For one moment he was back in the past, remembering how many times he had picked her up from the couch after she had fallen asleep in front of a film and settled her gently in bed. But all that had changed now; she was no longer his wife, and these days he probably wouldn't even be able to pick her up without overbalancing. He turned away.

'Must have been a bus going by.' He muttered to himself as he drew the covers over his head. 'Or I'm so short on sleep I'm starting to hear things.'

He came out much later on to find Chantelle wandering around the living room, ear glued to her phone. She waved a hello at him but kept on talking, although she did respond enthusiastically to his motions for tea. By the time he'd made them both a cup and poked his head into the living room to tell her that they were ready she'd finished and looked at him with a smile on her face. 'Isn't it weird how some people are so nice?'

'What do you mean?' Steven was puzzled.

'Well, the woman I spoke to sounded really doubtful when I first told her what had happened, but as soon as I mentioned that I worked for the police she said she'd see what she could do.' Chantelle shrugged. 'It happens some- times. A perk of the job I guess. She said that it'd probably be covered in my landlord's insurance, but if it wasn't then I'd be covered with my own.'

'That's great.' Steven couldn't help smiling. 'So what next?'

'I have to call my landlord now.' Chantelle rolled her eyes. 'That's not going to be such a pleasant conversation, I can tell you. He's a right tight arse when it comes to money.' She sat down on the sofa. 'Actually, I might just text him. I really don't fancy talking to him right now.'

Her telephone pinged again. 'Oh. That's the guys from work. I can get back into my flat. I'd better go. I need to pick up some stuff.'

'Hang on. You haven't even had any breakfast.'

'I'll get some at the shop.' It sounded like she just wanted to get out of the house and get things done.

'Don't be ridiculous.' Steven rolled his eyes. 'Surely you can spend five minutes to have a bowl of cereal.'

Her gaze finally focused on him and she bit her lip. 'There's a lot of memories in this place, you know.'

He was surprised by her directness, but glad of it. It was about time that they started being honest with each other. 'Come into the kitchen, have some cereal, and we can talk. I need some breakfast too.' He walked through the archway and started pulling things out of the cupboards. 'Cocoa loops do you?' She nodded and he pushed the packet towards her, followed by a bowl.

'You're right.' Steven grabbed a bowl for himself. 'I've been finding this whole thing a bit strange too. I mean, we haven't seen each other for years, and now we're suddenly spending all this time together. But surely we can be friends?'

She bit her lip again. The movement dragged his gaze towards her mouth and he felt a sudden urge to kiss her. 'I don't know. You hurt me a lot. We can't sweep all that under the carpet.'

'I hurt you?' Steven realized he had raised his voice and lowered it again. 'You were the one who walked away from our marriage.'

Chantelle was shovelling cereal into her mouth so she just frowned at him. It took her a couple of seconds before she could talk. 'Look. This is a conversation I don't have time for now. In fact, I don't even know if I want to have this conversation full stop.'

Steven held up his hands. 'OK. Let's not go there. But can we at least be friends? Because if not then all this is going to be really awkward.'

She considered his words for a full minute, as she almost inhaled the remainder of her cereal. 'I guess so. Only if you promise to be nice.'

He found himself mildly irritated by her comment. 'When am I ever not nice?'

'Yeah.' Chantelle muttered to herself. 'That's part of the problem.'

'Well, I was going to be nice by saying that you could stay here as long as you want, but I might not bother to offer now.' He stared at her accusingly, raising his chin. Then he realized what he was doing. Why was she bringing out the worst in him like this? Maybe he was still angry at her for leaving him. But if they were really going to be friends then he had to put all that behind him. He poured himself some cereal into a bowl, then looked over at her. 'Honestly, you are welcome to stay here. There's the spare room and all. Just until you get your flat sorted out.'

She placed her bowl back on the counter top. 'Thanks. I really appreciate that. And I will take you up on the offer. Only for a couple of nights though. I'm sure it'll be sorted soon.' Then she looked behind her. 'Are you sure your mum will be OK with that? It is her house too.'

A massive grin split Steven's face. 'Are you kidding? She loves having you around. She'll think all her Christmasses have come at once. But yeah, we can ask her if you like. You go do what you have to do and I'll talk to her when she wakes up.'

Chantelle checked her watch. 'I need to head.' Her phone pinged, and she swiped at the screen. 'That's my landlord. He says he'll meet me at my flat in half an hour.'

'Don't let him hassle you.' Steven touched her arm gently. 'None of this is your fault.'

'No chance.' Chantelle tucked her phone back in the pocket of her jeans. 'I won't be bullied by anyone.'

He leaned over to put her dishes in the sink. 'Do you want me to come and help?'

It was only when there was no answer that he turned around and realized she was already gone.

Chapter 9

Despite what she had said to Steven, Chantelle was still nervous as she neared the apartment. First she had to check the damage, rescue what she could and bin the rest. Then negotiate with the landlord and hope that he wasn't too annoyed.

The inside of her flat looked slightly spooky with the windows boarded up. She hugged herself mentally, thinking of her colleagues and how they had arranged it all for her. Another sign that she was in the right job. Working with people who cared about her that much was where she wanted to be.

She sighed as she surveyed her living room. Everything that had been out was a total write-off, including a spare uniform, which had been drying on the airer. She grabbed a couple of black bags from the kitchen and started clearing up.

Twenty minutes later most of the mess was gone, but there was nothing she could do about the sofa and carpet. She heard a brief knock on the front door and then it opened. The landlord always did this, almost as if he was making the point by using his key that it was actually his flat. She didn't know what it was about the man, but she really detested him. It could be his little constant digs at her that he claimed were jokes, or the way he always called her girl, as if she were fifteen years old.

Chantelle felt her skin prickling at the confrontation she knew would ensue but she squared her shoulders and turned to face him. She was going to give him a false smile, but decided on a worried frown instead. Much more appropriate for the situation.

His lips pursed as he surveyed the carnage. 'Well.'

'Yeah.' Chantelle pursed her lips too. 'Sorry about all this.' She didn't know why she was apologizing; like Steven had said, none of this was her fault.

'Hmm.' The landlord was drawing it out, she could tell, trying to make her feel bad. It wouldn't work. There was no way that anyone was going to make her feel guilty for doing her job, so she waited for him to make his move. He finally spoke. 'What actually happened?'

'The girlfriend of some guy I lifted smashed the windows and then poured a couple of bottles of bleach inside.' Chantelle pointed at the relevant places.

'Hmm.' The landlord spent a couple of minutes taking photos of the damage.

'My colleagues have already taken some photos as evidence.' Chantelle didn't know what else to say. 'I don't doubt they'll charge her with the damage and may even get her to pay compensation. And if not then my insurance should cover it.'

'OK. In that case, I won't ask you for any money for all this.' The landlord shrugged.

Chantelle felt her shoulders relax. That had been easier than she expected.

He wasn't finished yet though. 'I have workmen coming in tomorrow to clean up all this mess. Will you be able to move out by then?'

'Fine.' Chantelle nodded. 'How long do you think the work will take?'

'Ah.' He pursed his lips again. 'You see, I've had to think about this very carefully. I've already had complaints from some of your neighbours.'

Shit. She had forgotten that he owned most of the tenement block. No doubt people had been complaining about the racket.

'It's hardly my fault if someone comes round and knocks my windows in.' Chantelle crossed her arms, staring him down.

'Not exactly. But it's not the first time I've had complaints about you and we can't have people bringing down the tone of the neighbourhood. I'm afraid I'll need to give you your twenty-eight days notice.'

'What?' Chantelle's stomach twisted. This wasn't the battle she had been expecting to fight. She had thought he would grumble about the furnishings, that maybe they would have to split it and then she would claim on the insurance. Not that he would make her homeless. And not only that, to find out that some of her neighbours had it in for her? It was as if the rug she was literally standing on had been pulled out from under her feet.

'Wait.' She tried to regain some control over the situation. 'You can't do that. I'm a good tenant. I always pay my rent on time and this is the first time in more than two years that anything has been damaged. And who's complained about me before, and why didn't you say anything at the time? I know I work all hours, but I always try to keep things down when it's late at night.'

The man smiled, a triumphant look in his eyes. 'I couldn't possibly reveal my sources. And regarding the notice period I think you'll find, if you look at your contract, that I can do exactly that.'

Chantelle didn't often get angry, but at this point she really wanted to punch him in the face, just to wipe the smug smile off it. 'Tell you what. Take your sodding flat. My rent is due in a week and you're not getting it. I'll give you back your keys tonight.' That would only give her three hours to pack everything up before work, but it was worth it. She wouldn't play his stupid games. 'Do we have a deal?'

The man pursed his lips again. Would he stop doing that? It was really annoying. He let her stew there for a while before he replied, but she could see in his eyes that it was just too tempting for him. Given the way rental prices were going he would be able to get much more money from a new tenant.

'OK. It's a deal. Post them through the door when you leave tonight and I'll get them when I let the workmen in on Monday.' He almost couldn't hide his glee.

She couldn't work out what he had against her. Was it that she worked for the police? Or did he just not like strong women? Either way, it seemed like he couldn't wait to get rid of her. And if she was really honest with herself, the feeling was mutual.

He let himself out, and she surveyed what she still had left to do. Then she picked up her phone. There was only one way she was going to do this. 'Stevie? I really need your help.'

When Steven turned up at the door she almost cried with relief.

'I've brought Sean, and Sean's brought his car.' Steven took one look at her and held out his arms. 'Come here, you. Everything's going to be fine.'

She almost fell against him, grateful for his warmth, and found the tears running down her face.

'Hey. It's OK.' Steven held her tight and stroked her hair. 'It's all going to be just fine.'

She breathed in the smell of him, feeling the softness of his puffy jacket under her cheek. This took her back. How many times had she cried on his shoulder? Too many to count. She missed him. He had always understood her need to have a good weep when something happened. Had held her close and supplied her with tissues until the waterworks stopped. Until the time had come when he'd been so wrapped up in his own problems that she'd had to do her crying on her own.

'I've brought half the boxes, the rest are - oh.' Sean's voice came from right behind Steven.

Chantelle lifted her head and stepped away, wiping a hand across her eyes. 'Don't mind me. I'll go and find myself a tissue.'

It took them three trips in Sean's car to transport everything across to Steven's flat. When they were finally done the spare room was squashed to the brim. Sean declined the offer of either lunch or a cup of tea, saying he'd promised to visit his own mum, and disappeared.

Chantelle surveyed the box mountain. 'It'll only be for a few days. I'll sort something else out after that.'

'Don't worry about it.' Steven came to stand beside her. 'You might be sleeping on the sofa again tonight though.'

She nodded. 'I've managed to get the day off tomorrow, we can go through everything then and rearrange it all.'

'Sounds like a plan. Have you got time for lunch?'

Chantelle checked her watch. 'Doesn't look like it. I need to be at work in less than an hour. I'll have to grab some on the way.'

He nodded. 'Oh wait. Here. Keys.' He tossed them to her with a flick of his wrist and she grabbed them automatically, but not before the flash of green had caught her eye.

'Oh. That's the Nessie key ring we got when we were on our honeymoon. You kept it.' The trip had been the first time that Chantelle had stayed in a proper hotel. Her mind strayed to the other things they had done that week and she felt herself getting slightly warm. Now that she looked at it, this was the same set that had belonged to her. She remembered the scrape along the front door key from when she had used it to open a bottle of beer.

Steven raised his hands. 'Not me. This wasn't even my place until a couple of months ago. Blame Mum.'

'What's your plans for the rest of the day?' Chantelle knew she should be going, but she couldn't help asking.

'To be honest, I might just go back to bed.' Steven rubbed his eyes. 'I'm shattered and my stump's killing me after carrying all that stuff. No, don't.' He pointed a finger at her as she opened her mouth to apologise. 'I'm a grown adult and I can make my own decisions.'

Chantelle blushed, feeling embarrassed. It was all too easy to fall into the trap of being ableist without thinking. He did look tired though. Dark circles ringed his eyes, probably a mirror of her own. She felt a sudden urge to go to him and give him another hug, but instead she picked up her stuff and fled.

The news she got at work that day did nothing to improve her mood. The house was dead when she got home in the small hours of the morning, although someone had thoughtfully made up her bed on the sofa. But try as she could, she slept in little more than snatches, interspersed with very strange dreams. She was almost thankful when she heard Irene's gentle tread and had an excuse to open her eyes.

'Need a cuppa, dear?' Irene was looking down at her, a slightly concerned look on her face.

'Oh, please.' The thought of curling her hands around a hot container of milky liquid was heaven.

It wasn't long before Irene came back and handed her a mug, then eased herself down beside Chantelle.

'Where's yours?' Chantelle spoke quietly, aware that Steven was probably still asleep.

'Oh, silly me.' Irene got up. 'I forgot it in the kitchen.' She was soon back and lowered herself down onto the sofa again. 'Forgive me for saying this, but you look awful.'

'I feel awful.' There was no point trying to hide it. 'We got told at work yesterday that lockdown is probably going to be soon. That means everything closed. Offices, hairdressers, and probably most of the shops. Next week probably. And I've been trying to work out what to do. If I stay here, and lockdown happens, I'll be stuck for as long as it lasts.'

'Lockdown for...' Irene's forehead furrowed for a minute, but she held up a hand when Chantelle started to speak. 'Oh yes. The virus.' She looked pleased with herself, as if she had solved a particularly difficult crossword clue.

'Yeah. That.' Chantelle nodded. 'And so I'm stuck. There's no way I'll find another flat right now, the way the prices are going I'd need time to wait for a cheaper one to come up, and no-one will be moving until all this is over. I could go and stay with Sarah, but they don't have a spare room, so a couple of days would be fine, but any more than that and it would drive us both crazy. All of my other friends are in the same position; they either live in a tiny flat or have too many kids.'

The joke was a bit weak, but Irene smiled nonetheless. 'You know you're welcome to stay here as long as you like.'

'I know.' Chantelle reached over and squeezed Irene's hand. But I also have to think about what I'm doing in my job. I would never forgive myself if I brought the virus home to you or Stevie. Especially you; you're in the category that's now supposed to shield themselves from it.'

Irene did laugh then, almost spilling her tea in the process. She took a couple of sips to reduce the danger of her full cup, then turned to Chantelle, a resolute look in her eyes. 'You were the daughter I never had.' She blinked a couple of times, then cleared her throat. 'I always wanted another baby, even though I was almost forty by the time I had Stevie, but not long after he was born I realised what kind of a man his father was and swore I would never bring another child into that house.' Another sip of her tea, and she cradled the mug in her hands, staring into space. 'It didn't help me, of course; the night he discovered the contraceptive pills was one I don't care to remember.' She shuddered, but then a small smile crept over her face. 'I just made sure I hid them better after that.'

Chantelle felt her own skin crawl. Steven had told her some bits about what his dad was really like but in the main he had glossed over events, telling her he didn't like to relive the past. It sounded even worse than she had imagined.

'The day you married my Stevie was the proudest day of my life.' Irene took Chantelle's hand again. 'And I don't know what happened between you after that, but what I do know is that you're family and always will be. So if you need a place to stay, it doesn't matter what you might be bringing home. I'm dead proud of you and the job you do so I'll do anything for you.'

'Thanks, Ma.' Chantelle leaned over and rested her head on the older woman's shoulder. 'I love you so much.'

'I love you too.' Irene reached up and patted her cheek. 'And don't you worry about that virus. If it's my time to go then it's my time.' She looked furtively towards the doorway and lowered her voice. 'Don't tell Stevie, but if I did go, in some ways it would be a relief. I can feel things getting a bit more difficult every day. To go before I end up being totally helpless might be a blessing.'

'You're not at that point yet.' Chantelle squeezed Irene's arm. Then she lowered her voice. 'To be honest, Ma, Stevie is one of the reasons I don't feel comfortable staying here.'

'He's not been unkind to you, has he?' Irene took another sip of her tea.

'No, not that, exactly the opposite. He's been really considerate. But that's the problem.' She lowered her voice even more. 'I'm still in love with him, while he's made it totally clear that he wants nothing more than to be friends. And I don't know if I can live here, seeing him every day, knowing that fact.'

'I think-' Irene had no time to say any more, because Steven's bedroom door opened and he appeared in the entrance to the living room, rubbing one eye and yawning.

'I thought I heard voices.' He yawned again.

Chantelle's heart jumped in her chest. Had he heard their discussion? No, there was no way he could have; their voices had been quiet, and sound didn't carry that far. She took a large gulp of tea to hide her embarrassment. 'Kettle boiled not that long ago.'

'Great. I could really do with a coffee.' He wandered into the kitchen and Chantelle couldn't help admiring him from behind. What was it about this man that turned her on so much? Even the way he swung around capably on his crutches looked sexy somehow. She shook her head. Would that be an acceptable chat-up line?

There was going to be no chatting up of anyone, she reminded herself. 'Come sit down with us. Irene and I have got something we need to talk to you about. Lockdown's imminent and we need to sort out where I'm going to stay.'

Chapter 10

'So it's really happening?' Steven knew he should have seen it coming, but he had been so busy with everything that was going on he had pushed the thought away.

'Yeah.' Chantelle swung her feet up on the low table. 'They're going to put out an announcement this week encouraging everyone who can work from home to do so. Full lockdown still unsure, but it's definitely coming. It has to. Otherwise cases are going to run away with us.'

Steven shifted on the couch, his mind racing. 'What do you mean by full lockdown? You mean people not allowed to go out of their houses and stuff, like they've got in Italy? Are they really going to do that?'

'It's not clear at the moment, but I think so, yeah. Shops and restaurants closed, no travel, the works. They're saying it's the only way to contain it.'

A mix of emotions ran through Steven and to his surprise the largest one was relief. His weekend plans for the next few weeks would be a write off. But the thought that he wouldn't have to juggle everything was a definite bonus.

And if he was working from home then he could also keep an eye on his mum. 'I'm going to have to call Nick and let him know. I guess we can't do anything about it.' He shrugged. 'We'll just have to take things one day at a time.'

'Yeah, but there is one thing you're not considering.' Chantelle bit her lip. 'If we do get a proper lockdown, no-one will be moving so I won't be able to find anywhere to live. I'll be stuck with you until lockdown lifts and I can find another flat. Could you put up with me for a few weeks at least?'

It was true, he hadn't considered that. The thought of living in close quarters with her for such a long time sounded tortuous. But perhaps it would allow them to get to know one another again. If they could actually live together for a while then there could be a possibility of her giving him another chance. 'Is there someone else you'd rather stay with?' He tried to keep his voice neutral.

Chantelle bit her lip. 'It's not really about wanting, it's about options. You're the only person I know of who has a spare room. If I ended up at anyone else's place then I'd be crashing on the sofa. That's fine for a few days, but a few weeks? I can't ask them to do that.' She looked across at Irene. 'But we were discussing my job, and the risk of bringing the infection home. I'll be interacting with members of the public, and I can't deny it, it's pretty high risk. I'm not too happy about it, but Irene said she's OK with it.'

The first words that wanted to come out of Steven's mouth were that his mum was in no fit state to make those kind of decisions, but looking across her he realised that wasn't the point. He always got angry when people assumed that his disability meant that he couldn't make decisions for himself so the least he could do was afford her the dignity of making up her own mind.

'OK, that's settled.' He spread his palms out. 'If she's not bothered I'm not bothered either; if you bring it home we'll deal with it.' He hadn't noticed the worry lines in Chantelle's forehead until the moment they disappeared, but it was clear that he had just taken a weight off her shoulders. 'I'm going to get some breakfast. You want some?' He crossed to the kitchen and opened the cereal cupboard.

'Sure, since you're asking.' Chantelle crossed her legs and leaned back, arms tucked behind her head, giving him a small smile. 'I think I could get used to this.' He relished the sound of the laughter that came from both her and Irene.

It was later in the day that Steven called Nick to give him the bad news. 'Chantelle says there's going to be a proper lockdown. They're going to be taking it week by week, but she's been told to prepare for it being a couple of months. Although I'm assuming that's a pessimistic worst case scenario.'

'Really? I guess I could have seen this coming.' Nick's voice was glum. 'Still, it won't be that long, will it? We'll be back up and running by the summer. So it's only a couple of weekends we'll be missing, and we could probably reschedule them for the autumn. There's a few we were going to run that haven't been totally filled yet, so we could probably move people to them. Spread them across and it might work.'

'If you say so.' That did sound like a decent plan. 'Are you going to call round and cancel, or do you want me to do it?'

'I don't mind.' Nick sounded resigned. 'I might just email them all. Are we giving them a refund?'

Steven considered for a moment. 'I guess we have to really. But we should probably find out before we do that whether the accommodation will let us move the booking, or if we need to pay something for it.' He sighed. 'And here I was hoping that we wouldn't need to eat into any more of my savings.'

'I know.' Nick's stoic facade crumbled suddenly. 'Damn it, I was really looking forward to all this. Why does life have to be so screwed up?'

'It's not been officially confirmed yet.' Steven found himself wanting to find some positivity in the situation. 'We should probably wait until the official announcement. Then contact the accommodation and see what the story is. But we'll have to probably offer everyone a refund.' He considered the situation again; it was bad, no matter which way he looked at it. 'Actually, why don't we offer a refund, or a rebooking onto another weekend later in the year? And give them the dates so they can take their pick.'

'That's a good strategy. I knew it was a good idea going into business with you. I'm giving you a virtual high five right now.' Nick sounded slightly more cheerful.

'Oh.' Something else suddenly occurred to Steven. 'What about Jade's book? Is any of that going to be affected?'

'Jeez, I hadn't even thought about that.' Nick let out a long breath. 'I hope not. Surely they'll be able to work from home on everything the next few weeks. And the book launch isn't until the autumn. We're bound to be back to normal by then.'

Steven couldn't shake off the feeling that possibly it wouldn't be that simple. But what else could they do? 'OK. Let's keep an eye on the news. Wait until we get the official announcement and then we'll do what we've planned.'

'Great. I'll catch you soon.' Nick rang off, and left Steven turning his phone around in his hands. Surely in a few weeks time they would all be back to normal. Wouldn't they?

The door to the spare bedroom barely opened and Chantelle bit her lip, wondering how best to tackle the mess. There was no way she wanted to spend another night on the sofa; it was too short to be comfortable and the narrow width had seen her losing the covers a number of times. 'Why don't we get my stuff into the living room first before we go through all this? Then at least we can see what we're doing.'

It didn't take them long to get everything out and stacked in the corner. 'Let's go for it.' Steven went to heft some of the junk off the single bed, but Chantelle touched him gently on the arm.

'We need to involve your mum in this too.' She pointed with her head towards the living room. 'It's not fair to go through her things without asking.'

Steven nodded. 'You're right. Tell you what, shall we have a bit of a rummage to see what's in here first? Then we can take stuff next door for her to have a look at.'

Chantelle smiled at him. 'That's a good idea.' She poked her head out of the door and called through to Irene. 'Ma, do you want to sit on the sofa and we'll bring things out to you?'

'Sounds like a plan.' He heard his mum's voice answer back.

Steven surveyed the scene. What would be easiest to deal with? 'I never knew she was such a hoarder. I mean, she always liked shopping, but this is crazy.'

'These clothes first.' Chantelle pointed at the massive heap that lay on the bed. 'I'll bet there's loads of things there that are either the wrong size or don't suit her. It's an easy place to start.'

'Okey dokey. Let's do this.'

They left Irene sorting through a huge mound of clothes and surveyed the rest of the mess. 'One box at a time I guess.' Steven flipped open the lid of one that was perched on the corner of the bed. 'Oh. This is all my old school stuff. I'll have to have a look through.' He sat down beside it and started leafing through the papers. 'I don't think I'll keep much of this. It hardly covers me in glory. I remember my reports always said I was good at sport but could try harder in the classroom.'

'Yeah. You were always messing around. Do you remember when you let that bat free during French?' Chantelle had to smile at the memory. 'I remember poor Miss Raymond was terrified. And half the class. The other half thought it was hilarious.'

'Yeah.' Steven grimaced. 'Not really stuff I'm proud of these days. For starters, that poor bat! And I'm not even talking about Miss Raymond.' He met Chantelle's eyes steadily, and was rewarded by a snort of laughter.

It didn't take him long to extract the few things he really wanted to keep and then he reached for the next box. 'Oh. This is kiddie clothes. This can go to the charity shop, unless Mum wants any of them.'

'I guess she was keeping them for when we - I mean you - have kids. Maybe you should hang onto them. You never know what might happen.' Chantelle's voice sounded falsely cheerful and Steven looked up at her quickly, but she had her back to him and was rummaging at the bottom of the cupboard. 'How did your mum manage to keep this flat with two spare rooms anyway? It's a pretty big place for one person. I'm surprised the council didn't want her to move.'

Steven shrugged. 'I'm actually not sure. She probably never told the council that we'd moved out. And no-one ever asked.'

'Oh well.' Chantelle sat back on her heels. 'Chuck me that empty box, would you? This is all shoes and I'm going to take them out to Irene.'

He lobbed it over to her. 'What else is in there?'

'More clothes.'

Steven groaned. 'She could never wear all this stuff. I don't know what she was thinking. How did she afford it all?'

'Oh, you know how she would always go through the charity shops. She could never resist a good bargain.' Chantelle filled up the box. 'I bet that's where most of this comes from.'

The realisation struck Steven that he didn't really know his mum at all. It was amazing how you could spend so much time with someone and never get down to the real side of them and since he had moved out he had hardly been in touch at all. Guilt washed over him. He could have been spending time getting to know her, and instead he had been actively avoiding her. And now it was too late. Or almost too late. He would simply have to devote his efforts to making whatever time she had left as special as possible.

'Well, Irene is swimming in clothes, but she's making good progress.' Chantelle's voice made him jump. She'd cleared all the shoes out without him even noticing. 'And now this cupboard is empty I can put some of my stuff in it.'

They made a few more trips with boxes. Chantelle started pulling out her own things and hanging them in the cupboard.

'I'll help you.' Steven reached for a box.

Chantelle put out her hand. 'No, wait -'

It was too late; he had already flipped off the lid. His own laughing face stared back at him, caught up in an embrace with Chantelle by his side. It was the same photo that he had in his bedside drawer. The one she had lovingly stuck on the front of their wedding album. Which had been placed on top of her carefully folded wedding dress.

'You kept them.' His eyes met Chantelle's across the room.

'What, you expected me to burn it or something?' Chantelle was clearly trying to make a joke, but her voice was off again.

'Seriously? The way we parted, I wouldn't have been surprised.' He picked the album out of the box and turned a few pages. He saw himself waiting nervously at the altar with Pete beside him. The next photo was them saying their wedding vows. That day had been so full of promise and laughter it made his brain ache thinking about it.

'Where did it all go wrong, Chaz?'

Chantelle sagged against the cupboard. 'I don't know, Stevie. Maybe we were never right for each other and we simply hadn't realised it yet.'

'You don't really believe that, do you?' He leafed through another few photos, then gently closed the book and held it up facing towards her. 'Look. Look at this photo. Do you really believe all this was fake? That after knowing each other for eight years before we got married we were wrong about this?'

'People change, Stevie.' Chantelle's voice sounded tired and he knew he was pushing it. 'Can we talk about this another time? We've still got a load of stuff to do and I'm losing the will to live already.'

'Sure. Aye. Sorry.' He put the album back in the box and pushed it towards her. 'You get your clothes sorted. I'm going to see how Mum's getting on and make us all a cup of tea.' As he reached the door he stopped and turned back to her. 'But can we make sure we do talk about it? Because I really need to understand.'

Chapter 11

Something roused Steven and he blinked blearily at his clock. It was almost six thirty in the morning. His mind struggled to focus, and then he remembered. Chantelle was on an early shift today. Probably the sound of the door closing as she left had woken him up.

Now that everyone was working from home he missed his bike rides into the office. A new mandate had come through that they were only to leave the house for essential purposes or for exercise. Thank goodness Irene's volunteer work at the foodbank was considered essential so she could still get out. And Chantelle had her job. But apart from his daily run or cycle then Steven was stuck in the house and it was killing him. The spring was his favourite time of year to go walking, in the cooler months before the midges started to swarm. It was only just getting light and for a moment he considered rolling over and going back to sleep, but instead he stretched and yawned. Since he was awake, why not go out on the bike before work?

The quiet calm of the roads that were normally so busy filled Steven with joy and by the time he returned to the house his good mood had returned. He had forced himself to go back to road riding after his accident but still had a slight twinge of panic every time a car brushed by slightly too close to him, so the absence of traffic felt like a real gift. Grabbing his towel, he headed to the bathroom for a shower. He had to admit that sharing a flat with Chantelle was both the most wonderful and probably the most tortuous thing he had ever done. Like now, for instance, with the smell of her peachy-flavoured shampoo still in the bathroom. It was the same one that she had used when they were together, and it brought back memories of when they were living here before. Some steamy times in this very shower actually. They would always make sure one of them sneaked in so that his mum wouldn't notice, but he suspected she had known all along. There was that one time when he had made Chantelle come so hard that...

He became aware of just how hard he was himself, and groaned. This was madness. Sharing a flat with his ex-wife who he still had the hots for? Was there anything more screwed up? They still hadn't talked since the day they were sorting out her bedroom and the last two weeks it had been playing on his mind. Something about her had been off that day and he really wanted to know what it was. At the time he had thought she was just uncomfortable, but the more he thought about it the more he was convinced that it was almost like she had been trying to hide something. Had there been someone else? Was that why it had all ended? He dearly wanted to get to the bottom of the puzzle, but he also knew how stubborn she was. The more he pushed her, the less she would reveal.

It was time to stop using up hot water and get to work. A few swift strokes brought him to some sort of release and as he washed the jizz off he mentally let his frustrations flow away down the drain as well. It was going to be a busy day; the IT department had roped him into testing out some of the new videoconferencing software they were trialling and there were also endless health and safety discussions to be had. There were some good things about working from home. Being around meant he could nip out and get a cup of tea and check up on his mum at the same time. Her foodbank work got her out a couple of days a week and she spent the rest of the time either watching TV or reading the massive stash of books they had collected from the local library before it closed. He had been worried that dementia would affect her reading, but the romances and thrillers that were her usual choices seemed simple enough not to be causing problems yet.

Steven opened up his laptop on the desk in his bedroom. It was strange how going back to old things brought back old memories. How many times had he sat at this desk trying to concentrate on his homework while his parents were arguing? For one moment he imagined he actually heard them in the next room, but when he closed his eyes everything was quiet. Sometimes it was so hard not to be angry about it. To put it all in the past. Strive to make himself a better man than his father had been. He opened his eyes, staring at the login screen of his laptop, and took a deep breath. This wasn't going to get the day's work done. He typed the letters of his password and set to work.

A few days later phantom pains woke Steven in the middle of the night and he lay in the darkness with his face in the pillow, trying to breathe steadily. It was nothing new, but it was a while since they had been this bad. Although in some ways it was also a blessing they had woken him; he had been dreaming of lying on the road in agony while worried faces peered down at him. No doubt the real pains in his leg had made up the dream in his head while he was still sleeping.

When the stabbing finally subsided he looked over at the clock, now wide awake. It was almost three. He could get up and watch some late night TV for a while. It was Saturday tomorrow. Today. So no need to get up for work. If he took refuge under a blanket on the sofa there was every chance he would fall asleep again and wouldn't wake until someone else disturbed him. It was a solid plan.

Except when he got to the living room the blanket was already taken. Chantelle was sitting on the sofa in her pyjamas, staring into space. Steven sat down beside her, placing his crutches quietly down on the floor, conscious that his mum was still sleeping down the hall. 'Rough shift?' He had to stop himself from reaching out to place his arms around her shoulders as he had done so many times in the past. Instead he interlaced his fingers and rested them lightly on his thighs. 'Want to talk about it?'

The room was dim, but there was enough light from the street that he could see her shake her head. 'Not really.' She turned toward him. 'Sorry, I didn't mean that the way it came out. I just need a few minutes before I go to bed, you know? To separate things out in my mind.'

'I know.' He ached to reach out and touch her and searched for any excuse to distract himself. 'Fancy a cuppa?'

She smiled at him gratefully. 'That would be wonderful.'

Steven levered himself up and crutched towards the kitchen. 'I'll make it a decaf, then at least we might have a chance of getting back to sleep. I'll give you a wave when it's ready.'

They ended up back on the sofa and when Chantelle took her first sip she sighed with pleasure. 'I don't know what it is about tea. It seems to make everything look better.'

'That's what Jade says.' At Chantelle's enquiring look, Steven elaborated. 'Nick's girlfriend. I'm trying to remember if you've ever met.'

Chantelle shook her head. 'You've talked a fair bit about Nick, but I don't think I've met either of them.' She grimaced. 'I was going to say you should invite them round for dinner sometime, but that won't be happening in a while.'

They sat in silence for some minutes, sipping at the hot milky liquid. And then Steven couldn't take it any more. He opened his mouth to say something like *I still love you* or *Can't we give this another try* but Chantelle got there first.

'Stevie, I had a miscarriage.'

He stared at her, dragged out of his cosy fantasies about their relationship and wondered if this was a recent event. 'When?'

'When you were in the hospital.' Her face was cast down at her mug so he couldn't see her expression, but his heart ripped into pieces and he couldn't help himself. He pulled a cushion from beside him and placed it across his lap. 'Come here. Lay your head down and tell me all about it.'

She looked at him for a minute, obviously weighing up his offer, and then moved across and snuggled up against him. He caught the faint scent that taunted him in the bathroom every morning and breathed it in, letting it calm his racing mind. One hand found her shoulder, and with another he gently stroked her hair. 'Tell me everything. And tell me why you didn't say anything before.'

He felt Chantelle take a deep breath and let it out. 'Shit, I don't know really. Looking back it all seems so stupid, but when you're caught up in everything you just make the decisions that seem best at the time.'

Her shoulder rose and fell again as she collected herself. 'I can honestly say it was the most horrible experience of my life. To go through that sort of thing when you know what it is must be heart-rending enough. But I didn't even know I was pregnant. I had no idea what was happening to me. I spent an hour thinking it was my period coming, until I realised that it was far more serious than that. I'd missed a couple of periods, but I assumed that was to do with the stress of you being in hospital. Seeing as we were always careful about condoms and stuff.'

It had been a very stressful time. Steven didn't really remember the accident, but Chantelle had told him that the car had knocked him down and then somehow managed to drive over his leg. The collision had not only left Steven minus most of a limb but with significant internal bleeding. She had also said that in the early days there had been discussions about quality of life and what it might be when - or if - he came out the other side. For six weeks of his stay in hospital he had been barely conscious, drugged up on a massive cocktail of pain killers. No wonder he hadn't known what was going on.

A fuzzy memory came back to him. 'I remember one evening you disappeared and no-one seemed to know where you were. Was it then? Did it happen that night?'

'Yeah. The bleeding was so bad they had to take me in for an emergency operation. It was the following afternoon before I could get back to see you.'

Steven thought of how it must have been for her, to be lying there alone, knowing that he was only a few floors away but unable to help her. He curled a strand of her hair around his finger. 'I realise now why you didn't tell me. It would have killed me to know that you were going through all that and I couldn't even move from my hospital bed.'

Chantelle twisted around onto her back so she could look up at him. 'So you're not angry? I thought you'd be angry with me.'

Steven took a deep breath while he considered the idea. 'I don't know. I mean, I am, sort of. It's a big thing to keep from me. We almost had a baby? That's pretty major. I feel like I had a right to know. But what good would it do? When has anger ever helped anything?'

'I wanted you to get angry.' Chantelle's reply surprised him. 'After you got home from the hospital. I watched you lying in bed bingeing endless TV shows and stuffing your face and I wanted some of that anger back. Anything to drive you up and out and back into being the person you once were.' Her breath caught and he felt the wetness of tears beneath his hand. 'I know that it was a hard time for you, especially when that tosser who knocked you down tried to blame it on you and then started harassing you to drop your compensation case. But some days I just want our old life back. I want my fairytale romance with the boy I met. That day we got married…I ache for it. I ache for how happy we were, even though I know it will never be the same.'

The longing in her voice made Steven's eyes fill with tears, and he gathered his courage to speak the words that had been waiting in his heart. 'You're right, we can't go back. But I still love you. I never stopped loving you. So do you think there might be some hope for us to go forward?'

There. It was done. And now his fate was out of his hands.

'Are you being serious? I mean honestly?' Chantelle sat up, dragging the blanket with her, and he felt the loss as something more than a lack of warmth.

He nodded, and then realised it might not be visible in the dim light. 'Yes. A hundred percent.'

She was silent for a few moments. 'I don't know. I mean, the things that split us up haven't changed. I'll always be the one who wants to think ahead, while you just seem happy to let life flow around you. I love your spontaneity, but life doesn't always work like that. Sometimes you have to plan. And I worry we'll be straight back into the old patterns as soon as something else hits us.'

Steven shrugged. 'Isn't life always full of compromises? I'm not the same man I was three years ago. And from the looks of things you're not the same either. Do we always have to plan? Can't we take this one day at a time and see how it goes? Especially now, with everything that's going on. We don't even know how long it will be before they'll let us out of the house.'

Chantelle looked like she was going to say something, but a massive yawn split her face face instead. She snuggled back down onto his lap and pulled the blanket around herself. 'Maybe.'

Steven rested a hand on her head and stroked her hair with his thumb. 'Let's do one day at a time. I like having you back in my life.'

'Are you OK?'

Steven woke to find himself slumped awkwardly on the couch. His mother was peering down at him. No sign of Chantelle.

He sat up, rubbing a stiff muscle in his neck and feeling where the crease of a cushion had formed a deep line across his cheek. 'Yeah, I'm fine. I woke up in the middle of the night and came out for a drink. What time is it?'

Irene looked at her watch. 'Just after eight. Sorry, I didn't mean to wake you.'

Chantelle must have gone back to her bed, but she'd been kind enough to cover him with the blanket. His stomach rumbled. 'No, it's fine. I'm starving. Want some breakfast?'

Irene nodded. 'Let me get it for you.'

'You sit down here and I'll give you a shout when it's ready. I'll put the kettle on. Cocoa loops or frosted flakes?'

Irene sat down and reached for the remote control. 'That's nice of you. I'll have frosted flakes, please.'

Steven stared at the kettle as he filled it. Lockdown seemed to pale into insignificance compared with what Chantelle had told him last night. A dad. He had been a dad. For a couple of short months. And he hadn't even known about it.

Had it been a girl or a boy? Had it been too early to tell? He pictured a little copy of Chantelle running around in a play park and smiled to himself, then felt his throat close. They had agreed it was too early to have kids but there was never any doubt about the fact that they both wanted them. He was still struggling to come to terms with the news and the fact that Chantelle hadn't told him. If he was honest with himself, he was a little angry with her. To keep something like that from him...was it right?

The water overflowed out of the top of the kettle and into the sink, disrupting his thoughts. Huffing an exasperated sigh at himself, he turned off the tap and drained the extra water, then set the kettle to boil. Breakfast was easy; just two bowls and milk. His mother came to fetch everything and he finally sat down next to her with a sigh of relief.

'So what's this you're watching?' He peered at the screen, where some politician seemed to be getting a grilling about the current crisis.

'I would tell you, but I've forgotten the poor presenter's name.' Irene was happily making her way through her cereal. 'I do like to keep up with these things though. It's important to keep a grasp of current affairs.'

She had always been very vocal about her views, out of his dad's earshot at least. For himself, he had been trying to keep out of the constant news cycle, only dipping in for long enough to keep abreast of the latest lockdown regulations. He simply found it an all too depressing reminder of how his life had been turned upside down. Still, he had promised he would spend some more quality time with his mum, so he tried to focus on the programme as he ate his breakfast.

'Would you like to go out for a walk with me today, Mum?' He reached across and touched her arm.

She looked at him, surprised. 'If you like. Where do you want to go?'

'I don't know. Anywhere. Up to the woods. Round and about. Anywhere to get out of the house.' He slumped back on the sofa.

'You're feeling it too?' She reached out and put an arm around him, and he accepted the hug. She had always been a hugger. He felt himself relax slightly.

'Yeah. I'm going mad in here. Some days I simply want to get on my bike and cycle away and not come home.' He gave a wry laugh.

Irene frowned. 'It's not because of me, is it?'

'Oh no. It's just being stuck inside all day. Not seeing people. I miss my friends. Friday nights in the pub. I can't even go to the gym any more. And I can't see any of the guys. It's totally shit. I want my normal life back.'

'Don't we all, darling.' Irene's voice trembled a little, and he instantly felt guilty. Here he was, stuck at home for just a few weeks, and she was facing never having her normal again. He put his arm around her and squeezed hard. 'Come on, Mum. Let me get these dishes washed up and we'll go up to the woods. It's a beautiful day and I bet the daffodils are out. We'll leave Chantelle to sleep, she's working again tonight.'

'I'll need to get some clothes on and do my hair.' Irene put a hand up. 'I can feel it sticking out all over the place.'

'Do what you like, Mum, but you could always put on a hat.' He smoothed down the offending hair tenderly.

She grimaced. 'I've got to maintain some standards. I don't want to end up like one of those people you see who've dropped their breakfast down them and haven't noticed.'

Underlying it all was the fear of losing herself, he realised. He kissed the side of her head. 'You go do that. I'm going to take a shower. My neck's all knotted up from sleeping on this sofa.'

Chapter 12

They left a note for Chantelle and took a walk along the canal and up into the woods. Steven loved this little strip of land, hidden away on the top of the hill between two rows of back gardens. One of his first memories was of making mud pies in a hollow up here somewhere.

'Look at those orange ones, Mum.' Steven pointed. 'Such a pity we can't pick a few and take them back to the house.'

Irene knelt down to sniff them. 'They always have such a lovely scent. I don't know why I never thought to plant some of them in the garden.'

'Your mini daffodils are lovely, though. They've been cheering me up all week.' Steven helped her back up to her feet and they strolled on. He had noticed recently her sense of balance wasn't as good as it used to be, which was one of the potential symptoms that the doctor had warned him about. An arm offered with the excuse of keeping himself steady was a good way to preserve her dignity.

'Are you finding this very hard?' Irene turned to look at him. 'I know you're usually out and about at all hours of the day.'

'Kind of.' He found himself unwilling to admit the extent of his frustrations, maybe because he knew she would worry about him. 'What about you? How are you dealing with all this? On top of everything else?'

'I don't know.' He could sense she spoke honestly. 'I'm still trying to take the full scale of this in. People are saying it won't be long until we get back to normal, but I can't help feeling that somehow things will never be the same again.' She snorted. 'I heard someone on the TV the other day saying it was like the Blitz. Well, both my parents - your grandparents - lived through the Blitz and I can tell you it's nothing like that. We weren't forbidden from hugging our loved ones like we are now.' She shook her head slowly. 'That's the thing that cuts me up the most. I can't hug anyone. And we're not even allowed to get near our neighbours.'

'I'll hug you whenever you want, Mum.' Steven reached across and pulled her in for one. 'And let's face it, you've never got on well with the neighbours. Those ones on the other side of you were really horrible when I first moved in. It's only Brenda who seems decent. She's been really great passing food in through the door at all hours of the day.'

He kissed her gently on the cheek. 'You're doing pretty well with your memory if you can remember all this stuff.'

He had meant it as a joke, but Irene just sighed. 'I don't know. My brain seems to remember what it wants these days. I have no control over what it does or doesn't do any more.' She stopped and pointed at another patch of daffodils. 'Aren't those white ones beautiful?'

'You're still you. And I still love you.' Steven didn't know where those thoughts had come from, but he decided to run with it. 'Let's take one day at a time. That's all we can do at the moment.' It was starting to be a bit of a mantra. There were worse ones, he supposed. He pulled her gently to a stop. 'Stand here and listen to all the birds singing for a second. Isn't it beautiful?'

Chantelle was up when they got back, although she hadn't bothered to change out of her pyjamas. 'It feels dead weird not being able to pop out to the shops at all.' She yawned.

'I take it you mean the shops in town? The one on the corner is still open.' Steven suddenly remembered their conversation from last night. They really had to talk, he realised. Did the last words they had shared mean they were an item again? It really hadn't been clear.

'Yeah.' Chantelle crossed her legs underneath her. 'I sometimes meet Sarah in town when we're both off. Have a good blether and a bit of a wander around the shops. Now

I don't know what to do with myself. There's only so much TV a body can watch.'

Irene looked at them both. 'I can see we're all three of us feeling the same way.' She took out the little black notebook that she now always carried around in a pocket, and flipped to an empty page. 'We're going to have to put our heads together and think up some activities that can be done indoors.' She looked at them expectantly.

Chantelle bit her lip and thought for a minute. 'Well, I've got that bejewelling kit that Sarah and Simon gave me for Christmas. I've barely opened it yet. It's got stuff for making birthday cards and such. We could have a bit of a crafting session at some point.'

'Be...jewl...ing.' Irene wrote in careful letters on the pad. 'That's a start. And it reminds me I should have my sewing machine somewhere. If I haven't got rid of it. I'll have to have a look.' She nodded at Chantelle. 'I could teach you how to use it, if you like.'

Chantelle put a look of mock horror on her face. 'Oh no. I'm hopeless at these things.' She pointed. 'Stevie's the one who's always wanted to learn how to make clothes. Teach him.' A sly smile appeared on her face. 'Maybe then he might be able to make me something.' She winked at him.

Irene turned to him. 'Is that true?'

He could feel himself blushing. 'Not totally. It's just...you know...it would be useful to be able to alter some of the stuff I buy. No-one makes clothes for short guys.'

'Sewing lessons. Stevie.' Irene wrote on her pad. 'Anything else?'

Chantelle pulled out her phone. 'I'm going to message Sarah. She's always full of good ideas.'

'Have you still got all those jigsaws we used to do?' Steven wanted to know. 'I don't mind a good jigsaw. Especially all those ones with loads of sky.'

'Ugh.' Chantelle pretended to shudder, and they all laughed.

Irene looked thoughtful. 'I don't know where they'd be, if I've still got them. Probably somewhere in my room. But we can have a look.'

'Baking is supposed to be a big thing right now.' Chantelle was looking at her phone. 'Sarah wrote me that someone gave her a sourdough starter but with everything that's going on she probably won't have time to do anything with it, so if we want to have it we can.'

'Oh, so we're going all hipster now?' Steven stroked an imaginary beard and was rewarded with another laugh from Chantelle. 'Yeah, why not. It will keep us busy.'

'Bread.' Irene was still keeping track on her pad. 'Well, that's a good start. I would say other baking, but if we start that we'll all end up as round as barrels.'

'No. Endless cake is so not a good idea.' Steven shuddered. 'But we could try experimenting with some new recipes. Like real food, I mean. I feel like I always do the same things over and over again.'

'I know what you mean.' Chantelle nodded. 'I'd love to have some different meals to take to work. Something that's not just sandwiches all the time.'

Food went on the pad as well. 'The only other thing I can suggest is going through the cupboards.' Irene pointed vaguely in the direction of her bedroom. 'I'm sure there's a whole host of things which we can either throw away or make some use of.' She wrote that down. 'Well, I don't know about you, but I'm parched for a cup of tea with all that thinking.'

It wasn't until later that Steven managed to catch Chantelle alone in the corridor. 'You know what you said last night? We need to talk more about it. I want to know everything.'

'Everything?' Chantelle frowned, then she slumped back against the wall. 'You're right. I owe you at least that. But can we talk later? I need to get my stuff together for work.'

'Sure.' More avoidance, but if it was part of her then he was going to love her for it. 'You're off tomorrow, right? Could we go for a walk and talk then? I could take the afternoon off probably, there's not much for me to do now that we don't actually have people in the office.'

'You memorised my schedule?' The surprise showed in her voice, but he could tell she was impressed.

'What else am I going to do kicking my heels around the house all day?' He smiled at her. 'Took me forever. I don't know how you keep track of it.'

She waggled her phone at him. 'I don't.'

'Chaz...what you said last night...does that mean you want to give us another try?'

The smile disappeared. 'Shit, Stevie, I don't know. Can you give me some time to think about it?'

If he had ever seen someone who wanted to escape more it would be hard to describe it. But he wasn't going to make this work if he didn't have patience. 'Go on. We'll talk tomorrow.'

'See you later.' She flashed him a quick smile and disappeared into her room.

Chantelle clipped her mobile device back onto its holder and turned to her colleague in the van. 'Right, that's all done. Let's get out of here. I'm starving and I need my snacks.'

Donny, however, made no move to start up the engine and just looked at her, his blue eyes steady. 'Are you going to tell me what's going on?'

Chantelle had gone to reach for her water bottle but jerked around in surprise to look at him. 'What do you mean?' With his mouth hidden behind the medical mask it was hard to tell if he was joking.

'You've been all over the place this afternoon, which is really not like you. You asked that woman three times back there what her name was, so I need to know what's going on. It's fine to be a bit off on a call like that, but if we get something critical I can't have you in danger if your mind's not in the game.'

Chantelle opened her mouth to protest, then closed it again. It wasn't surprising that Donny had picked up on her mental unrest; he had been doing the job for more than ten years and his uncanny ability to read people had saved them both from some very hairy situations in the past few months. He already knew about her weird living arrangements and what was going on with Irene. 'Steven asked me last night if we could get back together. I've been thinking about it all day.'

'Ah.' The single syllable was one of the most expressive Chantelle had heard in a while. She waited to see if Donny would say anything else, but he just looked out through the windscreen, where a mother and child were crossing the street in front of them. The little girl waved at them enthusiastically and they both waved back.

Chantelle turned to Donny. 'Can you give me any advice? I mean, you're so much older and wiser than me.' Suddenly aware of how that might come across, she scrambled for more words, flustered. 'I didn't mean it like that, honest. I really don't know what to do. Has it ever happened to you?'

Donny was silent for a bit longer, and she could tell he was pondering her question. 'I can't say as it has, really. When I split with my wife we traded enough insults to make sure that going back was well nigh impossible.'

'He says we should take things one day at a time and see how it goes.' Chantelle fiddled with the lid of her bottle, opening it and closing it repeatedly. 'But I can't work like that. I need stability and certainty in my life. If I went back to him and it didn't work out again, I don't think I could bear it.'

Donny adjusted his mask slightly. 'Seems like, though, what you need is not to go back.' He held up his hand to forestall any further comment from her. 'From what you've said already about the way things were the first time, it's a situation that you don't want to go back into. But that doesn't mean you can't go forward. And go forward together.'

'That's pretty much what he said, and I get that.' Chantelle pulled down her mask briefly to take a swig from her bottle. 'But I need to know that it's what I want before I commit to it. And I simply don't.'

'It's always hard to find the balance between living for today and planning for the future, and you're the only one who can decide what combination is right for you. But with this pandemic, who knows? We could all be dead in a few weeks.' Donny shrugged and started the engine. 'Just talk to him. And keep on talking. Explore what a future together might look like. That's the best you can do.'

'Thanks.' Chantelle reached across and touched his shoulder gently. 'I mean really, thanks for that. I don't know what I'd do without you.'

Steven tried to lose himself in the television that evening, but Irene wanted to watch her favourite detective show and he just couldn't get into it. When he got up to fetch himself a drink for the third time in half an hour her patience finally snapped. 'For goodness sake, Stevie, you'll be pissing all night if you have another one.'

Steven huffed out his impatience, sinking back on the sofa. 'Sorry, Mum. I'll go and watch the football in your room.'

Irene looked at him for a couple of seconds, then nodded decisively and switched off the TV. She pulled out her notebook from her pocket and leafed through it until she got to the page she wanted. 'Right. I'm getting that sewing machine out and teaching you how to do it. You go and get those clothes you want altering from your room.'

'Oh Mum.' He knew he sounded like a teenager, but he couldn't help it. 'On a Sunday night? Are you kidding me?'

She waggled a finger at him. 'Anything to stop you mop-ing around. And if you won't tell me what's eating at you then the least I can do is distract you.'

Steven grumbled, but pushed himself up off the couch and went to do as he was told. A quick rummage in his cupboard turned up a couple of things that could definite-ly do with a bit of adjustment. He took them back into the living room, to find his mum unpacking the sewing machine onto the dining table. Bags of material and a box filled with brightly-coloured spools of cotton sat on the wooden surface. He passed the clothes over to her. 'Here you go. These jeans are a bit long, they always pool round my ankles. And this shirt I've always wanted to wear outside my trousers, but that's a bit long too so it looks ridiculous at the moment.'

She took the clothes from him. 'Hang on, I need to get my sunglasses first.'

He looked at her, confused. 'Sunglasses?'

She pointed at the bright orange shirt. 'You're a bit slow, aren't you? The colour on that one is enough to make anyone need some shades.'

'Oh, Mum.' Steven rolled his eyes, but couldn't help laughing as well. This was going to be so much more fun than he'd expected.

'I'm going to load it up with some random thread so you can have a practice. I'm sure I've got some scraps of material somewhere.' Irene plugged in the sewing machine and sat down in front of it, pulling up a chair for Steven to sit beside her. She lifted her hands but then froze.

'What's wrong?' Steven looked at her in concern.

'I've forgotten how to thread it up.' She turned to him and the expression on her face ripped at his heart. 'Oh Stevie, how could I forget such a thing?' She burst into tears.

He pulled her to him and held her tightly, rocking gently. 'Shh.' He reached across for his shirt. 'Here. Have the world's brightest hanky to blow your nose.'

She shook her head. 'Don't be ridiculous, I can't use that.' She patted her pockets, then pulled her handkerchief out with a small satisfied smile and blew loudly.

'It'll still be in there somewhere, Mum. You've got this.' Steven rubbed her shoulder gently. 'You must have done it so many times, I bet you could do it with your eyes closed. So don't think about it. Do it with them closed. Or do it while you're not concentrating. Your fingers will remember.'

Irene took a deep breath. 'I guess you could be right.' She stroked the top of the machine uncertainly.

'Do it while you're talking to me. Or thinking about what you want for dinner tomorrow.' He handed her a reel of white cotton. 'Here you go.'

She took it in her hand and placed it on the spool holder. 'That's a start, at least.'

'When did you first start sewing?' Steven had intended to distract her, but suddenly found himself actually wanting to know.

'Oh, almost before I can remember.' Irene looked at him. 'First it was the family mending and then when I was about ten I progressed to making clothes. It was much cheaper those days to make your own because there wasn't any of the cut-price Chinese stuff you get these days. I was never as good as my mum though. She had a real talent.' She looked down at the machine in front of her, now completely threaded and ready to go. 'Oh. It worked.'

'Told you.' Steven leaned over and kissed her on the cheek. 'I love you.'

'I love you too.' A small tear squeezed out of her eye and she dabbed at it with her hanky. 'Right. Let's swap over and you can have a go with this machine.'

After measuring him up Irene showed him how the foot pedal would control the speed of the machine, and left him practising on a scrap piece of fabric while she cut a strip off the bottom of his shirt and pinned it up. When she was satisfied he was fairly competent then she pushed the shirt at him. 'Go on. Give it a go.'

A sudden fear rushed through him that was totally out of proportion with the task in front of him. 'But what happens if I mess it up?'

She rested a hand reassuringly on his shoulder. 'Don't worry. You can always unpick it. But it's a bit of a pain, so do try not to. Go slowly and it'll be fine.'

He threaded some orange through the machine, copying the way he had seen her do it, placed the fabric in the right place, and pressed the pedal. He was so intent on what he was doing he forgot to breathe and halfway through he stopped and straightened, taking in a deep gulp of air. Irene laughed at him. 'It'll get easier as time goes on.'

He bent to the task again, and when he had finished he cut off the trailing threads carefully, then held the shirt up to examine his handiwork. 'Wow.' A grin spread over his face. 'That actually looks pretty decent.'

Irene smiled at him. 'Not bad for a first attempt.'

He gave her a nudge. 'What do you mean, for a first attempt? That's quality sewing right there.'

The look on her face told him she was enjoying this as much as he was. 'Thread up some blue and I'll help you with the jeans. I'll show you how to cut and pin them so you know how to do that too.'

Twenty minutes later he had a new pair of jeans as well. He stood up. 'Gimme a mo, I'll just go try them on.' He dressed quickly in front of his mirror, then came out to show her. 'They do look so much better now. Thanks, Mum.' He leaned down to kiss the top of her head. This was a gamechanger. He was unlikely to start making his own clothes any time soon, but how many times had he had to put something back on the rail because they were made for someone taller than him? He settled himself comfortably on the couch, smiling as Irene sat down beside him.

'You're looking very pleased with yourself.' She sounded pretty pleased with herself too.

'I was just thinking I can go out shopping and really pick out what I want now.' His smile faltered slightly as he realised that it wouldn't be an option for a while. 'I mean, when all this is over and the shops reopen. When things are back to normal.'

Irene gave him another fond smile and switched back on the TV.

'Shit, is that the ten o'clock news already?' Steven checked his watch. 'I'd better get myself off to bed. I've got work in the morning.'

'Night, love.' Irene reached over and patted his hand. 'Sleep well.'

Chapter 13

Steven managed to negotiate the afternoon off the following day, just as he'd hoped, and at twelve thirty came out into the living room to find Chantelle and Irene eating their lunch. Chantelle waved a hand in the direction of the kitchen. 'We've made a couple of extra sandwiches for you. Ham and cheese. I hope that's OK.'

'Aye. Magic.' He wandered into the kitchen and picked up the plate, then came to sit with them at the dining table. 'I've managed to get my holiday approved, so our walk's still on, if you're up for it.' He looked expectantly at Chantelle.

She glanced at Irene, who shook her head. 'You go for it. It's a nice day. Bit windy, but the sun's shining.' She frowned. 'I'm sure I was going to do something important this afternoon, but I can't remember what it was.'

Chantelle nudged her. 'You found those jigsaws and said you were going to get one started while we're out.'

'I was wondering what all those thumps were this morning.' Steven waved his sandwich. 'Thanks for these. They're really good. Did you put mustard in them too?'

Chantelle nodded. 'Can't have a ham sandwich without mustard.'

'Well, you can, technically...' Steven couldn't help teasing her, but she didn't rise to the challenge and only rolled her eyes. He switched topics. 'So where do you want to go for a walk?'

Chantelle shrugged. 'Why not along the canal? It's nice and flat.'

'I've kind of been avoiding the canal, because you're supposed to keep two metres from other people, and it's not even that wide.' He considered for a few moments. 'Do you think if we hold our breath every time we walk past someone then it would be OK?'

Chantelle regarded him as if she didn't know whether he was being serious. To be fair, he almost didn't know if he was being serious either. Who knew what the virus was capable of? 'There won't be that many people on a Monday afternoon. It should be fine.'

She was right; when they reached the canal it was almost deserted. They made their way in silence past two sets of locks before Steven couldn't bear it any longer. He turned to Chantelle. 'Go on. Tell me everything.'

'What do you mean, everything?' She frowned, confused.

'I know that it's hard to talk about it, but I want to know everything about the miscarriage. What it felt like. What you felt like. And I also want to know the real reason why you didn't tell me.'

She had been studying a pair of ducks feeding in the reeds near the opposite bank, but at his words her head jerked around to meet his gaze. 'What do you mean, the real reason?'

'When we spoke you seemed to imply that it was because you wanted to spare me, but you've never been one to avoid the difficult news.' He met her gaze with a smile. 'I remember you were the one who broke it to me about my leg, but you didn't mince your words then, so tell me. What really happened?'

Chantelle bit her lip and looked away again. It was so hard to find the right words to say, especially when she had kept everything bottled up for so long. Their feet crunched on the gravel path for a good twenty paces before she replied. 'I don't know. I guess, if I'm really honest, I think it was all tied up in my reaction to what had happened to you. I know this sounds weird, but sometimes having bad things happen to someone I'm close to is almost worse than going through it myself. Watching you go through all that in the hospital, knowing that it would mean you wouldn't be able to do the job you loved any more? I would have swapped places with you just to spare you that.'

'You would?' He glanced at her in surprise and then nodded slowly. 'Of course you would. And I would have done the same for you.'

'Thanks.' Her brain was already trying to piece together the words she wanted to say next. 'I guess...I guess I didn't tell you because I knew what it was like, to be powerlessly watching you go through something that I had no control over. And I didn't want you to feel the same about the miscarriage, especially when you were so ill and felt so vulnerable yourself.' She took in a deep breath and let it out again. 'I know that may seem a bit weird, but it's the best way of describing my feelings at the time.'

Steven shrugged. 'I guess that makes sense. I'm still not sure if I can forgive you though.'

She glanced at him in surprise, and noticed his specific smile he put on when he had made a joke and was expecting someone to acknowledge it. 'Shit, Stevie, I thought you were being serious there. Don't do that to me.'

'Sorry.' His face fell. 'I can't seem to help it somehow. Emotion always makes me uncomfortable and I can't help trying to break up the mood. I think it goes back to my parents fighting when I was younger.' He was silent for a few moments. 'I still don't understand why you didn't tell me later though.'

Why hadn't she? Chantelle tried to think back to exactly how she had felt at the time. 'I thought I would tell you when you came out of hospital but it always seemed like it wasn't the right time, or something happened, or someone came to visit. And then Sarah announced she was expecting Aileen, and it really hit home that she would be having a baby and we wouldn't. And I thought you would see that something was wrong then, but you were so wrapped up in yourself that you didn't. And then I got angry at you.'

'Oh.' She could see Steven thinking hard. 'Was that when you started to get all shouty and complain that I wasn't getting out of the house?'

She nodded. 'I'm sorry, I couldn't help it. You kept missing physio appointments, and I didn't feel like you were the same man I married. The one who was up for anything and would keep pushing through no matter what. And then Mum got told that her treatment had failed and she only had a few weeks to live and it seemed like you cared more about yourself than how I was struggling.'

Steven looked up to where a couple of seagulls were floating overhead. 'Mum had a right go at me the day you left. Some of the things she said still hurt. Mainly because they were true.'

Chantelle had to smile at the thought. 'Sorry about that. I told her when I got to work that day. You remember how she always used to do the lunchtime shift and I did the evenings? She couldn't wait for work to end before she stomped back home to give you a piece of her mind.'

He winced. 'Aye. There was a lot of stomping. And a lot of shouting. Which told me how serious things were. The only other person she ever shouted at was my dad.'

They passed under a bridge and by another couple of locks in silence.

'Look, I'm sorry I didn't talk properly to you about how I was feeling.' Chantelle stopped walking and turned to him. 'But I was pretty young back then. I don't know if I really had the words to express things like I do now.' Talking like this was hard. It was like ripping a manky plaster off; painful, but definitely the right thing to do.

'Will you tell me about the night you lost the baby?' Steven fiddled nervously with the zipper on his jacket. 'Fuck, that wording doesn't seem right. Losing it sounds as if you were careless or something.' He collected himself. 'What I meant to say is, I'll always feel bad that I wasn't with you, although I also know it wasn't my fault.' He spotted a bench. 'Shall we go over there? I could do with a bit of a rest, even though we're not really supposed to.'

'Sure.' They made their way over and Chantelle sat down gratefully. They had come a fair way, now that she thought about it. Strange how when you were walking and talking the time could pass without you noticing. She realised that Steven was waiting for her to speak and tried to collect her thoughts. 'Let me think. I'd been feeling a bit rough, but didn't really think anything of it, because my sleep was all broken up what with being at the hospital all the time and being worried about you. I kind of assumed that it was something to do with that. And missing my period. Maybe if I'd had morning sickness, I would have twigged, but to be honest, I'd kind of lost track of the days by then. And I knew that stress could knock them out; it had happened before when I was at school for exams and stuff.'

She reached out a hand towards Steven, wanting some support, and he took it and held it in his. A deep breath helped to steady her somewhat. 'I think when I started bleeding I was happy, because that was one thing that was back to normal. I managed to get a couple of sani pads off a nurse, but when they bled through I went to ask her where I could get some more, and she said that using them both up in an hour simply wasn't normal. She insisted on getting someone to give me an examination, and that was when they told me what was going on. I was pretty shocked. Like I said, to have to take in all that information in one go...' Her voice trailed off as her throat closed.

'Come here.' Steven's arms came around her and she rested her head on his shoulder, feeling the warmth from him seeping into her body.

'Thanks,' she mumbled into his neck.

Chantelle could feel him shake his head. 'No. I should have been there for you. If not on that night, then after that.

I'm sorry I was so selfish, leaving you to handle everything on your own.'

She raised her head and looked at him. 'I don't know. I think also I felt a bit guilty myself, wanting things from you that you clearly weren't able to give. You had just lost a leg, after all.'

'Saying it like that makes me sound like I carelessly left it somewhere too.' Steven's face slid into a hesitant smile, as if he wasn't sure how the joke would be received.

Chantelle did laugh, glad of an excuse to break the tension. 'I guess that's much more likely these days. With your prosthetic I mean.'

Steven shuddered, clapping a hand to his forehead. 'That's my worst nightmare. It has almost happened a few times.'

'Perish the thought.' Chantelle made a face. 'Was it very expensive?'

'More than I'm willing to reveal. But luckily that tosser's insurance paid out in the end and I bought it with that.'

'Yeah. I heard.'

'You did? Have you been keeping tabs on me? Getting the goss from my mum?'

'Well, we did work with each other until I swapped jobs. She always used to talk about you. I think she always hoped we'd get back together.' Chantelle didn't know why she was defending herself.

Steven smiled, but then his face grew serious. 'I still love you, Chaz. And I need to know, do you want to give this another try? Or do you just want to stay friends and call it a day?'

Chantelle had known this question would be coming at some point, but somehow her brain had carefully avoided thinking about the answer. She frowned. What did she want? Was she still the same person with the same feelings as when they had been married? She wasn't at all really, but looking at Steven she realised how much she still liked him. 'I don't know, Stevie. Like I said, I'm worried the things that drove us apart in the past will still come between us. But we've both changed in the last three years, so perhaps we could give it a go? I'm still not sure though.'

She saw the hope flare in Steven's eyes at her words, and he took her hands in his. 'Like you said, I'm not the same person that I used to be either. I'd like to think it's a better model, but we will just have to take things a day at a time. And I think that's all anyone can do at the moment, with things as uncertain as they are right now. I mean, either of us could be dead from this fucking virus at any time. Once lockdown is over we can start talking about what we want life to be like. But can't it wait until after then?'

He was looking at her, waiting for a response, and in answer she just leaned forward and kissed him gently. She must have taken him by surprise, because he froze for half a second, and then he was kissing her back, their tongues sliding against each other in a delicious movement that she had missed for too long. It wasn't until someone nearby hooted at them that Chantelle realised she had swung her leg up over Steven's thigh and they were properly entwined. They both pulled away, smiling sheepishly. Chantelle could feel her heart pounding and there were definitely good feelings going on in her lady parts. 'I see you haven't lost your skills, even after three years.'

Steven's smile widened. 'I see you haven't lost yours either.'

'So what happens now?' Chantelle looked at him. 'Are we going to date, or do we just screw each other until our brains fall out?'

Steven laughed. 'Could we do both? Is that allowed?' He picked up her hand and kissed it, and then his face fell. 'Not that there's much we can do for dates at the moment, with everywhere shut.' His eyes sparkled suddenly. 'Maybe we're going to have to spend our time screwing after all.'

Chantelle found a laugh escaping her. She had not felt this happy since her job offer from the police had come through. 'While I'm not against the idea, it would be nice to do some other stuff together. We're still allowed to go out and exercise, so just walking and talking would be great. I'd be happy to go running, too, although I'd be surprised if you'll be able to keep up with me.' She suddenly realised that he might take it the wrong way, and winced. 'Sorry. Sometimes I forget, you know? I just meant because you're shorter than me.'

Steven curved a hand gently around her neck and stroked her cheek. 'Hush. Don't worry about it. I'd be happy to go running. But you had better watch out - once I get my blade on I'm pretty fast.'

Chantelle lifted her chin. 'Is that a challenge? Because I'll have you know I was third fastest in my class when I was at the police college.'

'Ah, it's like that, is it?' Steven stroked an imaginary beard for a couple of seconds, then gave up and collapsed into laughter. 'Oh, it's so good to have you back, Chaz. I've missed you something chronic.'

'Me too.' Chantelle rested her head on his shoulder.

They sat like that for a few minutes, listening to the faint sounds of the occasional car rumbling down Great Western Road, and then Chantelle checked her watch. 'We'd better get moving, I guess. To be honest, with the regulations as they are even sitting on this bench isn't something we should really be doing. We've still got to get back and I always feel wary about leaving your mum alone for too long.'

Steven's gaze jerked around. 'You too? I thought it was just my paranoia.'

Chantelle shook her head. 'I don't know. I know that most of the time it's fine, she seems to get caught up in watching the TV for hours on end, but occasionally she seems to go off and do something that's totally unpredictable.'

'Aye.' Steven sighed. 'I still haven't got used to all this, you know? The idea that I'll never get her back to her normal self. That it's all downhill from here.'

'Yeah.' Chantelle didn't really want to consider that. 'I went through all that with Mum, of course. We were hopeful for so long, but then I finally had to accept that she wasn't going to make it.' Her mouth twisted and she took a deep breath. She was not going to cry right now. 'But in some small way it was also a relief, if you know what I mean? It meant that we could stop fighting and start making the most of the time we had left.' Her thoughts went to that day, and exactly how she had felt. 'I remember that day when we got back home from the doctor we both just lay on her bed and cried for hours. But then we dried our tears and started to make a bucket list. It might be a good idea. Even if you don't, you've got to have a honest conversation with her at some point about the future.'

'I thought about doing a bucket list.' Steven's shoulders slumped. 'But much good it's going to be now when we can't even go anywhere.'

'I don't know.' Chantelle desperately tried to be cheerful. 'It can't go on forever. Besides, you don't know what would be on her bucket list. It might be simple things, like learning how to cook properly, or having a nice dinner with people she loves. Which reminds me,' she suddenly remembered, 'I could have sworn she was engineering things to try and get us back together. So maybe that's on her list as well.'

The sparkle was back in Steven's eyes. 'You noticed it too? I was thinking the exact same thing.'

'She wasn't all that subtle about it.' Chantelle stood up and pulled on his hand gently. 'Come on. I want a cup of tea. Let's go home.'

When they got back Irene was sitting on the sofa, watching home improvement programmes. She looked at them appraisingly and a small smile appeared on her face. Then she pointed at the TV. 'Come and have a look at this. This couple, I can't believe it. They've flown them all the way out to goodness knows where for this programme, and they can't agree on what kind of house they want. Wouldn't you have thought that they would have actually talked about that before they got there?'

Chantelle just smiled. 'I'll go put the kettle on. Do you fancy some tea, Ma?'

'What? Oh, yes please. Thanks, love.' Irene turned her attention back to the TV. 'I mean, look. This is the umpteenth place they're looking at. He thinks it's too small, and she says it's fine. What are they expecting for that kind of money?'

Chantelle hummed to herself as she filled the kettle. One day at a time. She could do that. Put aside her planning brain for a while and simply live life as it came. Could she?

Chapter 14

The three of them were watching TV that evening when Chantelle felt her phone ring in her pocket. She jumped up from the sofa. 'Be back in a mo.' When she pulled it out it was Sarah. This would need some privacy. She swiped the screen. 'Hey.'

'Hey you.' Sarah sounded tired, but two small kids could do that to you. 'How's things?'

'Is that how's things in the general sense, or how's things apart from all the shit pandemic stuff that's going on?' Chantelle toed her feet into her trainers, grabbed her keys and coat and quietly closed the front door.

'Ugh, tell me about it. The nursery's closed, so Aileen's home with me again. Thank God I'm still on mat leave, otherwise I don't know how we'd cope. Simon's working from home, which is also a nightmare because he's had to set up his laptop our bedroom. Which just feels weird. Who wants to work in the same room where you have sex with your wife?' There was a pause. 'Sorry, that was probably TMI. Blame it on the lack of sleep. Sex is non-existent at the moment anyway so there's nothing to share. I'm too shattered. I usually have a kip when Effie's down for her afternoon nap the two days that Aileen's in nursery, but with her at home that simply isn't happening. And I can't even drink myself blotto because I'm breastfeeding! My life's a mess right now.' Another pause. 'Chaz, you still there?'

'I'm here, I was listening.' Chantelle had wandered along the road and up into the park. It had become one of her favourite places now they couldn't go further afield; set on the side of a hill, it had a lovely view of the hills beyond. 'It does sound a bit shit.' The sun had just set and the clouds were beautiful shades of pink and orange. 'And I can't even come over and help you out. We've been told to stay local, and Airdrie's not that.'

'How is it, sharing with Stevie and his mum? Are you doing OK? Is it not too weird?' Sarah's voice sounded half concerned, half intrigued.

Chantelle's mind jolted into consciousness. Should she tell Sarah what had happened? Was it too early? She didn't want to jinx things when they'd barely started.

It was too late. She had forgotten Sarah had a radar more sensitive than a military grade installation. 'Oh Chaz. You didn't. Tell me you didn't.'

'We just kissed!' Chantelle didn't know why she felt so defensive. 'It was one kiss. And we didn't only kiss. We talked a lot beforehand. About a lot of stuff we should have talked about before. I don't know why we didn't really.'

'Can I remind you that you tried to get him to talk, and he was tighter than a ram's arse about it?' Sarah sounded exasperated, but Chantelle knew her well enough to know that she was worried.

'Sarah! You know what Mum would have said about language like that.'

'Oh fuck it.' Chantelle could almost see her sister flicking her hand dismissively. 'The kids are both in bed and I am seriously at the end of my tether. Besides, arse hardly qualifies. Even Aileen's picked that up from someone at nursery.'

'So when does your maternity leave finish?' Chantelle tried to change the subject, hoping that Sarah would be tired enough not to notice.

Sarah sighed. 'I've only got another eight weeks. And there's no way that they'll let me extend it, not with the way things are at the moment.' There was another pause. 'Nice try, Chaz. But I want you to tell me about you and Stevie.'

Chantelle stopped walking and looked out at the remains of the sunset, wondering what she should say. She didn't know what the story was really. They'd agreed to take things one day at a time, so where did that leave her? 'I've told you pretty much everything. We went for a walk today. We talked about how we still like each other. And we kissed.'

'Hm.' Sarah's voice was sceptical. 'So what happens next?'

Chantelle shrugged, which she knew Sarah couldn't see, but her sister would hear it in her voice. 'We've said it might be worthwhile having another go of things. But we'll have to see how we get on.'

'Well.' Sarah still sounded doubtful. 'I can't say I'm keen on this new development, but I do trust you. Just take care of yourself, OK?' She sighed again. 'I miss you. I can't wait until all this is over and I can see you again.'

'I miss you too.' Chantelle turned to head home. 'Look. I'd better get back. Call me on video when you've got some time tomorrow, OK? Then we can catch up properly.'

'Will do. I'm going to go and spend five minutes with Simon before we both drop into bed exhausted.'

'Night night. Love you. Love to everyone.'

'You too.'

Steven lay in bed, wondering what to do. Chantelle's eyes as they had parted for bed had been full of promise, but now he was wondering if he had read the signals wrong. Or was she waiting for him to come to her?

'Fuck it.' He sat up in bed, ready to make his way next door, but before he could get any further the door stealthily opened and then closed again.

'I thought your room would be better because it's not right next to your mum's. These walls aren't that great for cancelling out sound.' The corner of the covers lifted and Chantelle slid in beside him. 'I feel like I'm sixteen again, creeping around behind her back.' He could feel her quiver with silent laughter.

Steven had to laugh too. 'Yeah. I remember we thought we were so clever, sneaking you in through my bedroom window. And then it turned out she knew all along.'

'She was always pretty switched on, your mum.' Chantelle rolled herself against him and he shifted to put his arms around her.

Steven gently brushed his lips against the back of her neck and was rewarded with a quick intake of breath. 'Did you come here for talking? Because I had something else in mind.'

Chantelle squirmed around until she was facing him. 'No. Definitely not talking. Not talking at all.' And she didn't say anything more for a very long time.

Afterwards they lay in each other's arms, listening to the silence outside. Chantelle was the first to speak. 'That was good. The sex I mean. Better than I remembered.'

Steven shifted slightly. 'I've had a lot of time to think about it. All the things I'd like to do to you, I mean.' He backtracked. 'That sounds wrong. I meant, do with you.'

Chantelle stroked along his arm. 'I know what you meant. I'm definitely not complaining.'

Steven glanced over to the window, as if he could almost see through the curtains. 'Do you know, I think I've never heard it this quiet? There's always the rumble of the traffic, or some people walking by, or something going on. I'm not sure I like it. It feels like the apocalypse might have happened.'

'This could be the apocalypse, you know. People are dying at a scary rate. Sometimes I wonder where it will all end. If we'll ever get back to something we call normal.' Chantelle bit her lip.

'At least you're out and doing stuff, though. Helping people. I feel like I'm going crazy, stuck in this flat. I like my colleagues. That was pretty much the only thing that kept me in my job. And now we have online meetings and all the office banter has disappeared.' Steven groaned. 'I don't know if I can cope with it. And what good is an office manager without an office?'

'Why don't you ask to go on furlough? Then you could spend your days doing what you wanted.' Chantelle rolled over until she was lying on her back and folded her arms behind her head.

'I know it sounds great, but with nothing to do?' Steven thought about it for a couple of minutes. 'I guess it would let me do some proper planning for when things open up again. I'm hoping we might be able to run a couple of weekends over the summer. But who knows? Things are so uncertain at the moment.' He looked over at her in the dim light. 'Anyway, I don't want to talk about this stuff when I've got you lying next to me. It feels like a waste of time.' A massive yawn split his face. 'Shame I've got work tomorrow. I guess I'd better get some shuteye or I'll be shattered.' He paused. 'Are you sneaking back to your bedroom as if this never happened, or can I convince you to stay with me?'

Chantelle snuggled against him. 'Don't need much convincing for that to happen.'

Steven yawned again. 'Night night. Sleep well.' He leaned over lazily to give her a kiss and managed to catch her ear.

'You too.' He barely heard the words before he disappeared into oblivion.

Steven had thought it would be a good idea to get all of his friends together for a video call, but looking at the four other slightly worried faces on the screen he had no clue where to start. 'Why don't we go round and everyone gets a turn, then we can devolve into chaos after that?' His attempt at a joke did win him a grin from Sean but only faint smiles from the others. A round of thumbs up signs did follow though, so he pressed on. 'Nick, you're furthest north, let's start with you. How are things up in Fort William?'

'I feel a bit bad saying this, but it's pretty decent up here.' Nick leaned a bit closer to the screen. 'It seems really weird with no tourists around, but with us allowed to go out walking locally then it's been amazing really. Jade and I go up Glen Nevis a lot.'

'How is Jade?'

'A bit mixed. As you might expect the go-karting place she works at is closed so that's why she decided to come with me. We went through quite a lot of angst about whether to give up our flat in Glasgow, but in the end I'm glad we did because obviously my parents haven't got any money coming in at the moment from the B&B so it's good to be able to support them a bit. Jade originally said being on furlough was great because she had loads to do in preparation for her book launch, but apparently the publishers are now saying they might want to put things off until next year. So that's all up in the air too.'

There were a few moments of silence while everyone digested the information.

Steven pointed at Pete. 'What about you?'

'If you point at the screen, you do realise none of us actually knows who you're pointing at?' Nadeem's voice held a note of humour.

Steven felt himself go slightly warm with embarrassment, but then he realised that if anything he did made people smile in such stressful times he was willing to sacrifice his self-image all the way. 'I meant YOU.' He put his finger close to the camera so that it looked massive and was rewarded by a general laugh. 'Go on, Pete. You next.'

'Well, we're a bit similar with the nice walks, although obviously Faslane isn't quite as remote. And our flat being on the base means that if we're out then we do bump into quite a lot of people, so it doesn't feel too lonely.' Pete took a sip from a big red mug. 'It is weird though being stuck in the same place with each other for such a long time during the day. David and I do get on really well together, but it still feels very strange.'

'Sean?'

Sean gave a big sigh. 'I'm starting to wonder how wise a decision it was to move back in with my mum. I know she desperately needs someone to help her around the house but we seem to have reverted to the relationship I had when I was about fourteen and I don't like the person I'm turning into.'

'You do realise that your mental health is the most important in all this?' Nick was the one to speak this time. 'All this stuff, I mean it's easy to get caught up in it, but some day it will all be gone and surviving with your sanity in tact is really the most critical thing.'

'I know, and thanks for the reminder.' Sean sighed again. 'I'm doing a bit of a rethink and I am keeping an eye on it.'

'It's a bit shit that you're not that far from me and we still can't meet up.' Steven frowned. 'In fact, this was massively poor planning, guys. We're all stuck in different locations and can't really support each other properly.' He tried to keep his tone light so that they would know it was a joke.

Nadeem waved to show that he wanted to speak. 'That's not entirely true though. Just being on this call and able to talk to you all is doing wonders for my mental health right now. I've been a bit worried about you and knowing that you're all surviving and still able to crack a joke is great.' He paused. 'Couldn't you and Sean meet up for a socially-distanced walk somewhere? Like some kind of cold war East-West standoff?' This time everyone did laugh.

'I don't know, actually.' Steven had never considered it. 'The rules are changing so much I've kind of lost track. I think at the moment they're saying stay local but I don't really have a clue what that means. I've only been going out for essential stuff and for the occasional bike ride or a run. But it's a good shout, we should look into it. How are things down in London, Deem?'

'Weird down here too. London seems a bit like a ghost town with so many people working from home. But it's actually quite interesting in some ways, it feels as if all the people who come into London merely because they need to have gone, and everyone who actually likes being in London is left. Living on the canal we've found that people are really trying to support each other. So in some ways it's not such a bad thing, although I hesitate to say that while there's so many people ill and dying of course.'

Sean shook his head vigorously. 'Not at all, we should find the good things in amongst the bad, it's the only way to survive. I've finally managed to clear away all the brambles from the old raised beds in my mum's garden and we're planting some veg. I have no idea how much will grow, but we're giving it a go.'

'Aye, and I've finally learned how to sew on a machine.' Steven couldn't help chiming in.

'Sewing?' That was Nadeem. 'Jenny will be impressed. She tried to get me to do some dressmaking at one point and had to give up in defeat. Sewing on buttons and mending torn seams is about the limit of my talents.'

'Oh yeah, what about the wedding?' Pete interjected.

A wry smile crossed Nadeem's face. 'We've not talked about that yet. I'm hoping that since it's not until November we'll be OK. But if it has to get moved, it has to get moved. We've decided we're not going to stress about it. And Jenny has such a backlog of orders for her business that she's not been impacted yet either. So we're both doing OK really. Although living with her is a bit of a nightmare.' He looked off to the side with a smile and Steven could tell that Jenny must be in the room. She must have flipped him a finger because Nadeem did the same in return.

The call devolved into a chat about lockdown activities and other random topics until finally Nadeem yawned and said he had to be up early for a work call in another time zone. 'But before I go, I just wanted to say to you all, this will be over at some point, and we will all be able to meet up again in 3D. Hopefully at the wedding, if not before. So hang in there, OK?' There was a general murmur of agreement. When they finally finished Steven rang off feeling much more upbeat than he had done for a while.

It was a Saturday morning and the three of them were sitting in the living room in their pyjamas, watching the latest news on the spread of the virus.

'It's terrifying.' Irene's cup of tea sat forgotten on the coffee table, while Chantelle sipped glumly from hers. 'I feel like there's absolutely nothing we can do.'

'That's not true, Ma.' Chantelle tried to find a positive angle. 'Your work at the food bank is even more needed now that a lot of people aren't working, and my job is as busy as ever.' She sighed. Now wasn't the time to mention how cruel she felt for moving people on from sitting in the park and splitting up groups of people. Or the increased number of domestic incidents from people stuck in their homes with abusive partners. She felt a big black cloud of negativity threatening to bring her down.

'Right, this is ridiculous.' Steven grabbed his crutches and jumped up. 'We're going out, and we're going to have a picnic. Look at this gorgeous weather and we're all inside moping around.'

'How are we going to have a picnic if we can't actually sit down?' It was one of the downsides of Chantelle's job that it didn't feel right to even bend the rules. Surely there was no harm to anyone from the three of them, who already lived together and were already sharing germs, sitting down outside somewhere for half an hour to have something to eat? But no, it wasn't permitted.

'I don't care about that, if we need to eat while we're walking we'll do it. Besides, when they say walking, they never say how quickly, do they?' He started to move infinitesimally slowly across the room, an innocent look on his face. 'Sorry, officer, I'm terribly disabled, I can't move any faster than this.'

Chantelle had to laugh at that. 'But where are we going to go?'

'We're going to leave this flat and walk away, and just go where our feet take us. And we're not going to come home until we feel like it.'

Irene threw up her hands. 'I feel like I'd be happy never to see this flat again at the moment.'

'Exactly.' Steven turned back towards them both. 'So let's go on an adventure. You both go and get changed while I make us some sandwiches.'

Chapter 15

Carrying a couple of small backpacks, they set off in the direction that would take them to the nearby woods. With no cars about it was easier to walk along the middle of the road, as it meant they could all walk side by side. This time it was Chantelle who took Irene's arm.

'Amazing how neat people's gardens are at the moment. Look at that gorgeous one with all those pink flowers.' Irene pointed. 'It makes me want to try a bit harder with our bit at the back.'

'The grass is easy maintenance, Mum, but we could go up to the garden centre and get you some stuff.' Steven stopped to look at the colourful display, which was full of bees making the most of the nectar harvest. 'What sort of flowers would you want?'

'Oh, I don't know. Pretty ones?' Irene laughed. 'Honestly, I know nothing about gardening at all!'

'I saw some lovely pink flowers outside the supermarket the other day.' Chantelle suddenly realised that this could be an opportunity for them all to do something together.

'But Stevie's right, I think the garden centre's still open at the moment.'

Steven resumed his steady pace along the road. 'What I'd really like is to grow some veg. But I don't know anything about that either.'

'There's a woman in the next street who has a couple of veg boxes in her front garden, I often see her out there when I'm on my way to and from work.' Chantelle shrugged. 'I don't know if she'd be willing to tell us what to do.'

'Veg boxes?' Steven sounded puzzled.

'You know, those sort of square things made out of wood filled with soil. They're full of green stuff at the moment so she must be good at it.'

'Oh, that's what Sean called raised beds the other day. That would be great.' Steven's face looked happy for the first time that day. 'How amazing would that taste.'

'Totties,' Irene interjected. 'Just think about freshly dug totties. My Da said they used to grow their own veg during the war, especially a good crop of those.'

Chantelle squeezed Irene's arm gently. 'He never passed on any of his skills then?'

Irene shook her head. 'Unfortunately not. Once rationing was over then not having to grow your own veg became a bit of a status symbol, you know, that you had enough money to buy food in. We never had a lot, but with both Ma and Da working then we had enough to get by.'

'So totties.' Steven pretended to write on his hand with an imaginary pen. 'Anything else?'

The thought of food was starting to make Chantelle feel hungry. 'I know it sounds a bit healthy, but I'd love a bit of salad. A nice crispy lettuce or some mangetout peas or something.'

'Mangetout.' Steven pronounced the word with a ridiculously fake French accent. 'Are you sure, Madame, zat zat is what you want?'

Chantelle rolled her eyes but had to smile. After weeks of stress and worry it was so nice to fool around a bit. She put her free hand on her cheek in an affected manner. 'Oh yes, Monsieur, ze piz iz izzactly what I want.'

Irene's infectious giggle got them laughing and fooling around, and then they all jumped when a woman about Irene's age popped up from behind a low hedge right beside them wielding a small trowel.

'Sorry, we didn't mean to disturb you.' Chantelle was quick to apologise, and they stepped back to maintain the required two metre distance.

'Not at all, it's lovely to hear people having a good time.' The woman's voice sounded slightly wistful, as if it wasn't something she'd had much experience of recently. 'Go ahead and laugh as much as you want.' But the moment had passed, so they just wished her a good day and carried on up the road.

A circuit through the woods took them about half an hour and when they came back round Steven stopped and turned to the other two. 'So we could go down that way along the river if you like, the walk is pretty nice and we could meet the canal and come back along there.'

Irene looked where he was indicating. 'What are the other options?'

Steven pointed in the opposite direction. 'I heard from someone that there's a way out the back of the golf course onto the hills, if you want a bit of open space. If we wander up that way then there might be fewer people, and if I need to take my prosthetic off and sit down for a couple minutes while I do it then who's to complain if we just happen to eat at the same time?' He looked at Chantelle, one eyebrow raised.

Chantelle lifted her own eyebrow right back at him. 'You're bad.' Then she relented with a sigh. 'OK. But only if it really is a couple of minutes. And only if there's no-one else around.'

'You can blame me if anyone pulls you up about it.' Steven drew her in for a quick kiss. 'I'll tell them my stump was hurting so badly that I had to sit down for a bit. And you can tell them you didn't want to leave such a vulnerable person by himself on the side of a mountain.'

'Vulnerable, my ass.' Chantelle slipped her hand around and squeezed his bum gently.

'That's my ass you're touching, I hope you know the difference.' Steven found her backside and did some squeezing of his own. '*This* is your ass. And a very gorgeous ass it is too.'

'People are watching.' Irene spoke in a stage whisper that had them all laughing again.

'Come on then.' Chantelle took Steven's hand and started off down the road, her heart full of joy. 'Let's go find this golf course.'

Steven eyed up the sourdough starter that was sitting on the table as if it was going to jump out of the jar at him. 'I could have sworn you just said you feed it. As if it was alive or something.'

'Well, technically it is alive. That's what Sarah says. Apparently it's some kind of fungus.' Chantelle unscrewed the lid and sniffed it cautiously. It was a miracle it had arrived all the way from Airdrie with the lockdown restrictions on travel. Chantelle had suggested posting it but with the mail delivery times increasingly unreliable then Sarah had sent it via a neighbour of hers who worked in Glasgow, who had passed it onto a colleague of Chantelle's who lived nearby her work, who had dropped it off at Chantelle's police station. With the supermarket shelves empty of flour due to people stockpiling, a woman across the road had offered to get them some from a wholesale supermarket. So now a twenty kilo bag was sitting in their kitchen ready to go.

'What are the instructions?' Irene motioned towards the jar.

Chantelle pulled out her phone and scrolled through it. 'Let me see. She's sent me the amounts we need to make the bread, but she's also said to watch some video that she said will really help. A sexy Irish guy, she says. She's sent love hearts.' She rolled her eyes.

'I take it Simon doesn't know about her crush on the Irish baker?' Steven waggled his eyebrows suggestively.

'Given that they've been locked down together for weeks already he probably does.' Chantelle laughed and brought it up on her screen. 'Here we go. Let's take a look. It's only ten minutes long.'

They squashed next to each other on the sofa while Chantelle held out her phone so all three of them could see. Silence fell over them for a while.

'Well, I think he is quite sexy.' Irene folded her arms when the video had finished. 'I might have to watch it again. It is a lot to take in.' Her mouth quirked upwards.

'Mum! He's way too young for you.' Steven made a shocked face, pretending to be disapproving.

'There's no harm in looking at the scenery.' Irene reached towards the phone and pressed replay.

'It's weird, he makes it sound incredibly simple and really tricky all at the same time.' Steven thought it seemed a bit complicated. 'Does it matter we haven't got one of those bumpy tray things he put it in to rise? A banne-thingy, whatever it was?'

Chantelle shook her head. 'Sarah said something like a Pyrex dish will be fine.'

'Well, we've got plenty of those.' Steven nodded. 'How do you stop it sticking? I know what those things are like. You remember when I tried to bake you that birthday cake without putting any butter round the tin and it stuck so badly we had to prise it out one spoonful at a time?'

Chantelle smiled at the memory. 'It wasn't so bad. Not after we squirted a load of cream over the top of it.'

'Still, I can't imagine we'd be able to do the same with a loaf of bread.' Steven frowned.

'I think we've got some of those greaseproof sheets. And we can add plenty of flour. At least we're not short of that.' A snort of laughter escaped her. 'Oh, the only other thing Sarah wrote is that you should always leave some of the starter behind. And feed it flour and water every day until you need it again.'

'Oh aye. The feeding. If we're going to have a pet, the least we can do is give it a name.' Steven pointed at the jar.

Irene had finished re-watching the video. 'I had an Irish boyfriend when I was younger.' Her voice was all soft and dreamy. 'Very handsome, he was.'

'You did?' Steven turned to his mum in surprise. 'What happened to him?'

'Oh, we had to break it off. He was from a very well-off family, so of course his parents would have never had me. It simply wasn't done in those days. But it was good while it lasted.' From the smile on her face it was clear that the memories she was re-living were good ones.

'What was his name?' Steven couldn't help asking.

'Mmm...' Irene frowned. 'Oh, Robert, that was it. But everyone called him Bob. Apart from his parents of course.'

Steven picked up the jar and waved his hand over the top of it. 'By the power invested in me, I hereby name you Bob.' He tapped the top of the jar as if he was casting a magic spell.

'Really?' Chantelle looked him sceptically. 'And it's not weird to have a sourdough starter named after one of your mother's ex boyfriends?'

Steven just looked at her with a wicked smile. 'Are we turning Bob into something we can actually eat or not?' He pushed himself up off the couch, still holding the jar, and headed towards the kitchen.

'Oh, one more thing Sarah did say.' Chantelle's words made him turn back towards her. 'Apparently it may take a few goes to get this right. She's been warned that the first one may come out looking like a pancake.'

Sarah's warning had been well-advised, Chantelle reflected a couple of weeks later, as their first effort came out looking like it had been run over by a steam roller. Things had got better though and now they were turning out quite decent loaves which were perfect for soups and sandwiches. And Chantelle was finding she really enjoyed doing it. The kneading of the dough seemed to focus her thoughts and make her happy. Irene had taken to watching bread-making videos on the internet, and every now and then communicated a tip to them which seemed to improve things. It was great to be making something physical that she could actually touch.

The sunny weather had continued, which was a boon now that you were only allowed to do things outdoors. It was a glorious Monday and Chantelle had taken the advantage of her day off to have a long lie in and make some bread for lunch. She placed it in to bake and then made her way out into the garden where Irene was sitting in her deckchair reading a book.

'Do you want a drink? I've just put the bread in the oven and I'm going to put the kettle on.' Chantelle looked down at Irene, feeling the sunshine starting to heat her back already. 'It's pretty warm out here. Have you got sun cream on?'

Irene fished out her little black book and leafed through it. 'Let me see. Suncream went on about eleven.'

'Oh, you should be fine then, it's only eleven thirty.' Irene's book was something along the lines of her own police notebook, Chantelle suddenly realised, in which times and details of events were carefully noted down for reference later. The thought made her smile. 'Did you want a drink?'

'Just some water, thanks love. It's too hot for tea at the moment.' Irene lifted up her book again.

Chantelle delivered tea to Steven, who thanked her gratefully, and she took her own drink and the water outside. Steven still seemed to be busy at work, which she was grateful for. If they hadn't furloughed him, it meant he still had things to do, which meant there was a smaller chance of him getting made redundant when all this was over. He had mentioned something about an office move, which again was a good thing, surely, because if they were keeping an office in town then it meant they'd want him to go back at some point to run it. The other thing she was thankful about was her job, because the order it imposed on her life was what was kept her going at the moment. She had always been an obsessive planner, with every moment of her free time scheduled for something, and without anything to do with her day she knew she would have felt entirely lost. Although, if she was totally honest with herself, her job wasn't the only thing keeping her going. Rediscovering her relationship with Steven was magical and she was falling in love with him all over again. They had been going out on long walks almost every day and talking, exactly like they used to do. The nights they spent sleeping next to each other, and not always sleeping either. The sex was amazing and she had to admit she had missed that too. Her heart was so happy it almost hurt.

'What are you smiling about?' The question from Irene startled her out of her reverie. Chantelle had been so wrapped up in her own thoughts she hadn't noticed the other woman had put down her book and was looking at her.

'Oh, I don't know. Maybe how in the middle of all this death and destruction there are still good things to be found in the world.' She wrapped her arms around herself. 'How are things down at the food bank?'

'The food bank.' Irene's forehead wrinkled. Chantelle was coming to recognise it as as sign of struggling to remember something, so she just waited patiently until Irene continued. 'Mixed, really. We're getting loads more donations because of all the stuff that's been on the news, but we've had so many more families coming in. For some of them the twenty percent of their salary that they're losing on furlough is making all the difference.'

Chantelle bit her lip. That was another reason to be happy that she and Steven were still working; it gave them a half-decent income that even meant they could save a little at the moment with them not going anywhere. Now if only this darned lockdown would lift so they could all go back to normal. She shook her head to clear those thoughts. 'I just wish I could do more, you know?'

'You're already doing so much.' Irene looked at her sternly. 'Don't think I haven't seen you coming in exhausted after a shift when you've been out all night with hardly a break to eat or drink.' She went back to her book for a few seconds, then looked up again. 'Sorry, I don't want to be rude, but you caught me in a really exciting bit. The guy's hanging off a train by one hand.'

Chantelle couldn't help a smile. 'Don't mind me. I'm just going to sit here and enjoy the sunshine until my timer tells me the bread's ready.' She leaned back and closed her eyes. Things were pretty much as good as they could be with a pandemic on. There was only one cloud on the horizon and that was her headaches, which these days sometimes developed into full-on migraines. They were threatening to flare up a couple of times a week now and she'd already had to get a repeat prescription from the doctor, which seemed to be helping somewhat. She couldn't afford to take time off work because too many days absent would be a black mark against her record. The doctor had referred her to a specialist for a proper assessment in case it was anything serious, but with the hospitals diverting staff to deal with the virus he had warned her it could be a while before she got an appointment.

She was glad when the sound of the back door slamming disturbed her from her thoughts and Steven came round the corner. He pulled out another chair and sat down with a sigh. 'Thought I'd take an early lunch seeing as you're both out here. It's a tragedy working inside with all this good weather.'

'It would also be a tragedy to get sunburned.' Chantelle felt her worry lift. 'Did you see the neighbour across the road yesterday evening? He looked as if he'd been dipped in a vat of pink paint.'

'I thought it was more of a lobster hue, if I'm honest.' Steven's eyes sparkled at her.

Chantelle sniggered. 'I'll give you that. It must have been dead painful.'

'I'm sure he'll live. He's out in the sun again today.'

'Shall we go in for lunch, or do you want to eat out here?' Chantelle was already pretty warm, but she didn't want to take Steven out of the sun when he'd been inside all morning.

'I don't mind eating inside.' Steven rescued his crutches and stood up. 'I can feel myself toasting already. But it would be nice to go for another walk when I finish work. Fancy it?'

'I've got to take a look at what I still need to do on my probationary evidence portfolio, my deadline is coming up soon. But I'm sure I'll find some time.' Chantelle stood herself and gave him a quick kiss. She turned to Irene. 'You coming? Or is the guy still on the train?'

Irene looked up. 'Give me two minutes?'

The perils of a good book, thought Chantelle. 'Alright, we'll go and get some food sorted and give you a shout when it's ready.'

Chapter 16

Steven closed the lid of his laptop gratefully. Not that he minded being busy, but there was so much to do. The office move was next week and there was a long list of things he had to get sorted. At least he had managed to get a charity to agree to take away all the desks and chairs they didn't need. That was one less headache to deal with.

He rubbed his temples with his fingertips. A bit of exercise would do him good. And Chantelle too; she had been looking far too stressed lately. He put on his prosthetic and poked his head around her door. 'You up for a walk?'

She was sat on the bed, papers all around her in an untidy sprawl. She looked up, pushing a strand of hair out of her face. 'I can't. I've got to prepare for my final assessments. There's so much stuff to learn.'

'I'm sure you're further on than you think you are. Anyway, didn't you say that you also had a fitness test coming up? That means you need to get out of the house. We could go for a run instead if you really want. You'll be better off for a break and you can get back to it later.'

'I guess you're right.' Chantelle sighed. 'I just can't afford to screw it up, you know? I couldn't bear the humiliation if I failed.'

'You're not going to fail.' Steven reached over and took her hand. 'Come on, up. We'll just do a quick walk around the block and then I'll get the food on for our tea.'

They left the house, squinting into the bright sunshine. Chantelle looked at him. 'So how was your day?'

Steven frowned, wondering how much to tell her. 'A bit weird, really. I mean, I'm flat out sorting things out for this office move, but that will all be sorted soon, and then I have no clue what's going to happen. The new office is a serviced one, so that's a big part of my responsibilities redundant, although they haven't said anything about it so far. I've tried asking my boss if that's what the plans are, but apparently he hasn't heard anything from higher up. He says if it does happen then he'll do his best to convince them to retrain me in something else, but to be honest he doesn't sound hopeful.' It was something which had been worrying him ever since the plans for the office move had been finalised. 'I have to say I was possibly hoping for redundancy at some point, because I'd get more money than leaving, but I was thinking more like in a couple of years time. Once Nick and I have been able to build up the other stuff a bit and when I'd get a bit more of a payout.' He rolled his eyes. 'Sorry. All I seem to be doing is complaining.'

'It's fine. I get what you mean.' Chantelle shrugged. 'I hadn't realised the new office would be different and your job might be at risk. I'm sorry myself, I've been so wrapped up in my own stuff that I haven't talked to you properly these last few days.'

Steven stopped and pulled her in for a quick kiss. 'Look at us both, apologising. I love you. And you're the most important thing in my life. Everything else is immaterial.'

Chantelle melted towards him. 'I love you too.'

Steven laughed. 'That's my stomach rumbling. We'd better get back.' He took her hand and wrapped it in his. 'It'll all work out one way or another. We're going to be just fine.'

It had been a busy day for a Wednesday and Chantelle logged out of her machine at the end of her shift with a grateful sigh. She was getting tired of the constant regulation changes and the dirty looks they got for enforcing the lockdown rules. The weather was better than she had ever seen it in May and she felt bad for stopping people sitting down in green spaces when some of them didn't even have gardens of their own. But it was time to go home and stop worrying about things. The trouble was she couldn't stop herself. She was worried about her probation being approved and despite Steven's apparent faith that everything would work out then she knew he was worried about his job. They were both worried about Irene, whose mental capacities seemed to be ever diminishing. Sarah was worried about Chantelle too, being out on the front line without enough proper PPE. But what little there was had gone to the hospitals and the police had to wait and hope. And on the shift there were tensions too; it was hard to have camaraderie with your colleagues when you were forced to be at least two metres apart. The entire situation had knotted her shoulders up tighter than they had ever been and her headache was pounding at her temples again.

She rubbed her forehead and checked her watch. It was still officially another hour before she could take another painkiller, but did it really matter? She felt in the pocket of her high-vis vest for her packet of pills and swallowed one, washing it down with a swig from her water bottle. She looked at the packet. Only five left, and her prescription didn't get renewed for another five days. She thought about the illicit Valium stash that they had recovered from someone's house yesterday and sighed again. Right now she almost wished she had filched one while she was counting them up. One of them and she would have been knocked out blissfully all night.

'Still here, Chaz?' A voice behind her made her jump. 'You should be gone by now, unless you've got paperwork to do.'

She turned, feeling as if her guilty thoughts were written all over her face. One of the shift sergeants stood behind her.

Feeling her face flush red, she grabbed her bag, mumbled a goodbye and almost ran out of the room. Of course she wouldn't have taken anything. It wasn't wise. Things like that could look legit but you never knew what could be in them.

Her guilty feeling stuck with her all the way home and as soon as she got through the door she headed towards the bathroom, grabbing the laundry bag she always put her uniform in at the end of a shift. Irene might have said she didn't care if she got infected, but if Chantelle could possibly help it she wasn't going to let it happen. The bag always went straight in the washing machine, to be hung up and dried for the next time it was needed. There was no sign of Steven, although she could hear talking coming from his room, so he must be in a meeting. She ran a hot bath with lots of bubbles and climbed gratefully into it. Hopefully the heat would do something to unwind the tension in her shoulders. Possibly even a stiff drink, although half three in the afternoon was a bit early for a gin and tonic. She lay back blissfully and closed her eyes. If she could only stay in here forever and never come out...

A door banged somewhere in the house and she opened them again, reality flooding back. With another sigh, she sat up. Falling asleep in the bath really wasn't a good idea. Washing her hair only took a couple of minutes and then she wrapped herself in her big fluffy bathrobe and opened the door. A bit of afternoon TV with Irene would sort her out.

To her surprise, Steven was already on the sofa, flicking between channels. Chantelle dropped down beside him. 'Isn't it a bit early for you to finish work?'

Steven just grunted, his finger still moving on the remote.

'Where's Irene? I thought she'd be here.'

'She went for a walk.' Steven didn't even look at her. He stopped for a minute on a cop documentary, then, as if remembering she was beside him and wouldn't want to watch it, he carried on flicking through the channels.

'By herself? Is that a good idea?' Chantelle looked at him in surprise. 'I thought you were the one who said you didn't want her to go out on her own.'

'Look, I don't, OK?' Steven turned to her. 'But what do you expect me to do? Use your handcuffs to lock her to the table?'

The harshness in his voice made her blink and she stared at him for a few seconds. It was then she noticed that he was literally shaking. She laid a hand on his arm. 'Don't be angry at me. I only asked.'

Steven sagged suddenly, dashing a hand across his face. He flicked the TV off. 'I'm sorry. It's not you. I found out just now work are casting me off.'

'Oh.' Chantelle was surprised at his anger. 'I thought you said it was possible though? So why get that het up about it?' She placed a hand on his arm and squeezed it gently.

He sighed. 'I know. It's not that they're letting me go, it's the way they've done it. They did tell me a while ago that my position was disappearing, and were promising me that with all the remote working that's going on now I'll be able to do something else in the company, but they've suddenly changed their mind. Now it's just a letter with a redundancy package. And it's the usual week for every year I've worked there. Just two weeks. It's not even a grand.'

'Well, that's a good thing, right? You'll also get your four weeks' notice for doing absolutely nothing, or almost nothing. You said now that the office move is done then there won't be very much to do. Will they stick you on gardening leave?'

Steven's jaw tightened. 'That's what I'm angry about. A couple of weeks ago they gave me my official redundancy notification. My manager promised me it was just a formality, to keep the big bosses happy while he found something else for me, but this afternoon he said things had changed and they would have to let me go. So by the end of next week I'll have no money coming in. I feel like such an idiot for falling for it.'

'The bastards.' Chantelle felt her own anger rise up. 'Can't you put in a formal complaint?'

Steven shook his head. 'He's been too clever. The only thing I've got in writing is the redundancy notice. Everything else was on phone calls while we were discussing other stuff. He's been so friendly to me the entire time I've been working there I never expected it.' His face crumpled, and for one minute Chantelle thought he was going to cry. 'Do you know what he said to me? "Business is business, Steven. You wouldn't understand."' His fists clenched.

'Tosser.' Chantelle rolled her eyes. 'Sounds like you're well shot of them, if you ask me.'

'I know.' Steven deflated again. 'But I still worry. About Mum, and about money. And about you too.'

'What are you worrying about me for?' Chantelle felt her eyebrows go up. 'I'm doing fine.'

Steven's eyes captured hers. 'Really? Because I'm not so sure about that. You've been looking really tired, and I can't help thinking you've been stressing about your job too much. Some days when you come home you look almost white when you walk through the door.'

'You know I've always been pale.' Chantelle tried to laugh his comments off, but he kept up a steady gaze. She did some sagging of her own. 'OK, I am struggling. All this is too much. I mean, people are dying out there. Every time someone goes off sick from the shift I wonder if they're going to come back. The morgues are getting full. And in the middle of all this I'm trying to pretend as if everything is normal and finish off my probation as if none of this is happening.' She curled up into Steven's warmth, feeling again like she wanted to close her eyes and ears and never resurface into reality.

Steven kissed the top of her head. 'We'll make it through this, Chaz. There's no denying things are a bit shit right now. But this pandemic can't last forever, and you will pass your probation, and I will find another job.'

'And there's other things, too, I think.' Chantelle found herself buoyed up by his positivity. 'You're worried about Ma, but she seems happier than I've seen her for years. She likes having you here.'

'She likes having us both here.' Steven corrected her. 'You know she thinks of you like a daughter. Remember how upset she was when you moved out.'

Chantelle stiffened, the old hurt resurfacing. 'You make it sound like it was my fault.'

'Hell, no. In fact, possibly more my fault than yours.' Steven was silent for a while, tracing a gentle pattern on her arm. 'That's one of the other things that worries me. If I lose my job, I'll be stuck here in the house and the last time that happened was after the accident. I can feel it all flooding back. What happens if I become that same person and drive you away again? It could be Groundhog Day.'

Chantelle thought for a bit. She didn't want to dismiss his fears, especially as she had some matching ones of her own, but what else could they do? She suddenly found inspiration. 'Yeah. Groundhog Day. Why did I never think of that before?'

'You what?' She hadn't realised that she had voiced her thoughts out loud until Steven spoke himself.

Chantelle looked up at him. 'You're forgetting the most important thing about that film. The guy got the chance to try again and again until he finally got things right. So we do just that. We take things one day at a time. And if we screw up one day, we start afresh the next. Of course, we won't get the chance to do exactly the same things over again, but with things the way they are at the moment every day does feel a bit like Groundhog Day. Eat, sleep, work, watch the awful stuff on the news, repeat. So it might not feel much different.'

Steven laughed, and squeezed her gently. 'I hadn't thought of it like that. I do love you.'

'I love you too.' She turned her face up to his for a kiss, which he willingly gave her.

His hand moved up to caress her neck, then down onto her shoulder, where the bathrobe had fallen away. 'Oh.' His voice sounded surprised. 'Are you not wearing anything underneath?'

'It's a bathrobe, silly.' She laughed, giving him a suggestive raise of her eyebrows.

He shifted so that his hand could travel further down inside, and she felt a stab of desire as his fingers caressed the side of her breast. His lips curved in a smile. 'I see.' He gently squeezed her nipple and she sucked in a breath. She thought he was going to say something else, but instead he bent down his head to kiss her again.

It was only when she felt his hand move down to reach between her legs that she suddenly remembered where they were. 'Hadn't we better take this to the bedroom? If your mum walks through the door it it could be slightly embarrassing.'

'True.' He reached for his crutches, but she put a hand on his arm. 'I'll carry you. My privilege.'

He frowned at her. 'Are you sure? I've put on a lot of weight in the last few weeks.'

She waved a hand dismissively. 'I'm not the waif that I once was. I carried a man out of a building last week because the fire service hadn't managed to get on the scene yet.'

'You went into a burning building?' He looked at her as if the thought horrified him.

She shook her head. 'That one wasn't burning. The one next to it was. I was never in danger.'

He still looked terrified. 'I do worry about you.'

She stood, scooping him up as she did so, and held him tight to her chest. 'Don't think about that now. Just make love to me. We can talk about it later.'

He nestled his head into her neck and sucked at the sensitive skin there. 'I can manage to do that.'

She almost ran for the bedroom, only just remembering to slam the door closed with a foot, and dumped him unceremoniously on the bed.

Chapter 17

Steven cycled slowly back though the centre of town, wanting to savour the unique experience. Having a valid reason to be out and about took away all the guilty feelings he had developed in the past few weeks every time he went out of the house and left Irene by herself. Dropping off his laptop at the empty office had been a strange experience, but the sunny day lifted his spirits, along with the lack of traffic. He normally used routes along canals and rivers as much as he could, but the novelty of having two lanes pretty much all to himself made him take the main roads home. If only it could be like this more often.

The empty roads had given him another gift as well; Sean and he had finally decided that if they met at some point on their circular cycle rides and stayed at least two metres apart it could hardly do any harm. They didn't tell Chantelle what they were doing, as it wasn't strictly legal, and had decided to pretend they had met 'by accident' if anyone pulled them up about it. So at least once a week they enjoyed taking deserted back streets and chatting. It was small things like this that were keeping Steven going. Sean seemed to have improved things with his mum and the vegetable garden was reportedly doing well.

Irene was in the living room when he got back, watching some sort of crime drama. She flicked the remote to pause when she saw him. 'How was your day, love?' She looked at her watch. 'Isn't two o'clock a bit early for you?'

'That's me finally finished with work, Mum.' He sank into the sofa beside her. 'Feels a bit strange, but I'm sure I'll get used to it. I'll have to call up the job centre tomorrow.'

'Oh.' Her face looked as if the information was news to her, and he steeled himself to have to explain the situation to her yet again, but instead she only asked, 'So what are you going to do next?'

'I'm not sure. It'll depend on what's available. It might be tricky to get something straight away, if I'm honest. Everywhere is closed and loads of people are on furlough already. I'll have to see what comes up.'

She got up without speaking and went into the bedroom and Steven wondered if she was upset. He was just debating about whether to go after her when she reappeared, dragging a couple of big plastic tartan storage bags. She dumped them in front of him. 'Here you go. I knew it was a good idea to keep them.'

Steven warily unzipped one of them. 'What is it?' He lifted the top item out of the bag. Was it more clothes that she had stashed away? Then he realised it was a carefully folded piece of bright red fabric, a sort of rough cotton a bit like a workwear shirt might be made of. 'What's all this for?'

'You always said you wanted to make your own clothes, now you've got the chance. And it would be good for someone to finally make use of all this, it's been lying around for years. I kept meaning to make things but never really found the time.'

'But I don't know anything about sewing. Just because I managed to turn up the bottom of that shirt doesn't mean I'll be able to actually make stuff.' He threw the fabric back on top of the bag. 'It's a crazy idea.'

'I'll teach you. It's really not that hard. Let's get some of these bits out of the bag, it'll be easier for me to remember what's what if I've got them in front of me.' She sat down on the sofa and took out the red cloth that he had discarded earlier.

Steven suddenly realised that she was more animated than he had seen her for a while. 'OK. But let me make a cup of tea first, aye? Do you want one?'

Irene nodded, still pulling stuff out of the bag. 'That would be lovely.'

When Chantelle came home at half past four she found them deep in a discussion about the difficulties of sewing thick fabrics. Steven waved a piece of red cloth at her. 'Look what I made!'

She took it and held it up; it was a simple but carefully sewn shopping bag, with two long handles made of the same fabric. 'Nice. Looks pretty swanky.'

'I made it with longer handles so you can sling it over a shoulder.' His face was full of pride. 'I always hate those short ones that you can't get your arm through properly.' He held up some blue denim. 'I really want to make myself some bike panniers next. I quite fancied this because I thought it would be hard-wearing, but Mum says it's going to be a pain to get it to sew properly, so I think I'm going to go for this black.' He hefted a large stack of black material across the table. 'It's a bit thinner but it's cotton, so it should still be tough enough.'

Chantelle fingered an edge thoughtfully. 'That is pretty nice. I wouldn't mind a bag made out of that.'

'Bit plain for a handbag, really.' Irene looked across at her. 'Although you could stick some sequins on it to bling it up a bit.'

'Bling it up?' Steven laughed. 'Now I know you have been watching too much daytime TV.'

'It's not like there's much else to do at the moment, is there? I've already watched everything on catch up at least three times.' Irene's face curved into a mischievous smile. 'I would have never said until this point that having a dodgy memory can actually have its advantages.'

'Oh, you two.' Chantelle sat down on the other side of the table, her stress from work falling away. 'But I didn't mean a handbag. My grab bag that I got when I first started work is falling apart. One of the handles is broken and it's starting to split so it would be great to have a new one. Do you think you could make me one?'

Steven looked dubious. 'Isn't a bag like that a bit hard? Doesn't it have lots of compartments and a zip and stuff?'

Chantelle picked up the red bag. 'My old one does, but I could probably do with just a couple, to separate things out a bit. If you made two of these somehow, but a bit bigger and flatter, and sewed them together and then did a flap over the top, it could be great.' She made movements with her hands to show what she meant. 'Would that be doable?'

'I see what you mean.' Irene looked thoughtful. 'Probably. You go have a shower and let me discuss it with my new apprentice.'

Chantelle laughed, then realised that she hadn't even thought about washing her hands when she came in and sprang up with a gasp of horror. 'You do that. I'll be back.'

By the time she returned the two of them were busy with their heads over a piece of paper. Steven had a pencil in his hand. 'I was thinking a flap like this. Over the top. A massive one, so when the bag's full it will stretch like this.' He made busy marks on the paper. 'You see?'

'But then how are you going to fasten it? And won't it look a bit rubbish when it's empty?' Irene pointed at what he had drawn.

'Don't worry, my bag's never empty.' Chantelle took a look over his shoulder. 'By the time I've got my big jacket, waterproof trousers, gloves and my posh hat in there it already weighs a ton. Then add to it snacks, my dinner for if we get caught somewhere and anything else I need to carry around and it's massive. And they've finally issued us all with full PPE in case we need to go into a house with the virus in it, so that's a whole load of extra stuff.'

'They've only just done that?' Stevie glanced up, then shook his head. 'I'm not even going to ask.'

Chantelle held up a hand. 'Don't get me started on that. But my point is that this bag is never going to be empty.'

Irene tugged at the pencil until Steven let go of it. 'You could have the flap like this.' She made some small adjustments to the drawing on the paper. 'Then you could have a couple of loops on the end and a series of buttons at different heights so that you can fasten it on the right one depending on how full the bag is. And that will stop you needing any zips or anything.'

It was the first time in a long while that Chantelle had seen Irene fully engaged in something constructive and she felt a strange tightness in her chest as she watched the two of them discussing the design. After a lot of wrangling they finally settled on something they were both happy with.

Irene looked up. 'Will you be wanting your name on it? I think there's personalised labels you can order off the internet, we could sew one of those on.'

Chantelle considered for a few moments. 'A lot of people do that, but it's mainly because they've all got similar bags. As long as it looks quite different from the others then it should be fine.'

Steven had taken another piece of paper and was still busy sketching. 'I want to make a clean copy so I don't forget what we've done. This one's full of extra lines and bits where we've rubbed things out.' A few minutes later he looked up and pushed the paper towards her. 'See what you think.'

Chantelle took the sheet and studied it. There were actually three different drawings on the paper; one was the whole bag from a front view and a couple looked like expansions of different bits. 'Wow, that looks amazing. Will it have separate compartments inside?'

Steven reached across the table and pointed with the pencil. 'Two big ones, like you suggested. And Irene showed me how we could do you a mini inside pocket so smaller things don't get lost at the bottom.'

'For secret snacks.' Chantelle looked up and met his eyes, her heart full of joy.

'Do people often steal your snacks?' Steven frowned.

'Oh no, I don't think anyone would do that.' Chantelle shook her head. 'But there's nothing better than rediscovering a snack that even I've forgotten about.'

'OK, so defo a secret snack compartment.' Steven took the pencil and drew an arrow towards the place and marked in tiny capitals SECRET SNACKS.

Things deteriorated from there as the three of them took it in turns to put ever more hilarious captions on various bits of the bag until they were laughing so hard Chantelle had to beg for a halt. She got up from the table. 'Are any of you hungry? I could do with my tea.'

'Yeah, starving actually.' Steven glanced at the clock. 'I'd totally forgotten the time. What do you fancy? We could do chips in the air fryer, and there's some steaks I got from the butcher on the way back from town this morning. I thought we could all do with a treat.'

'Sounds like heaven.' Chantelle wandered into the kitchen.

'Chuck me the potatoes and I'll peel them for you.' Steven called from behind her.

When she got back to the table Irene was busy clearing the leftover material away. Steven was still pondering his drawing. 'Only challenge is now, if I want to do my bike panniers as well this is going to take more material than we've got already, and where do we get it when the shops are closed? Ordering stuff like that off the internet, you never know what you're going to get.'

'Hang on.' Irene started to leaf through her latest notebook. 'I'm sure there was something in here.'

They waited patiently while she pored over a few pages, a habit they had got used to over the last few months. There was no point trying to rush these things as she would get flustered and stressed out. Finally she held up the book triumphantly. 'I knew it! The woman across the road, I was talking to her' - she consulted the page - 'yesterday, and she said that the big fabric shop in town is doing mail order. You order stuff on their website and they'll send it out to you. I didn't catch the name of it, but she said it's the big one just off Sauchiehall Street so it should be easy to find.'

'Oh well, that sounds like it could be a win.' Steven had been busy packing up the sewing machine and hefted it back onto the shelf behind him.

Irene was still reading from her notes. 'She said it came all wrapped up in tissue paper like a present to herself, it was lovely.'

Steven was looking at her notebook thoughtfully. 'Shame we can't digitise all that so you can do searches on your phone. Some sort of database.' He scratched his head. 'I might ask Nick. He's good with all that IT stuff.'

'Sounds like a great plan.' Chantelle chucked him the bag of potatoes, which he caught neatly. 'But not as great as food right now. So get to it.' She tossed him the peeler.

He caught it and flourished it theatrically as if it was a majorette's baton. 'Yes ma'am.'

Chantelle reached over and kissed him on the top of the head. 'I love you.'

He looked up at her and the softness in his eyes made her breath catch. 'Love you too.'

Steven felt the sweat dripping down the curve of his spine and pushed himself harder up the hill. Getting out on the bike did feel good, partly because it helped him to forget about everything that was going on. Thankfully things had settled into a fairly constant rhythm now that the sewing seemed to have captivated Irene in just the right way. Once Chantelle had taken her bag to work two more of her colleagues had put in requests and now those were done a friend had roped Irene into making a pile of face masks. Brenda was still taking Irene to the food bank twice a week and it was lucky that it was still open, because it gave Steven a break while they were out. Irene had deteriorated to such an extent that he didn't feel safe leaving her alone any more. With Chantelle usually picking up any shopping they needed on her way in from work Steven really valued these outings on his bike.

By the time he got back home he was reeking and desperate for a shower, but Chantelle had obviously been watching out for him, because as soon as his bike was back in the shed the door opened before he had even had time to get his front door keys out. Something good had happened, he could tell, by the way she was looking at him. He tilted his head at her. 'Yes?'

'How did you know?' Chantelle sighed. 'Never mind. My news is too exciting.' She held up a piece of paper. 'I've found her.' Her voice was lowered, as if it was some big secret.

'Found who?' Steven lifted off his helmet and leaned forward to give her a quick kiss.

'Abigail.' When he looked at her blankly she rolled her eyes. 'Irene's sister.'

Steven felt his happiness drain away. 'Will you stop with your interfering?' He pushed past her down the hallway. 'I told you they don't get on. Where is Mum anyway?'

'She's having a snooze. Went to her room about half an hour ago.' Chantelle followed him into the kitchen. 'I don't understand why you're so against Abigail. What's she done that makes her so terrible?'

Steven ran a pint glass under the tap and lifted it up to gulp from it gratefully. 'If I'm honest? I don't really know. I was only a kid the last time she came here and I was in my room playing games online. I thought the shouting was my parents arguing, so I didn't really give it any mind. It was only when I heard a bang and looked out the window that I realised it was Auntie Abigail. But I swear I've never seen Mum look so broken that evening, not even after the worst stramash with my dad. It took her weeks to get back to her normal self. And I do know they haven't spoken since.'

'Wouldn't Abigail would want to know about the dementia though?' Chantelle fingered the paper that was still in her hand. 'They are sisters after all.'

'Why would she care, when she hasn't all these years? I don't think she has that right.' Steven swigged the last of the water from the glass.

'People change? She might have been wanting to get back in touch but not really known how to do it.'

'She's not even in Glasgow any more. I think someone told me she'd moved to Yorkshire somewhere.'

Chantelle nodded and held up the paper. 'She's still there. I managed to track down an address.'

A sigh escaped him. 'Did you get that through your fancy police contacts?'

'No, silly.' Chantelle rolled her eyes. 'I said you watch too much TV. I'd be sacked for doing things like that. I tracked her down on social media. She's not a prolific poster, but it looks like her daughter is, and I've managed to find their house on Streetview based on photos that she's put up. I must have a word with her about that when we finally meet her; you can't be too careful on social media these days.'

'I've got a cousin?' For one moment Steven was tempted, but then he shook his head. 'There isn't going to be any meeting. Mum would never want Abigail to see her like this.'

'Like what?' Chantelle's voice grew suddenly harsher, and she grabbed the pile of neatly-folded face masks that was lying next to the sewing machine, waving them in his face. 'She's still a person, Stevie. And making a valuable contribution to the pandemic efforts, last time I looked. The only reason why I did it was because she's started talking about Abigail herself and the fun times they had together when they were younger. I thought it would be good for her.'

'She's regressing, Chaz. The doctor said this would happen. People with dementia tend to slip further and further into the past.'

Chantelle looked at him stubbornly. Steven placed his glass carefully onto the worktop, slightly frightened of how much anger he felt inside him. Almost like a copy of the glass itself, ready to shatter uncontrollably if the wrong type of force was applied. 'I'll think about it, OK?' He stalked past her and into the bathroom, equally careful not to bang the door behind him.

Chapter 18

'Are you coming?' Chantelle knocked on Irene's bedroom door. 'You said you wanted to see it.' They had started watching films together on rainy afternoons, when the weather made a walk an uninviting prospect.

Irene was rummaging in the top drawer of her bureau. 'I'm sure I put it here.'

'What are you missing, Ma?' When Irene didn't appear to hear her Chantelle walked forward and touched her gently on the arm. 'What are you looking for?'

'My purse. I'm sure I left it here.' Irene kept on searching.

'I thought you always kept it in the drawer by your bed.' Chantelle reached over and opened the side table. 'Here you go.'

Irene took it gratefully. 'Thanks, love. I was worried about that.'

'Do you want to put it away until you need it? Then you'll know where it is.' Chantelle felt her heart wrench. Irene seemed to have deteriorated a lot in the last couple of weeks and watching paranoia develop about losing things was really difficult. 'Come on, Ma. Steven's waiting for us to watch the film.' She eased the purse out of Irene's hand. 'I'll put this back for you.'

They all sat on the sofa together. It was a bit of a squeeze, but Chantelle liked it this way when they watched horror films. She always preferred having people on both sides so nothing could creep up on her. It was silly, she knew, but they simply scared her too much.

It was about half way through the film when Irene got up. 'Don't mind me, I'll be back in a sec.'

Steven looked up. 'We can pause it, if you want.'

Irene waved a hand. 'I'll only be a minute.'

Chantelle turned her attention back to the screen, then jumped as an attacker appeared around a corner. She curled into Steven. 'This one might be a bit too scary for me.'

Steven put his arm around her. 'Don't worry, I'll protect you from the scary monsters on the tiny screen.'

It was only once the imminent attack crisis had passed that Chantelle suddenly realised Irene wasn't back. She looked at her watch. 'Hang on, it's been a good ten minutes since she went to the loo. I'll go and check up on her.'

Steven pressed the pause button, his face worried.

There was no-one in the bathroom and Irene's bedroom was empty too. 'Shit.' Chantelle felt her heart speed up. She poked her head back into the living room. 'She's gone.'

Steven's eyes widened. 'Fuck.' He grabbed his crutches and stood up. 'What do we do?'

'She can't have got far in ten minutes.' Chantelle tried to project the calm exterior she normally used for work. 'She was looking for her purse earlier. Maybe she popped out to the shop?'

'Does she even remember how to get to the shop?' Steven sighed. 'I knew I should have locked the door and hidden the key.'

'No point beating yourself up about that now.' A sudden thought occurred to Chantelle. 'Try that phone finder thing. She could have taken it with her.'

Steven picked up his phone with a shaking hand. 'I can't even remember how you do it.'

'Give it here.' Why she was destined to always be the calm one in situations Chantelle didn't know. She tapped a few times at the screen. 'See, I'm right. There's a dot in the shop on the corner.'

Steven raised his eyes skywards. 'Thank God for that.'

'Well, thank technology, actually.' Chantelle poked him in the shoulder gently. 'I'll nip down there and check she's there. You stay here in case she comes back before I find her.'

She slipped her trainers on and grabbed her jacket, keys and facemask, and then on second thoughts added her purse, just in case Irene had tried to buy anything in the shop without money. Outside a light drizzle was falling.

Had Irene taken her coat when she left? Chantelle hoped she had.

When she entered the shop she couldn't see anyone inside, but then a man exited from a door at the back. Chantelle recognised him as one of the people who normally worked behind the counter. 'I've got her in the storeroom with a cup of tea.' He pointed backwards with a thumb. 'I was just going to call your colleagues, Officer.'

'Chantelle, please.' She shook her head. 'I'm off duty.'

'I knew she was yours, because I've seen you come in together, but I didn't know where you lived exactly. Otherwise I would have got the wife to take her home for you.'

Chantelle pressed her hands together in a gesture of gratitude. 'Thanks for taking care of her. We're straight on up when you turn right out of the door. Number ninety-three, if it happens again.' Her heart sank as she realised what she had just done, and she looked around quickly to check there was no-one else in the shop. 'I'd appreciate if you'd keep that information to yourself though. I don't really want anyone else knowing where I live.'

He just smiled at her. 'It's nae bother, hen. My auntie was just the same as your mam so I know what you're going through.'

Chantelle took a deep breath to dispel all the residual anger and worry and then popped her head around the door of the storeroom. 'Ready to go, Ma?'

Irene looked up from where she was sitting on a stack of big rice bags. 'Oh, it's you. What are you doing here?' She was cradling a half-empty cup of tea in her hands.

Chantelle sat down beside her. 'Waiting for you to come back so we can watch the rest of the film. Are you coming?'

'Just let me finish my cup of tea, love. I wouldn't want that nice young man to think I don't appreciate it.'

Chantelle heard a snort from the doorway and looked up to find the man in question standing there. Given that he was sporting a shock of white hair his mirth was entirely justified.

'Not so young these days.' He pointed at Irene's cup. 'If you leave that behind I'll grab it when you're gone. I'm just sorry our accommodations aren't more luxurious.'

Irene patted the bag she was sitting on. 'I have to say these are pretty comfortable. Do you ever come in here for a snooze?'

The man tapped the side of his nose and winked at her. 'I couldn't possibly say.'

Chantelle fished her phone out of her pocket, remembering Steven would still be worried. She typed in a message. *Found her.* Within seconds she got a relieved emoji in response.

'Come on, you.' Chantelle held out a hand to help Irene up. 'Let's get home. Did you want anything while you're here?'

Irene's face fell. 'I thought I did, but I can't remember.'

'Well, better take a list with you next time.' Chantelle tried to keep her voice cheerful, even though her heart was breaking inside. She slung an arm around Irene's shoulders and kissed her on the cheek. 'Love you, Ma.'

'Love you too.' Irene squeezed her back.

When Irene was settled safely back in front of the television Chantelle drew Steven aside. 'Are you sure you won't consider a home for her? Not even now?'

'This is her home.' Steven frowned at her. 'Don't even start.'

'OK, OK.' Chantelle held up her hands. 'I'm not going to argue with you any more. You do whatever you want. I'm going to have a lie down.'

'But what about the rest of the film?'

Chantelle shook her head. 'It wasn't that good anyway.'

She flounced off to her room, feeling hurt. It seemed that just because she wasn't related to Irene then Steven was leaving her out of decisions entirely. Was that really fair? In her heart she knew it wasn't but then she also didn't want to keep arguing with him. Even so, letting things deteriorate to the point where Irene got lost or hurt also wasn't something she could do. She'd seen too many examples of people who slipped through the cracks because their family either couldn't or didn't want to take care of them and there was no way she was letting that happen to Irene.

A few smacks of her pillow to fluff it up left her feeling no better. But what could she do? She considered the problem for a few minutes. Steven had said a couple of times that he didn't want to consider the two nearest nursing homes because he had heard some horror stories, but what if she did some research, talked to people there and found out the real truth? They might turn out to not actually be that bad. And then if she laid out those facts in front of Steven it might be enough to make him change his mind. She pulled out her phone and started tapping at the screen, suddenly feeling much more cheerful. Gathering information and intelligence wasn't going behind his back. It wasn't like she was trying to make the decision for him. They could make it together once she had everything to hand.

Steven draped the red and white striped cloth over the outside table and laid three sets of cutlery on it. Lunch with Brenda had become a bit of a regular event recently. Strictly it wasn't actually lunch with Brenda, more like lunch next to her, because in order to keep to the lockdown rules they had separate tables and separate food. It had taken Chantelle some time to become reconciled to the idea, but as Brenda had suggested, with their gardens only divided by a low fence then how was it anyone's fault if they happened to have lunch outside at the same time, as long as they kept their two metre distance apart? And if their tables happened to be positioned directly opposite each other then wasn't that just the best place to catch the sun at that time of day? Steven smiled as he thought about it. He enjoyed spending time with Brenda too; she had a keen wit and often made them laugh, which was definitely something much in need in these difficult days. The unusually good weather that had continued all through April and May had been in their favour too. It was easier to do without travel when your own back garden felt like being on holiday.

Chantelle appeared, bearing a big bowl of salad and a stack of glasses that she set on the table. 'Be right back.' She came back a moment later, her arms full of sauces and a carton of fresh juice. 'Ma's just carving the chicken.'

'It's so nice to have a proper sit down meal.' Steven fingered the edge of the tablecloth. 'Especially with weather like this.'

'You're not wrong there.' Brenda plonked her own cutlery and a glass down on her table. 'The smell of that chicken of yours has been tempting me for the last half hour.'

'So sorry!' Chantelle's face went pink. 'You know we'd share with you if we could.'

'I know.' Brenda grinned at her. 'And don't you worry. I've got myself a gourmet burger and a hefty salad. So I'm looking forward to that.'

By the time they had dished everything up Steven was starving. Silence reigned for a few minutes as everyone tucked into the food. Eventually Brenda put down her fork with a sigh of pleasure and reached for her glass. 'Well, that is one fine burger. I almost don't miss my real life at all.'

'This good weather can't last forever though.' Chantelle looked up at the sky.

'Look at you, searching for the worst in things.' Brenda wagged a finger at her. 'Cherish every moment, is what I say. Worry about tomorrow when it comes.'

Irene squinted up at the sky. 'Seems like you should be more worried about getting sunburn on a day like today.' She looked at Chantelle. 'Do you have sun cream on?'

'I'm not a child, Ma.' Chantelle tried to look annoyed, but Steven could see the curve of a smile at the edge of her lips. 'Of course I've got some on.'

'Good.' Steven decided to carry on the joke. 'I'd hate to see you shrivel to a crisp. I wouldn't be able to touch you then.'

Chantelle's eyes went wide as she registered the innuendo behind his words. Irene seemed not to have noticed, but a knowing glance from Brenda had Chantelle's face flaming. She poked him in the ribs. 'Stop that.' When Steven just laughed then Chantelle opened her mouth again. 'You know I wouldn't be able to touch you either. Especially not in that place you like so much.'

Damn. Steven should have known better than to play this game. Because now what he had was Brenda laughing her head off from the other side of the fence, while he was glad of the curve of the table to hide how hard he was. How did Chantelle have that effect on him, while she only seemed embarrassed by the idea? Having totally missed the joke, Irene was looking at the three of them in puzzlement, which only increased Brenda's laughter.

Chantelle leaned towards Steven. He thought she was going to kiss him quickly but instead she put her lips next to his ear. Her voice was barely audible, even at this close distance. 'Don't worry, you're not the only one who's a little bit moist.'

Her voice slammed straight through to his cock and he got up, grabbing the empty juice box to hide what she'd done to him. 'I'll go get some more.' There was no way he could sit innocently next to his mum with a hard-on creating a mountain inside his shorts.

Chantelle also stood up. 'I'll go get the dessert.' She followed him back inside the house. As soon as they were through the door Steven slammed it and pushed her against the wall. 'You tease. You knew exactly what you were doing out there.'

Chantelle's face creased into a satisfied smile. 'You started it.'

He touched his lips to her neck. 'How long do you think we have before they notice that we're gone?'

'Oh, I don't know. Two, three minutes?' Chantelle pulled his body closer to hers. 'Can you make me come before then?'

'I can do my best to try.' He bent his head again.

If the other two noticed their dishevelment when they reappeared they made no comment on it. Irene had left a portion of the trifle on Brenda's doorstep that morning, so at least they were able to all enjoy the same dessert.

'That was lovely.' Brenda licked her spoon and laid it down. 'Was that lemon and orange in it?'

'Yes, I zested it as well.' Irene nodded.

Brenda sighed. 'I'll miss your food when I go up north.'

'Up north?' Chantelle looked at her in surprise. 'Don't tell me you're leaving us.'

'Not for good.' Brenda shook her head. 'But my sister's going in for an operation on Monday and she'll need someone to take care of her when she comes out. She's got no-one else who can do it, you see, and I don't want her in hospital longer than she needs to. It'll only be for a few weeks, hopefully. Then I'll be back down here.'

'No, of course.' Irene nodded rapidly. 'We'll miss you, though.'

'I'll be back before you know it.' Brenda squared her shoulders. 'And this lockdown has to lift sometime soon. It can't go on indefinitely.'

Brenda's departure would see them even more isolated, Steven realised. Would Irene still be able to go to the food bank? He would probably have to take her now. Which would give him even less time to himself. He sighed, feeling the weight of everything settle in ever more deeply on his shoulders. He sent up a quick prayer for normal life to resume, and soon.

Chapter 19

The next day Chantelle waited until she heard the door slam behind Steven before reaching for her phone. She felt a bit bad for going behind his back, but only a little. If he wasn't ready to face up to facts then she would have to do it for him. She propped herself up on the bed with pillows and dialled the first number on her list.

'Ashburn Care Home, Sandy speaking.'

The voice that answered the phone was cheerful and Chantelle felt her spirits lift. 'Um, hi.' She felt her heart beating faster. Why was she so nervous about this? It was only a simple enquiry. She cleared her throat and started again. 'I, er, wanted to ask about possible care for my mother. She's got dementia and things are getting a bit too much to handle at home.' It was only a small bending of the truth from mother-in-law. And Irene was the only mother she had left. Chantelle still crossed her fingers just in case.

'I'm sorry to hear that.' Sandy's tone changed from cheerful to compassionate. 'And I'm sure we can do something for you, we do have a few beds free at the moment.'

'That's great.' Chantelle breathed a sigh of relief. Maybe this would be easier than she expected.

'You'll appreciate, of course, with things as they are, that we can't show you round in person. But we've just put a video on our website which gives you a virtual tour of our communal areas and a couple of the rooms, and we're happy to get one of the staff to give you a live video tour so you can see the room that she'll actually be staying in.'

'That sounds great.' Chantelle looked down at the list of questions she had written down on her pad. 'So you're not letting any family members in at the moment?'

'Unfortunately not.' Sandy's voice became regretful. 'But the main sitting room has a large window we've been opening so people can talk through that.'

It wasn't ideal, but it was something at least. And how long could the lockdown go on? Another month or so at the very most? Maybe they could delay putting Irene in the home until it lifted.

'So how much does it cost, and what's the procedure for paying for it all?' They didn't have much money, but between Irene's pension and Chantelle's salary it might not be too bad. The price per month made her wince, but Sandy's reassurance that the local authority would pay a large part of it had her breathing a bit easier. She thanked the woman and hung up, ready to do some more research.

Two hours later she found her stomach rumbling and she put down her phone, rubbing her eyes. Out of the two nearest care homes then Ashburn definitely seemed the best. It was only ten minutes walk away, and near a lovely small park which gave a great view from the windows. Steven still hadn't returned from his bike ride, but that was nothing unusual; on the days that Chantelle was off work he often went out for long periods. She knew he was frustrated about being at home all the time, but his search for jobs had so far proved fruitless and she did understand how he was feeling. If it wasn't for her job she would be feeling pretty desperate too. It was sad that they both seemed to be at their happiest when they were out of the house.

Chantelle realised the whirr of the sewing machine had stopped. She should probably go and see what Irene was doing. Still in the house, obviously, as she hadn't heard the door, but then what if she had been on the phone and missed it? The sudden worry had her scrambling off the bed. But when she poked her head into the living room Irene was sitting on the sofa, cradling a cup of tea in her hands.

'Kettle's just boiled.' Irene nodded in the direction of the kitchen.

'Thanks, Ma, I could do with one right now.' Tea made, Chantelle returned to plop herself down next to Irene. It was unusual for both TV and radio to be switched off, and Chantelle took a long searching look at Irene. 'Are you OK?'

Irene huffed a small mirthless laugh. 'What does that even mean these days?' She pointed at the TV. 'Couldn't stand it any more. The whole world's dying and we can't do anything about it.'

'But we are doing something about it.' Chantelle couldn't let that pass. 'That's what this lockdown is for. We're literally saving lives right now by staying at home. You could even be saving your life.'

'Well, that's not a major achievement.' Irene stared into her cup as if it would give her all the answers. 'I've started wondering if my life is really worth it.'

'No, Ma, no. Don't do this.' Chantelle curled up next to Irene's warmth, nestling her head on the other woman's shoulder. 'Your life means something to me. It means a lot. So don't even think that way.'

There was silence for a long time, and when Chantelle lifted her head to check on Irene she found tears rolling down the other woman's cheeks. 'Oh Ma.' She wrapped her arms around Irene and pulled her in for a hug, much like her own mother had done to her when she was little. While Irene cried her eyes out, Chantelle rocked her, stroking her hair.

'You've got this, Ma. No matter what happens, you've got this. We've got this. We're in this together. And we will get through it.' Chantelle found herself shedding a few tears of her own. How could she have thought that putting Irene in a home would be the best solution for any of them?

When Steven came home she met him at the door, putting a finger to her lips. 'She's sleeping. She had a bit of a meltdown earlier. I think she's just exhausted with everything that's going on.'

Steven leaned his head against the wall. 'We're all exhausted. I don't know how much more of this I can take. The constant bad news and the uncertainty, it's killing me off.'

'Wow. The live-for-the-moment guy has finally had enough of living for the moment.' Chantelle was trying to make a joke, but it fell flat.

'This isn't living, Chaz. This is barely surviving. And I don't know what to do. I can feel the panic rising in me every time I think about what's going on.' He pushed past her into the living room and plopped down onto the sofa.

She sat down next to him. 'How was Sean?'

Steven did a double take. 'How did you know? Who spilled the beans?'

Chantelle felt her spirits lift a little. 'It was just a hunch. These last couple of weeks you've come back from your rides looking so much happier, I suspected you were meeting up with someone. And Sean is the only one of your mates who is close enough to make it work. But thanks for confirming it.'

'Sneaky.' Steven spared her a small smile as he massaged his good leg gently. 'I thought you'd disapprove.'

Chantelle shrugged. 'There's sticking to the rules, and there's doing what you need to keep your mental health in order. There's been talk about easing the restrictions to allow two households to meet up outside, so it probably won't be long before it's permitted. I'm assuming you never go closer than two metres apart, so chance of infection is pretty limited?'

'Never. We're always careful.' Steven shook his head. 'And it has been a massive help, for both of us, I think. He's been really struggling, living with his mum.'

'More than you?' Chantelle looked at him searchingly.

'It's not a competition.' Steven was deflecting and they both knew it. His stoicism crumpled under her steady gaze. 'OK, I admit it. I have been struggling. This situation would be bad enough as it is, but with everything else that's going on? It's a fucking nightmare. But what what do you want me to do about it? What decent alternative do we have? Don't tell me a nursing home would be better right now, when we wouldn't even be able to go and see her.'

'No, you're right.' Chantelle sighed and laid an arm across Steven's shoulders. 'Come here. Give me a cuddle and we can pretend none of this exists for a few minutes.'

They snuggled down on the sofa and Chantelle pulled the green fluffy blanket over them. Steven mumbled something against her chest that Chantelle didn't quite catch. She bent her head down. 'What was that?'

Steven raised his head. 'I said I got some posh sausages from that nice butcher you like. I thought we could have them with mash and some frozen spinach.'

He was always thinking about her, she realised. Even in the middle of all this turmoil, he had thought to get her something nice. 'Are they those amazing pork and apple ones you got last time?'

His face broke into the first proper smile she'd seen for a while. 'I got a few of those, but they also had some venison and cranberry ones that sounded pretty awesome too.'

'Magic.' She gave him a squeeze. 'I do love you.'

He kissed her softly, then nestled his head back onto her chest. 'I love you too.'

Steven woke up with a start. Had that been the front door closing? If so it would be Chantelle back from her night shift. She always went for a quick shower and then came back to snuggle in beside him. He smiled in anticipation at the thought of her soft skin next to his and was just drifting back to sleep when the realisation hit him that he couldn't hear anything from the bathroom next door. His eyes snapped open and a bleary look at his watch showed that it was only four in the morning. Far too early for Chantelle to be home. He groaned as he realised what that must mean. It was the third time in two weeks that Irene had decided to go for a wander without telling them. To be fair, the first time she had managed to find her way home, so when she went out the second time he hadn't been too worried, but three hours later she had called him sounding distressed, having had a fall in the woods and forgotten how to use the mapping app. He had resolved after that never to let her out alone again but she obviously hadn't listened to his request. Or had forgotten that he had actually made it. Anything was possible. Her little black book had been working so well up until now, but recently she had started forgetting that it even existed, so it was no help. He had been resisting locking her in, feeling like he would be imprisoning her, but it was probably time to face the facts and just do it.

With a sigh Steven called up his device locator on his phone. He had bought two of the tiny buttons and slipped one in a pocket of each of Irene's jackets, with her full permission of course. That and her phone usually covered all bases. But this time all three of them showed their location firmly inside the flat. He groaned again and pulled aside the curtains so he could open the window. It was already light outside, so that's what must have confused her. And yes, the early June morning was warm enough that she wouldn't have thought to take her coat. He sighed again and reached for his prosthetic. If she had no phone then she had no way of getting in touch so anything could happen.

A quick search of the flat to check he hadn't been imagining things showed that Irene was indeed missing, and she hadn't taken her purse either. He splashed some water on his face to wake him up properly and went to grab his bike. It would give him a better chance of catching up with her. He found Chantelle's number and called it.

'Mum's gone missing.' He spoke as soon as she answered. 'I'm going out to search for her.'

'Stevie, I'm kind of in the middle of something here.' Chantelle's voice was tight. 'I know I keep my phone with me in case there's an emergency, but given how often this is happening recently it doesn't really count.'

'I'm sorry, I just thought you would like to know.' Steven realised his voice was snarky, but given his sleep deprivation he felt slightly justified.

'Look, if you're really worried about her then you should call 999, otherwise you're on your own. I'm not even supposed to have my personal phone on me when I'm out at work, so I'm going to get in trouble if I don't go.' She cut the call before he had the chance to say anything else.

Steven leaned his head back against the wall of the shed. On his own. Fine. His shoulders slumped as he felt tears start into his eyes. All this stuff was too much to handle by himself. He hadn't realised exactly how close he was to breaking point. With a great effort he pulled himself together and wiped his face with the hem of his t-shirt. *It's just tiredness talking. Now focus. You need to find her.*

He cycled in ever-increasing circles around the area, hoping that would help him catch her. It helped that with it being early morning there were very few people out, although he did see a couple of desperate-looking parents with prams which made him feel a bit better about his own lack of sleep. But an hour later, with a good few kilometres radius covered, he started to get worried. Surely she couldn't have walked this far. Unless more time had passed between the door closing and him waking up again? Surely not. Had he missed any of the streets? Again, he thought not. He adjusted his helmet to scratch his head as he wondered what to do. Best thing probably was to go home, just to check she hadn't ended up back there. And he could have a much needed drink of water and work out what to do. Just on an impulse he cycled back through the woods, thinking the coolness of the leaves would calm his nerves. And there, sitting on a fallen tree, was exactly who he had been looking for.

Steven pulled up next to Irene and propped his bike at the end of the log. He sat down beside her. 'Hello, Mum.'

Irene had been staring blankly into space, but as her gaze swung round to meet him her face lit up. 'Hello, love. Is that you out for a bike ride? That's nice.'

'I was looking for you. It's a bit early for you to be out. I got worried about you.'

Irene's face fell. 'I simply can't stay in that house any longer, Stevie. Those four walls make me feel trapped.'

'I can understand exactly how you feel. In fact, I feel a bit like that myself.' Steven put his arm around her. 'So next time you want to go out, why don't you give me a shout and I'll come with you? Then we can both escape together.'

Irene nodded. 'That would be nice.' She pointed up at the tree canopy. 'Birdsong seems to be wonderful today.'

'That's because it's not even six in the morning, Mum. They're all just waking up themselves.'

'Oh goodness! What are you doing up so early? More to the point, what am I doing up? I had no idea it was that sort of time. This summer light's got me all confused.'

'I don't know what you're doing up so early, and to be honest you're running me a bit ragged with all this.' Steven regretted the words as soon as they came out of his mouth, because Irene's face crumpled and tears spilled down her cheeks.

'I know I'm a burden on you, Stevie. I'm trying so hard not to be, but I just can't seem to make it work.'

Steven pulled her to him in a hug and rested his head on her shoulder. 'You're not a burden, Mum. Honestly. It's this whole pandemic thing that screwing everything up. I don't know how much longer I can take it. Having no job makes me feel totally worthless, even though I know that's a stupid way to feel. Everyone loses their job at some point. But with everything else that's going on I can't seem to power through like I normally do.'

Irene stroked his hair like she had done when he was younger. 'Is there anything I can do to help?'

'You can make sure you take your phone when you leave the house? Just so I know where you are and can come and get you if you get lost again? I don't want to have to lock you in, but I also don't want to have to repeatedly come out searching for you. I don't think my heart could take it.' Steven pulled back and gave her a kiss on the cheek, in the hope that it would soften his words.

'I will. I'll try my best.' Irene was silent for a few minutes and Steven listened to the sounds of all the different birds that were singing their hearts out in the trees. In some ways it was comforting to see this part of nature carrying on as if nothing was happening in the outside world. He should come up here more often to get some perspective on everything. He had been spending far too much time cooped up in the house, applying for jobs. Feeling like he should be doing something. But maybe it was OK to not do anything for a while. To relax into what was instead of worrying about the future. Go for walks with his mum. Cook nice meals for Chantelle when she came home from work. Spend some effort planning with Nick what whey were going to do when lockdown ended. He felt a weight lift suddenly from his shoulders and he took Irene's hand. 'Come on. Let's go home. How do you feel about pancakes for breakfast?'

'Ooh, sounds great. Can we make those fluffy American style ones? With blueberries in them?'

'If we've got any blueberries left. I'll have to check the fridge. You'd better not have snaffled them all.' Steven rescued his bike and wheeled it over. 'That way, Mum.' He pointed. 'That's the way home.'

'Me? Snaffle all the blueberries? A likely story.' Irene seemed to have caught the lightness in his tone herself, and her eyes sparkled at him in a way he hadn't seen for weeks. 'Chantelle is the one who loves her fruit the most. If they're all gone we'll have to blame her.'

'You're not wrong there.' Steven felt his spirits lift even more at the thought that his mum wasn't entirely gone yet. 'In fact, why don't we see if the corner shop is open on the way back. If I remember right they open at six and they might have some fresh fruit. And we can make some extra for Chaz for when she gets home.'

Irene pushed herself up off the log and smiled at him. 'Sounds like a great plan. Lead on, soldier.'

Chapter 20

When Chantelle put her key in the front door of the flat she was still fuming. It was partly frustration with herself for actually bothering to answer her phone, but she was mainly angry at Steven. Trying to deal with a major road crash was difficult enough without having to field calls from him at the same time. The only saving grace was that she had put her phone away seconds before her sergeant had shown up. And at least Steven had managed to find Irene; he'd confirmed it in a message that Chantelle had seen when she finished work. But in some ways that made her even more angry because it meant that he hadn't actually needed her at all. The laughter coming from inside as she pushed open the door only added to her irritation.

When she looked into the living room Steven and Irene were sitting on the sofa, mugs in hand. Steven smiled at her. 'We made pancakes for you. Do you want some?'

The unexpected offer made Chantelle falter for a second, and her stomach rumbled. Then she collected herself. She was not going to be bought off by pancakes when there were important things she needed to say. 'How many times have I said to you, only call me at work if there's an emergency? And did you listen to me? No.'

Steven blinked rapidly, obviously surprised at her outburst. 'It was an emergency. Mum was missing. I thought you would want to know.'

'Then send me a fecking message or something, so I can see it when I have the time!' Chantelle waved her hands in frustration. 'When I said emergency, I meant death, or serious injury or something.'

Irene stood up. 'I'm going to be in my bedroom having a snooze after all the excitement I've had this morning. I think this is something you need to have out on your own.' She pointed at the sofa. 'Have a seat, love. You'll be tired.'

Chantelle was tired, she realised, and the unexpected kindness from Irene in the face of her own rage made her suddenly feel like crying. She flopped down onto the comfy cushions and touched Steven gently on the arm. 'I'm sorry for shouting at you. It's been a difficult night. We had a major road crash right before you called me, two people died and two more probably have life changing injuries. That's why I'm so late home. And it was a drunk driver too, which always feels so futile.'

Steven put an arm around her and kissed the top of her head. 'I forgive you. I'll just put it down to you being tired and hangry.'

Chantelle's stomach growled again at the thought of food. 'Did you say pancakes?'

She felt Steven's chest rumble in a laugh. 'Blueberry ones, too. And there's some maple syrup and scooshy cream if you want it.'

Chantelle sighed. 'Heaven.' She pushed herself up off the sofa. 'I'll go and shower quickly before I have breakfast, then I can relax. And you probably should change your clothes too now, I might have contaminated you.'

Steven rolled his eyes, but by the time she got out the shower he had done as she suggested and was back on the sofa, swapping his shorts and t-shirt for a pair of blue jeans and the bright orange shirt he had altered a few weeks back. He pointed into the kitchen. 'Pancakes are on the sideboard. I'd stick them in the microwave for thirty seconds before you add on the other stuff.'

She piled food up high and came to sit down beside him. There was very little said until her entire plate was gone and Chantelle put it down with a groan. 'That was amazing. Why don't we do this more often?'

Steven shrugged. 'Probably because we're too busy doing other things. Looking after Mum is becoming a bit of a full-time job.'

Chantelle snuggled into him. 'We do need to talk about that. Things are getting harder and harder, and now she's starting to go missing regularly. Wouldn't it be better to have her in the care of people who actually know what they're doing? Then it might be less stressful for everyone, her included. We're all exhausted and it's not good for any-one.'

Steven jerked away from her, disgust forming on his face. 'How are we still having this conversation? We've had it once and I don't want to have it again.'

Chantelle sat up straight, gathering her feet underneath her. 'The point is that it wasn't a conversation. I made a suggestion that was open for discussion and you shut me down. That's not how things should work if this is a part-nership. We should make decisions together.'

Steven held up a hand. 'The point is that there is no discussion. How you can even think about putting her in a place like that is beyond me.'

'That's the thing, though.' Chantelle huffed out a breath. 'I'm not so sure that it's true. I spoke to the manager at Ashburn and it seems like a decent place. She even offered to do us a virtual tour so we could see what it was like for ourselves.'

She realised Steven was staring at her. 'You called a care home? After I told you it wasn't an option? You went be-hind my back?'

'I went behind your back because you refused to listen to me. I love her too, you know.' Chantelle felt her anger rising again.

Steven folded his arms. 'She's my mum, this should be my decision. I'm the one who takes care of her most of the time.'

'Yes, while I'm out earning money to feed all three of us.'

The look Steven flashed her told Chantelle it had been a mistake to bring that up. 'I never asked you to stay here forever. Mum and I can do perfectly fine on our own. You're not related so you have no power over what happens to either of us.'

'Fine.' Chantelle got up, feeling a speedy exit was necessary before she dissolved in tears. 'I'll be gone as soon as I can find myself another place. And you can see how you do without me.'

She slammed the door behind her and threw herself on the bed, trembling with anger. That last comment had been such a low blow, knowing as he did that Irene was the closest thing to a mum that she had left. She took a few deep breaths, trying to calm herself. Then the door clicked open and she looked up, ready for another argument, but it was Irene instead.

The older woman came and sat down next to her. 'Feel any better?'

Chantelle bit her lip. Then she gave up and buried her head in Irene's thigh. 'Oh, Ma. He said you were nothing to me because we weren't related.' Her body shook as she finally let the full force of all her pent up emotions loose.

Irene gently stroked her hair and said nothing until Chantelle's sobs died down. Then she gave Chantelle's shoulders a squeeze and pulled her into a hug. 'He can say a lot of things, but he can't say shit about that. You'll always be dear to me, and I've written it down in a special place so even when I don't remember you can read it back to me.'

Chantelle shed a few more tears on the red wool of Irene's jumper. 'I was so afraid that he would take you away from me.' She looked up into Irene's face. 'He can't do that, can he? Can he?'

Irene shrugged. 'Honestly? I don't know. I'll probably have to give him power of attorney at some point, but if I can I'll try to make sure you're included in some way. If you don't mind that, my love? I had hoped you would find your way back together somehow, but if it's really not working out I don't want your being able to see me to be dependent on him.'

Chantelle flopped backwards onto the bed, staring at the ceiling. 'I just don't know, Ma. I'd desperately hoped the same thing too, but if this thing between us is too much to deal with then we might just have to accept it.'

'Don't rush into anything, OK?' Irene stroked her hair once more. 'You get some sleep, love. You're clearly exhausted. And I'll give you one of my favourite quotes before I go. I can't remember who said it but that doesn't matter.'

'Tomorrow is another day?'

Irene laughed. 'Not that one. This one is "Avoid making any irrevocable decisions while tired or hungry."' She rolled her eyes. 'Although how I can remember that when there's multiple things spilling out of my brain every second I have no idea.' She leaned forward and kissed Chantelle on the forehead. 'Get some sleep. Things will look better on the other side.'

Irene had her hand on the door handle when there was a tapping and Steven poked his head around the door.

'She needs her sleep.' Irene's voice was stern.

'I know.' Steven's face looked miserable. 'It's just - well - Chaz - don't go. I love you. And I know we can work this out somehow.'

Irene flapped her hands at him. 'You can work it out later. Leave her alone for a bit. The poor girl's exhausted. She's been out all night.'

'OK, OK, I'm gone.' Steven's head disappeared, and a moment later Irene was gone too, closing the door gently behind her.

Chantelle snuggled under the covers, gathering them in around her. While Steven's words meant a lot to her, was love enough? Could they really work it out? Or were they heading back to the same old patterns that had driven them apart in the first place? The questions swirled around in her head until sleep finally overtook her.

Steven and Chantelle fell into an uneasy truce after that and things were still not right between them three days later when Steven finally managed to get out of the house for a bike ride. The weather was beautiful and it lifted his mood as he cycled along the mostly deserted roads. Sean was waiting for him at the usual place and Steven hailed him as he started up and they fell into an easy formation.

'So what's the plan today?' Steven glanced sideways. Sean was in his usual bright orange cycling jersey and orange and green shorts. Steven always said that it made him look exactly like an upside down fruit with leaves attached, but Sean remained stubbornly impervious to the teasing.

'Blairscaith Muir?' Sean looked at him hopefully. 'It's a good place to claim that we met each other by accident, with it being so popular and almost half way between our houses.'

'I thought they were doing forestry stuff up there? I'm way past the age where playing dodge with heavy machinery seemed like a good idea.'

'Hell, yeah. But no, the forestry stuff is all finished.' Sean looked momentarily alarmed. 'I take it you once did think it was a good idea? I would have never dared.'

'My lips are sealed.' Steven grinned at him. It had only been once, and there had been a particularly close shave which had put him off from ever doing it again.

'Anyway, as I said, it's all finished up there.' Sean grunted as the hill they were on started to really bite. 'And they've left a brilliant combination of gravel access roads and churned up dirt paths with enough mud to keep even you happy.'

'What, even in this weather? We haven't had rain for weeks.' Steven fell in behind the other bike.

'Oi! Stop slipstreaming me and get out and do some real work.' Sean swerved and slowed suddenly so he came back alongside. 'This hill is steep enough as it is.'

'Yeah yeah.' Steven grinned at him. 'You not fit enough?'

Sean stuck a middle finger up and Steven laughed. Getting out like this was so great. Exactly what he needed to take his mind off the situation back in the flat. But with that thought all his worries came flooding back in.

'OK, what is it this time?' Sean's voice sounded slightly resigned. Or was he teasing?

'What do you mean?'

'You suddenly shot off up that hill like you had the flames of hell trying to catch up with you. And you're scowling. I checked.'

'Scowling?' Steven felt his face draw into an even bigger frown before he managed to smooth it out. 'Just the usual lockdown squabbles, I guess.'

'Trouble between you and Chantelle?' Sean's voice changed from teasing to concerned in an instant.

'I don't know.' Steven tried to arrange his whirling thoughts. 'I can't help feeling like maybe it's just not meant to be, you know? We were perfectly happy until I got knocked down, and now life seems to keep throwing us these curve balls. The combination of the accident and everything else that was happening did for us the first time, and now it's the combination of fucking lockdown and what's going on with my mum. We never seem to catch a break.'

'You do realise that Chantelle never would have moved back in without lockdown though? And you may never have got back together. So every cloud has a silver lining, as my mum always says.'

'I know that. But now we've argued about Mum's care, and it seems such a petty thing, but it's actually a massive thing too. I could never put Mum in a home, even if it means giving up my own job to take care of her. But Chantelle doesn't seem to understand that.' Steven felt the sadness sink into him again.

'Just talk to her. And keep on talking. Chantelle's a problem solver, you know that. And she cares for you. She's probably worried about you taking on too much. And I'm sure she's stressed because of her job too. I wouldn't like to be in her shoes at the moment. Not only are they having to cope with all of the things that they usually have to deal with, but they're having to enforce all the lockdown rules that no-one wants to do.' Sean waved cheerily at a driver who was overtaking them slowly with plenty of room to spare.

'I know. But we still seem to have reached this sticking point we can't get past. She's still angry at me for some things I said, justifiably, I guess. I was pretty mean.'

'What did you say?' Sean looked over, eyebrow raised.

'I said that she didn't have a say in Mum's care because they weren't related.' At Sean's sucked in breath Steven felt embarrassment starting to heat the back of his neck. 'I know, I know. But she also went behind my back to talk to a care home, and that just feels wrong. Like I can't trust her any more.'

'So you're even. Call it quits and shake hands, agree to start with a clean slate.' Sean shrugged.

Steven huffed out a breath. 'I think, if I'm honest, it cuts deeper than that. I think that in some way it taps into my fears that maybe I'm not doing a good enough job with my mum. That at some point someone will come along and say to me "hey, you're disabled yourself, how can you possibly take care of someone else?" And then one layer deeper than that are all the insecurities I had around the time of my accident that somehow having only one leg makes me not good enough to deserve a partner. And I know I dealt with all of that ages ago and got through it. It's just this fucking lockdown messing with my mind.'

Sean was silent for a few minutes while they cycled down one small slope and up another. 'I actually think...' His voice sounded very thoughtful.

'Yeah?' Steven looked at him.

Sean frowned, as if considering something very important. 'I actually think, on balance, if I'm really honest...'

'Come on man, spit it out!' Steven was getting irritated now.

'I think that it's more like one and a third legs instead of one, although I'd have to take some measurements of both length and circumference to really make an accurate decision. I mean, does it depend only on length? Or should it take into account weight? And if so, how does one accurately weigh an object that's actually attached to something else? There is much to be considered.' Sean's face and tone was carefully serious, but his eyes were sparkling.

Steven found himself laughing, big belly laughs that forced him to head off the road and take a break while he bent over and clutched his stomach, holding himself up by clinging onto his handlebars. Sean stopped beside him and soon the two of them were whooping and wiping their eyes. They only recovered when another car passed them honking its horn, the driver obviously enjoying the moment as much as they were.

'Oh, fuck me.' Steven wiped his eyes a final time. 'I need you in my life more often, Sean.'

'You should have seen your face!' Sean went off into another fit of laughter, then eventually managed to compose himself. 'I could have sworn that you were expecting me to impart some priceless pearl of wisdom.'

'You do actually do that, more often than not, to be fair.' Steven was serious now. 'If I'm totally honest, these bike rides are pretty much the only thing keeping me sane right now. You're a good mate, Sean.'

'Aww.' Sean's eyes filled with tears again, but for a different reason this time. 'I could say the same thing about you. Things haven't exactly been easy with my mum either, and getting out like this has been a lifeline for me too.' He took a step towards Steven, then suddenly remembered. 'If it weren't for these damn regulations I'd be squeezing you so tight right now that you wouldn't know what's hit you.' He smiled broadly. 'How about we go cut up some trails?'

It was only once they were back on their way that Sean looked over at Steven again. 'You know what, if you're really struggling, the best person to talk to might be Nick. He's been to the depths of some places most people never get to and he might have some good advice.'

'Aye, you're right about that.' Steven nodded thoughtfully. 'I might just do that.'

Chapter 21

By the time Chantelle got home from work the following afternoon she already had the beginnings of a headache. Irene was in the living room, a pile of completed face masks already on the table. She looked up from the sewing machine. 'How was your day, love?'

Chantelle shook her head. 'Don't even ask. I'm going to go and soak in a hot bath for a bit, then probably go to bed.'

'I'll bring you a cup of tea if you like.' There was whirring for a few seconds, with Irene feeding the dark blue cloth through the machine gently.

'It's fine, I'll have one when I get out.' Irene's tea making was slightly erratic these days and she frequently added too much sugar, having forgotten that she'd added it in the first place. Normally Chantelle didn't mind so much, as hot sweet tea was very much to her taste, but today the thought of sugar on her unsettled stomach was nauseating. 'Do you know where Steven's gone? Did you put it in your book?' As Irene looked around, Chantelle pointed. 'It's up on the shelf.'

Irene consulted her notes. 'Out for a bike ride, he said. He left about two, so he should be back soon.'

Things had been slightly frosty between Steven and herself since their argument about the nursing homes, so it was time to get in the bathroom before he came back and demanded the shower. Chantelle started the bath and stripped off her clothes, making sure they went in the laundry bag. Slipping gratefully into the half-filled tub, she rolled her neck to ease some of the tension in her shoulders, catching sight of the laundry bag as it sat on the bathroom floor. These daily rituals seemed so much a part of her life now it was weird to think that it was only two months since this had all started. But then, two months of this sort of stress was a very long time. And when would it end? There had been lots of speculation about when the lockdown would be lifted, but the current reality was that there was very little end in sight.

Chantelle ran the bath until it was full and then shut off the tap, luxuriating in the feel of the water running over her skin. Irene loved bubbles but Chantelle preferred to use her favourite shower gel and give herself a good scrub with a flannel. Sadly no amount of scrubbing or hot water was able to wash away her headache and by the time she finished it was pounding away behind her eyes. She would just have to admit defeat and take another dose of painkillers. They were strong enough that they would send her to sleep for a few hours and she could hopefully avoid a full-strength migraine.

A pair of fluffy pyjamas felt like heaven, and with a grateful sigh she flopped onto her bed and reached for her handbag. Two pills would sink her into oblivion.

A cold sweat broke out over her body as she realised the packet she was holding only had one blister pack in it, which was totally empty. They normally came with two. Had one fallen out of the packet? She rooted around in the bottom of her bag, her dread increasing with every second. No, it was definitely not there. This meant she was out of painkillers, and with them being prescription she wasn't due to get any more until the end of the week. She knew that she had possibly been a bit over-ready to take them given everything that was going on, but had she really taken so much more than she thought?

Her gaze went to the front of the packet, where her name and address were printed along with the instructions. She was already struggling to focus, but the word 'one' jumped out at her. She rubbed her eyes and squinted at it. Take one, it clearly said on the front. But her old one had been exactly the same size, and she had always taken two. Then she realised with horror that these pills were double the strength of her old ones. With it being a blank white packet, and the blister packs looking exactly the same, she had just assumed. No wonder they had seemed to be working better, and no wonder her stomach had felt a bit off the last couple of weeks. She was on a double dose.

The problem was, what to do now? Chantelle pressed a hand to her throbbing forehead. The pain was getting bad enough that rational thought was starting to be too much. She was out of decent painkillers, and while she probably had some ibuprofen stashed somewhere, it would barely touch the sides. Could she ride this one out? Should she call the GP's surgery before they closed? She shut her eyes for a few moments while she tried to gather her thoughts.

A touch on her shoulder roused her from her pain and she opened her eyes, wincing as the light hit them. Steven was standing over her, freshly showered, his face looking concerned. How much time had she lost?

'Mum said you'd gone for a rest, but then I heard you moaning. Are you OK? Can I get you anything?'

Chantelle closed her eyes again; it was just too painful to keep them open. In as few words as possible she explained the situation. 'And now I don't know what to do. Not only am I stuck without anything to take away the pain, it's also really dangerous to take too many. Could I have damaged my liver?'

She heard the soft clunk of Steven's crutches and felt him sit down beside her on the bed. A cool hand gently stroked across her forehead. 'Let's take things one at a time. How bad is the pain? Out of ten?'

'About an eight?' Every time she spoke the vibrations increased the pain shooting through her head.

'Well, that's better than a ten.' The stroking continued. 'Is this hurting or helping?'

'Helping, I think.' At least it was distracting her.

'Your head does seem very hot. Are you sure this might not be coronavirus?'

The thought hadn't even occurred to her. 'No.'

The hand left her forehead and she winced as the door creaked open. It wasn't long before she felt the weight of his body back on the bed. 'I've got a cold wet cloth for your forehead, I'm going to lay it on for you. Just thought I would warn you beforehand.'

The cool dampness did seem to provide a bit of relief, but it was still not enough to open her eyes. 'Thanks.' She felt for his hand and squeezed it, trying to convey her gratitude.

'I'm going to call the NHS helpline, they'll be able to give us some advice. I know it will probably be just to stay put and monitor you, but at least I'll feel a bit better about it.'

The bedroom door creaked open. 'Are you OK?' It was Irene's voice.

'Chantelle's got a migraine, Mum. But I need you to stay out in case she's got the virus. Can you do that for me?'

'Of course. I'll get you some water.' The door creaked closed again.

'Just leave it outside the door, I'll nip out and grab it in a sec.' The sound of Steven's voice echoed around in Chantelle's skull. She squeezed his hand again. 'Yes?'

'Can you talk a bit quieter? And get rid of some of the light?'

'Sorry.' Steven's voice dropped to a whisper. He rolled over on the bed and she felt his shoulder come to rest next to hers. 'Do you want a cuddle?'

Chantelle was worried about him catching something, but with the amount of contact they'd already had it was probably too late. She rolled her head onto his shoulder, and sighed in relief as she felt his arms go around her. Steven rescued the cloth which was now slightly warm. Then he swore softly. 'I forgot to call.'

'Don't go. Stay here with me. If I pass out you can call an ambulance.'

'That's so not funny.' Steven's voice sounded strained, but he did as she asked and they lay there together for a while. It had been a long time since Chantelle had had to put up with the full force of a migraine, and at times she just focused on the pain as everything else went blank. At one point she vaguely remembered Steven getting her to drink some water. She had no idea how long it took before the pain began to recede, but by the time it felt safe to open her eyes light was filtering in around the edge of the curtains. She was still nestled in Steven's arms.

He stirred and opened his own eyes, looking down at her blearily. 'Feeling any better?'

'Like I went ten rounds in the boxing ring. Or that time I got smacked in the nose. But the worst of the pain is definitely gone.' She looked at the grey smudges under his eyes. 'Did you get any sleep at all?'

'I snatched a few minutes here and there.' Steven smiled wearily at her. 'I guess we know it's not the virus then. Which is definitely a bonus.'

'I don't know why this is happening to me.' Chantelle bit her lip. 'I never used to be like this. That's why I asked the doctor to let me see a specialist. There must be a reason behind it.'

'I know it was bad, because at one point last night you told me to go and get some Vallies from the drug dealer who lives two streets across from here.'

'I did?' Chantelle felt her face go hot. 'I don't remember that.'

Steven yawned. 'Don't worry, I didn't take you seriously. Anyway, about the migraines, I was reading articles about it, and some of them said there is sometimes a trigger. You know, stress, caffeine, that sort of thing.'

'Well, tick, tick, tick on the stress for all of us, with everything that's going on, so that doesn't help.' She was silent for a while. Thinking was slow when she was this tired.

'You don't have to go to work today, do you?' Steven's arms tightened around her.

'Today and tomorrow are rest days.' She felt him relax. 'We should probably tell Ma that I've not got the virus. She'll be worried.'

'If she's remembered. I never know these days. It's a fifty-fifty chance she'll either have forgotten about it and gone to sleep, or have been lying awake all night worrying about you.' His tone showed his bitterness. 'But I'll go and see what she's up to.'

'You do know that if this is all getting to be too much then it's OK to ask for help?' Chantelle hadn't meant to bring it up, but it somehow slipped out. 'Even if it's just mental support for yourself, a chance to talk about what you're going through.'

Steven slipped off the bed and Chantelle felt the loss of his warmth in more ways than one. 'I'll consider the mental support. But there's no way I'm putting her in a home. No way.'

Chantelle lay back on the pillow, thinking. She would have to call the doctor today, explain what happened and ask for advice. If stress was a trigger for her migraines then she was screwed. A stressful job with pandemic stress on top of that was no recipe for success. But then what else had Steven said? She suddenly realised that even though things had been frosty between them he had still been researching her migraines, trying to educate himself about them. Trying to find a solution. And then he had held her in his arms all night while she struggled with her pain. All of her irritation with him dissolved and she found herself bursting into tears. He really loved her. And in spite of his adamant views about nursing homes, she found she couldn't be angry at him any more.

She blew her nose and considered Steven's words. Caffeine. That was an interesting idea. What was it in? Chocolate, but there wasn't much in that. Tea, but she had always drunk that. Although weak, with lots of milk, so it barely counted. She did love a coffee. One of the favourite parts of her day was when herself and Donny set off in the van. Their first stop would always be to a local cafe to set themselves up for the shift. And coffee was something she had barely touched before. But would the occasional cup really be enough to trigger things? If that was the case then they would only be triggered on a day she was working.

Her heart sank as she realised that was probably true. And not only that, since the pandemic had started the cafe had started offering free hot drinks for key workers. Which meant that often it would not only be one coffee a shift, but often two. Yesterday they had even stopped onto the way back into the office and she had ordered an extra large just to get her through her paperwork. It all suddenly made sense.

The door creaked again and she looked up at Steven with a big smile. 'I might have cracked it.'

'What's that you said?' Steven cupped a hand to his ear, smiling for the first time that morning. 'You might be cracked? I'd agree with that after the night we've just had. In fact, I feel a bit cracked myself.'

Chantelle went to jab him in the ribs but then changed her mind and held out her hand instead. 'Why don't we both go back for a quick snooze, then I'll go and make us some breakfast.'

Steven flopped onto the bed and put an arm around her. 'Sounds like a fabulous plan.'

He was asleep in seconds, and as Chantelle listened to the soft sounds of his breathing she found herself drifting away too.

Chapter 22

Chantelle could feel her mobile vibrating for the third time in the pocket of her high vis vest. She ignored it; even if it was an emergency call from Steven then getting it out in front of the complainer who was currently narrating the entire daily habits of their neighbour was a massive no. When the job was finally done and she was safely back in the van she pulled it out and looked it. Three missed calls, all from the same number. 'Sorry Donny, got to call Steven quickly.' Her partner simply nodded and started up the engine.

Steven answered on the first ring. 'She's gone.'

'What do you mean, gone?' There was no need to ask who he was talking about.

'I literally popped to the corner shop to get some milk and when I got back she was gone. I've searched all over for her. She can't have gone far but I just can't find her. I've already done a full sweep of our area.'

'I take it none of the locator devices have managed to go with her?'

'She left her phone on the coffee table, and I found one of the buttons dropped on the floor of the hall. Although whether that was on purpose or by accident I just don't know.'

The pit dropped out of Chantelle's stomach. 'Is anything missing of hers?'

'I've had a good look through her room and it's hard to tell, you know how full of junk it still is. I can't find her purse anywhere, although I could be wrong about that too. I've checked all the streets round our house, and the takeaway in case she went back there, but if she's got bank cards and cash she could be anywhere by now.' Steven's voice was taut with worry.

By now Donny was looking at her with concern on his face and it dragged Chantelle's thoughts back into focus. 'You need to call the police. They'll log her as missing and start an investigation.'

'Can't you dial it in?'

'I could, but chances are we'll get assigned another job in the next few minutes and I won't get time. Ring 999 and they'll take all your details and kick things off.' Chantelle hated doing that to him, but there was no other option. And sure enough, right then her radio sprang to life. 'That's one coming in right now. I'm really sorry, Stevie, but I've got to go.'

'Trouble at the ranch?' Donny looked at her for a couple of seconds, his grey eyes assessing her. He responded to the radio message, then took off the handbrake and started down the road.

'Irene's gone missing. Stevie said he literally popped out for ten minutes and she was gone. It was almost as if she was waiting for her chance to break out.'

Donny frowned as he took in the news. 'I'm sure someone will find her. They'll get CCTV onto it pretty quickly. You're lucky it's during the day, there'll be more people around to notice her.'

Chantelle bit her lip while she thought about it. 'The trouble is, she's still got enough capacity on a good day to appear pretty normal and she's still relatively mobile if she's got her walking stick, so she's not going to stand out.' She held up her hands. 'I can't think about it now. What was that call we got?'

'Disturbance at a house on Lincoln Avenue. I know the address.'

'What, at this time in the morning?'

Donny shrugged. 'Want to pull up the details on your device and read them to me while we're on the way?'

By the time Chantelle got home at four Steven looked like he was on the point of tearing his hair out. He didn't even wait until she had taken off her uniform, just grabbed her and hugged her tightly. She breathed in the smell of his skin, so welcome after spending all day in a mask. 'Have you had any news?'

Steven grimaced. 'Nothing. They've checked the CCTV at the station up the road, so at least they know she's not got on a train. They said they've asked for the CCTV from the buses but it's going to take a bit of time to work out which bus she might have got and then access the CCTV from each one. Especially as there's a couple of services which go from our nearest stop. That's two different companies as well so extra work.' He sagged suddenly, perching on the edge of a chair. 'You were right about all of this. I've been burying my head in the sand.'

'No, you've been doing what you thought best.' Chantelle shook her head sternly. 'This hasn't been easy for any of us. Including her.'

Steven looked up at her gratefully. 'Your colleagues have been amazing today. And I'm holding onto the hope that if she has taken a bus she'll be easier to spot because there aren't that many people using them at the moment.'

'Someone will find her.' Chantelle went to flop onto the sofa beside him, then realised she should go and change. 'As you said, there are much fewer people travelling at the moment so she will be easier to find.' She sighed. 'I guess I'd better go have a shower.'

Steven sniffed his armpit. 'I could do with having a shower too, I've spent all day tearing around the neighbourhood.' He collected himself. 'I called up Brenda to make sure she lets us know if she turns up there and she's promised she will.'

Chantelle smiled at him. 'That shower...want me to wash your back?'

Steven looked at her, worry still creasing his eyes. 'Is that an innuendo? Because I really don't feel in the mood for ... you know.'

'It was literally an offer to wash your back, actually. I know that might surprise you based on my past record, but it's true. The last call I had before we finished was pretty intense and I just want to remind myself that there is such a thing as honest love in this world.'

'In that case, let my back be at your service.' Steven stood up and took her hand. 'Honest love is about all I have to give you right now.'

A shower did make Chantelle feel a bit calmer, and once they had a cup of tea made they sat at the dining table. 'Tell me everywhere you've searched so far.'

'Everywhere.' Now that she looked at Steven, he did look absolutely wiped. 'Your colleagues even looked through all the cupboards and under the beds to check that she wasn't hiding in the house.'

'You'd be surprised by how often it happens.' Chantelle nodded. 'But give me a list of the other places, just in case I can think of something you've missed.'

'Everywhere, really. The food bank, the takeaway, all the local shops. And every street within a couple of miles of here. I took my bike and just cycled around for a couple of hours. Searched through all the undergrowth in the woods in case she's had a fall. Went along the canal for a good few miles in each direction.' Steven sighed. 'Your colleagues have done loads, but they said once the local area was covered they need some better leads before they go and do anything else. Someone of theirs is chasing up more CCTV possibilities and they said they'd keep me posted as soon as they find anything. They did ask for more ideas about where she might be, but I honestly can't think of anywhere else. It's been more than eight hours now. If she's kept walking she could be almost anywhere.'

'And with decent weather like today no-one would question someone out for a walk.' Chantelle bit her lip. 'Hang on. What about the bingo hall?'

'It's closed because of lockdown.' Steven shook his head. 'And it's a good hour's walk.'

'Yeah, but if she was really confused she might have forgotten. And the bus would take her direct. Surely it's worth a try.'

'I'll go on my bike and take a look.' Then Steven's head slumped into his hands. 'I'm so tired, Chaz. I know that may seem stupid when I'm not even working, but it's true. And it makes me feel guilty to even admit it. Isn't looking after your parents something everyone is supposed to do when they get old?'

Chantelle reached across the table and cupped a hand gently around the side of his head. She felt him lean into it slightly as if drawn in by the warmth of her touch, and took some comfort from that. 'That's the thing though, she's not old, is she? None of us expected something like this to happen so soon. And doing it any time would be bad enough, but with everything else that's going on right now? I'm not surprised you're exhausted. I'm exhausted too. I think everyone is.'

One of Steven's hands detached from the side of his head to cover hers. 'I love you, Chaz. You always know what to say to make me feel better.'

She leaned over the table to plant a kiss on his lips. 'Come on, my love. We'd better get going.'

'We?' Steven frowned.

'Yeah, we. I've got the key to Brenda's shed and she said I could use her bike.'

Steven got up. 'How is it that woman manages to save the day when she's not even around?' A short laugh escaped him. Then his eyebrows drew together again. 'Wait a minute. So you're saying that all those times when you've said you can't come with me for a bike ride it was just an excuse?'

'Busted.' Chantelle drew him in gently for a hug. 'But also, I know you, and I know that if you don't get some time by yourself you get like a bear with a sore head.' She patted the item in question. 'Come on, love of my life. Let's go and do this together.'

'And here I was thinking your job was the thing you love best.' Steven sneaked a cheeky look at her as they walked towards the door. 'You certainly spend enough time talking about it.'

'Do I?' Chantelle felt a flush of embarrassment. 'Don't tell me I get boring.'

'Never.' He placed his hand on his heart as if he was making a vow. 'In fact, it's got to the point where I know if you come home and you aren't talking about it then it's been something really bad and that's when I need to winkle it out of you.'

Chantelle put a hand lightly on his shoulder, suddenly lost for words. This man, who she had been assuming was totally unaware of all her internal turmoil, had actually been quietly observing and doing the best he could to support her. She leaned forward to place a gentle brush of her lips on his. 'I do love you.'

'Love you too.' Steven stepped away from her and opened the front door. 'Are you ready to rock and roll?'

'I'm sorry for being so harsh on you. I was wrong to judge you about the decisions you were making about caring for her.' They were riding side by side along the canal, and Chantelle felt the need to say the words that had been in her head ever since Irene's disappearance. 'But it might be partly my fault that she's gone. Things have been frosty between you and I since we argued and I'm sure she's picked up on that. Maybe it is the reason she's gone missing.'

Steven looked sideways at her. 'Even if that is true, and I don't believe it is, I think you were the one who might have been right. I mean, look where we are now. She's gone and we don't know where to find her. I could have at least locked the door after me when I nipped out this morning. But then I always kept worrying, what if there was a fire and she couldn't get out? Maybe she is better off with someone else to care for her. Someone who can keep an eye on her twenty-four seven.'

'But locked away in a care home? We wouldn't even be able to visit at the moment. I'm just not sure any more that is the best option.' Chantelle dropped back to give an oncoming pedestrian space to pass, then pedalled faster to catch up again.

'Surely this virus can't last forever.' Steven didn't look at her this time. 'The cases are dropping off already.'

'Really?' Chantelle felt a note of disbelief creeping into her tone and made efforts to keep her voice normal. 'What happens when they relax the rules and everyone goes back to mixing? It could be a year or so before you're able to see her properly, and at the rate things are moving she might not even recognise us by then.'

'I thought you were the eternal optimist?' Steven looked at her with his eyebrows raised.

'That's your job.' Chantelle lifted a hand to poke him gently in the shoulder. 'I'm the obsessive planner and doommonger extraordinaire.'

'Not doom, exactly. It never hurts to have a bit of realism.' This time it was Steven who dropped back to make way for an overtaking cyclist.

Chantelle waited until he was back beside her to speak again. 'Talking about realism, do you realistically think we'll find her at the bingo hall?'

Steven made a disbelieving sound. 'Not really. But I do know if we don't go and look I'll be wondering about it all night.'

They didn't find her, of course, and when they dropped by the takeaway on the way back home to avoid having to cook then Jules said he still hadn't seen Irene. They thanked him profusely and cycled the rest of the way home, Steven riding one-handed so he could carry the bag. By the time they had forced down some of the food they were so depleted they shoved the leftovers into the fridge and crashed into bed.

Steven had thought he wouldn't be able to sleep, but wrapped in Chantelle's arms exhaustion overtook him. The next thing he knew it was daylight and Chantelle was stroking his head and calling his name softly. He rolled over to find her fully dressed in her uniform.

'Is that you off to work?' He yawned and stretched. Not that he minded her waking him up, but when she had an early start she usually just crept out of bed and tried to disturb him as little as possible.

Chantelle shoved a bit of scrap paper at him. 'Look what I found.'

Steven hoisted himself up to a sitting position and tried to focus his bleary eyes on the paper. It had his mother's spidery handwriting on it. 'Dear Stevie and Chantelle,' it began.

Dear Stevie and Chantelle,

I know things have been a bit difficult between you these last couple of weeks and I feel like it would be better if I gave you some space to sort things out between you. I have gone to visit my sister Abigail in York and will be back in a week or so. Hopefully that will be long enough, but if you do find you need some more time I'm sure she'll be happy to have me for longer.

All my love,

Your Mum

Steven looked up, feeling relief flow over him like a cool rain shower. 'Where did you find this?'

'Behind the clock on the living room shelf.' Chantelle hung her head. 'Oh Stevie, this is all my fault. I'd stashed Abigail's address there for safekeeping and she must have found it. The paper I wrote it on has gone.'

'She remembered! Last time she went missing I told her to write me a note if she was going anywhere. Well, at least we know where she's headed.' Steven pulled Chantelle towards him for a hug and kissed the top of her head. 'Do you want to tell your colleagues, since you're off in now, or shall I give them a call?'

'I'll do it.' But Chantelle made no move to get off the bed and Steven knew what was going through her mind.

'You honestly can't blame yourself.' He used the arm that was holding her to give her a gentle shake. When there was no reaction, he squeezed her tighter and used one hand to rub the top of her head until she squealed. 'Not the hair! Stevie! I spent ages doing my bun.'

'See? There are more important things in life than feeling guilty.' He planted a kiss on top of her mussed up hair. 'As I keep telling you, she's her own person. We can't keep her imprisoned inside her own home. Now get to work so your colleagues can do their job of finding her and bringing her back.'

It was midday before Chantelle rang to confirm that someone from the North Yorkshire police had visited Abigail and confirmed that Irene had indeed got there safely quite late the previous evening. It was only when she got home that afternoon that Steven got the full story.

'Abigail said that because it was so late it wasn't until the next morning that she realised something about Irene wasn't quite right, which was why she never thought to call anyone. She's also said that since Irene's there already she may as well stay for a few days so they can catch up properly.' The two of them were sitting on the sofa with a cup of tea each. Chantelle hadn't even bothered to take off her uniform, she was that exhausted, and Steven was so glad to have her close to him he couldn't have cared if there were a bajillion viruses in it.

'She does know what she's like, right?' Steven looked at her incredulously.

'Yeah, but Abigail says she's been lonely these last few weeks. Apparently her daughter's recently moved down to London so they haven't been able to see each other either. She says it will be great to have some company for a few days.'

'And after that?' Steven sipped at his drink, grateful for the hot sweetness of the sugar.

'We should talk to your mum about it. That letter shows she's still got the capacity to make decent decisions, even if she'd forgotten about the bust up with her sister.'

'I guess I could decide to not get another job and become her full time carer permanently. That might give me time to get this business off the ground when we're finally allowed to. And I could claim her carer's allowance, which would at least be something.'

Chantelle pushed her toes under his thigh. 'She has said many times she didn't want to be a burden on you. Have you ever thought that maybe she would like to go into a home? It's sometimes easier mentally if it's someone you don't know cleaning up after you.'

'I'm still not sure about that.' Steven shifted uncomfortably. 'But you are right, we should talk to her about it. I've just been on auto-pilot these last few months, making decisions based on assumptions I've made and not actually talking to people about things.'

'Well, there is a pandemic on.' Chantelle leaned over and pressed her lips to his. 'Making decent decisions is pretty challenging when there's all this other stuff happening. We just have to make the best of it.'

Steven sighed. 'I feel bad saying this, but can we not talk about everything that's going on in the world right now? The past couple of days have made me feel about ten years older as it is.'

'Well, that only makes you thirty seven now. You're still in your prime.' Chantelle laughed and kissed him again.

'Talking about making the best of things, you do realise that with Mum gone we have this flat all to ourselves?' Steven sighed again, feeling the tension finally start to flow out of him. 'I feel weird not having to constantly think about someone else.'

'Oh, and there was I hoping you were thinking about me.' Chantelle gave a theatrical pout. 'I was just going to ask you if you wanted to wash my back.'

'I take it that is an innuendo this time?' Steven looked at her, feeling a grin break out on his face.

'It most definitely is. Although I wouldn't mind a real back scrub too, if you're willing.'

Steven pushed himself up off the sofa and held out his hand. 'It would be my pleasure.'

Chantelle gave him a wicked smile as she stood up. 'There's no rush. Have you remembered that I've got the next two days off work?'

'Oh yeah, I had forgotten.' Steven quirked an eyebrow at her. 'Stuck in the house, unable to go out for anything except brief periods of exercise... I wonder how we're going to spend our time?'

Chantelle whispered something in his ear and Steven felt heat sear through his body. He looked at her. 'Really? You surprise me.'

She tugged on his hand, leading him in the direction of the shower. 'That's only my first idea. I've got more where that came from.'

'I can't wait to hear them.' Steven had already stripped off his t-shirt. The bathroom door slammed behind them and soon the sound of water drowned out everything else.

Epilogue

Two Years Later

'Let's have everyone together for a final group shot, please!' The photographer waved a hand at the milling mass of friends and family members. 'Then I'll do the individual shoots with each of the couples and the rest of you can go off and get the party started.'

As the guests wandered back across the grass to the marquee and Pete and David volunteered to go first, Steven took the chance to pull Chantelle in for a quick kiss. 'Have to say I never expected to be doing this a second time around.'

'You're happy about it, though?' Chantelle ruffled his hair gently.

'Oh aye. And Jenny's idea to combine all the weddings was genius.'

'I told Deem it was a good plan.' They both turned at the sound of Jenny's voice. 'Because of all the lockdown rules we knew we'd have to put the wedding back if we wanted to have a big party, so it made perfect sense when you told us you wanted to get remarried. And then when

David popped the question to Pete we knew we'd want to add them in too.'

'Did Jade and Nick not want to add themselves to the mix as well?' Chantelle asked with a smile.

'They seem very happy being not married together for the rest of their lives.' Steven gave a shrug. 'But then Jade has always been a bit of a rebel as far as convention is concerned.'

Chantelle drew Jenny in for a hug and kissed her gently on the cheek. 'You look stunning today. That dress is a work of art.'

Jenny twirled happily, the floor length ivory skirt spinning out as she did so. 'I know. I'm so proud of this design that I've already copied it in three other colours.'

The other two laughed at her obvious enjoyment. Jenny nodded towards the open side of the marquee where Irene could be seen swaying happily to the music. 'How are you getting on having her at home still?'

'Oh, good days and bad days.' Steven smiled wryly, thinking of what his life with his mum was like. 'But we've got an arrangement with a local care home where she goes to them during the day and it seems to be a good solution.'

'Oh yes.' Jenny bounced excitedly. 'Deem told me your outdoor business has really taken off post-lockdown.'

'Aye, it's really exploded now that everyone's doing local holidays, we've got more bookings than we can handle this summer.' Steven nodded. 'Mum's still sewing and apparently has been teaching quite a few of the care home residents, so it works both ways. Let's just say we're managing for now. And she does seem so much happier sleeping at home. I guess it's because she's been living in that flat more than thirty years now. There's a lot of memories there.' He felt Chantelle squeeze his fingers and knew she was thinking of all the ones they shared themselves, both good and bad. 'Her sister Abigail has even started making noises about moving back to Glasgow now that her daughter's decided to stay in London, so you never know.'

'And thank goodness the lockdowns are finished, so people can actually come and visit.' Jenny shuddered theatrically. 'I mean, I know there's other challenges on the horizon, but it's so amazing to actually be able to have a party like this and get everyone together! And the rain stayed off as well.' She raised her eyes upwards, as if giving a prayer that it would stay that way.

'And even more of a miracle, I still fit into my old wedding dress, and Steven managed to get rid of all the lockdown flab he put on. I was really worried he wouldn't actually fit in this posh kilt you'd had made for him.' Chantelle shot a wicked side glance at her new husband.

Steven gasped in mock outrage, but any reply he might have made was forestalled by the photographer shouting 'Next!'

'You two go.' Jenny pushed them both gently. 'Deem seems to have wandered off somewhere, probably chatting to someone. I'll go and find him.'

Steven and Chantelle walked towards the photographer, who pointed out where they should stand. When the formal photos were done Steven turned towards Chantelle. 'So are you going to pick me up again?'

She hefted him into her arms in a fluid move and kissed him soundly. 'Good enough for you?'

'You'll always be more than good enough for me.' Steven smiled up at her. 'And I'll always be grateful for the day you picked me up.'

'Urgh.' Chantelle put him down with a roll of her eyes. 'You airing out your dad jokes already? You might need to get some practice in.'

Steven's mouth fell open. 'You're not?'

Chantelle smiled. 'No, not yet, don't worry. But I would like to try sometime soon, if you're up for it.'

'Another corny joke!' Steven crowed triumphantly. 'You see, you can't help yourself either.'

'Wait, what?' Chantelle frowned in puzzlement, then groaned as she realised what she had done. 'Let's get off to the party before you do any more damage. I want to introduce you to some more of my police colleagues.'

Steven pulled her in for one last kiss. 'I love you, Chaz.'

She cupped her hands on either side of his head, her dancing blue eyes locked with his. 'Love you too.'

Other books

Happiness: Glasgow Guys Book 1

Can a simple list save a life?

Glasgow used to be Jade's happy place, but a family tragedy the night of her twenty-second birthday stole away her joy for the city. Now she spends her free time wandering the streets, desperately searching for some peace of mind. Nick's move to Glasgow was supposed to be a bold new start, but instead is just grinding away his mental health. A chance meeting with Jade when Nick is at his lowest point gives him hope for something better. Because Jade claims to have a list which can unlock the key to happiness...

What readers have said about Happiness:

"I found this book really absorbing"

"A moving love story"

"It painted a vivid picture of areas of Glasgow and The Highlands"

"A wonderfully written book that shines a light on mental health"

Trust: Glasgow Guys Book 2

When someone else tells a different story...how can you be believed?

After resisting the advances of a senior colleague loses Jenny her job, she escapes from London to visit friends in a small Highland village, hoping the distance will provide some respite from the trauma she has suffered. Meeting Nadeem, a considerate ex-Army medic, helps her start to rebuild her confidence and begin legal action against the company. But Nadeem is fighting his own battles with grief over the loss of his best friend in Afghanistan, and when he and Jenny discover that their lives are connected back in London the two of them find out just how far trust will stretch before it snaps.

What readers have said about Trust:

'I highly recommend this lighthearted, but deep read.' J M McQueen

"'I loved the relationships between all of the characters' Kirsty Hopkins

'The book was easy to read and flowed' Courtney Lewis

'I loved this book...the characters are the shining star in all this' Reading With Wine

Keep an eye out for the Marriemuir series, coming in 2026!

Acknowledgements

This is the third book I've published and everything I do wouldn't be possible without the wonderful collection of family, friends and colleagues who give me so much joy in my life and support me when things get tough. There are a few special mentions though:

My neighbours, who helped me through all the lock-downs and went for socially distanced walks when things were permitted.

Mairi MacMillan, who was the one who told me to publish the book, and for all her continuing support and encouragement on my writing journey.

Nikki Maxwell, who gave me invaluable advice on living as an amputee, although any errors or inconsistencies remain my own.

My wonderful editor Ali Williams, for giving me feedback on the story structure.

Amanda, for doing an eagle-eyed read through of the final manuscript and spotting some things I'd missed.

Fully Booked Design, for creating a cover that was so gorgeous it made me want to finish the book before the others that I'd planned.

All libraries everywhere, for creating welcoming spaces that are great for writing, and for doing so much to champion books, especially by local authors.

All the people I've had conversations with about dementia, particularly Ruth, who has gone above and beyond in her caring responsibilities while also experiencing challenges of her own. We wouldn't have met if lockdown hadn't happened, so this book is also partly for her.